I0551872

BITTERSWEET
RETRIBUTION

Also available by **Nicholas P Boyland**

BITTERSWEET SACRIFICE

BITTERSWEET HUMILIATION

NICHOLAS P BOYLAND

This novel is a work of fiction and the characters and events in it exist only in its pages and in the author's imagination. They are not even distantly inspired by any individual or group known or unknown to the author. All incidents herein are pure invention.

First published in Great Britain 2015 by Rhino Trikes Church Street Winsham Nr Chard Somerset TA20 4JD

www.rhinotrikespublishing.com

Published by Rhino Trikes

ISBN 978-0-9576285-7-1

Cover photograph by Kelly Boyland

To my wife Tracey

without whom there would be no Natasha

PROLOGUE

Satanic pact

The Arab alighted from the Aer Lingus plane at Dublin airport. He wore a conservative business suit in charcoal grey, his dark hair, beard and moustache were trimmed more towards the Western style than would be considered the custom of his native Bahrain; a predominantly Muslim country. Temporary diplomatic status saw him breeze through customs without a hitch. The driver held up a handwritten sign bearing the letters BAPCO, an acronym for the Bahraini Petroleum Company who were in legitimate venture talks with the Irish Development Authority.

"Yazan Rahimi?" the driver questioned.

"Yes, I am he," the Arab answered in perfect clipped English.

"Mr Doherty sent me, I'm to take you to the hotel," the driver replied.

"Thank you. Mr Doherty is most kind," he said, gesturing to the driver to organise his baggage which was following on behind on a porter's trolley.

"I'll get that then shall I?" the driver suggested with a hint of sarcasm, before escorting Mr Rahimi to the waiting limousine.

The meeting was scheduled for later in the evening. Yazan Rahimi had been delayed on the connecting flight between Shannon International Airport on the western coast and his final destination at Dublin, and was taking the opportunity to catch up on his sleep and watch a little porn on the hotel's cable TV.

Yazan was well rested and relaxed by the time security escorted him into the conference room. Mr Doherty was seated, but courteously stood up as the other man approached him.

"I trust you had a good flight Mr Rahimi, and that your room is adequate?"

"Yes, yes Mr Doherty, quite sufficient for my humble needs."

Doherty grinned and thought, *this man's needs are anything but humble.*

"Can we get straight down to business Mr Doherty?" the Arab asked abruptly.

"Yes of course Mr Rahimi. I'm all ears, go right ahead."

"Two years ago, your man, Mr Dix, failed in his mission to carry out a little clean-up operation on my client's behalf, as you will no doubt remember?" The Arab's manner was somewhat patronising.

"Yes, I also remember that it was at your client's insistence that the task was trusted to Mr Dix, a man not from what you might call our 'inner circle', a man who was something of a mercenary, at best a loose cannon. Not a man loyal to 'the cause'."

"I cannot comment on my client's reasons for this preference, but needless to say the situation, it would seem, has arisen in which my client feels that the need for this 'tying up' of 'loose ends' has become somewhat imperative and he would like to engage your expertise to further these ends."

"Mr Rahimi, this is our hotel, it's as safe a venue as exists anywhere in the world. If you have business to discuss, please don't talk in riddles. You want me to arrange the demise of the woman Natasha Curland?" The question was clearly rhetorical; Doherty left it hanging awhile before continuing. "We are not mercenaries Mr Rahimi; we do not kill for profit. We are an organisation founded on a cause. Frankly, I find the whole suggestion somewhat insulting."

Slightly humbled by the remark, the Arab appeared on the back-foot. "Please forgive my impertinence Mr Doherty, it is not my intention to insult you, however, if you could be persuaded to use your considerable expertise to facilitate our objective, my client would be prepared to make an extremely generous donation to your cause, or indeed to any cause you cared to proffer."

"Were your employer's generosity to extend to the region of two million dollars US, I could probably find a suitable operative to carry out the task discreetly."

"Discretion is not what my employer requires sir, in fact, he would very much like the, uh, assassination to be most un-subtle, most un-subtle indeed. It should look like a revenge killing, a trademark IRA 'hit' I believe you would call it. Would this be a problem?"

Doherty smiled. "Not a problem at all Mr Rahimi, the army has broad shoulders so it does. The killing of an ex British soldier's wife will not cause a ripple in anyone's conscience."

"Very well Mr Doherty, the price is acceptable. How is your reach abroad sir? I may have another contract for you in mainland Europe. Would this be possible?"

Doherty laughed. "Where there's British soldiers, you'll find my men, no problems there. Who's the new mark?"

"A Dutch woman; another loose end. You'll find all the details in this envelope. This killing however should be handled with the utmost discretion; a mugging perhaps. No signature. This woman is nobody of substance or significance, my client would like it to remain this way." He took a brown A4 envelope from his attaché case and handed it to Doherty. "If you'd like to put a figure to this contract too, I will see to it that funds are transferred to the account of your choice."

Doherty glanced at the documents inside the envelope before catching the Arab's eye and holding him in an intense stare for a few seconds before declaring, "Three million, US for both marks, bank transfer to an offshore account, in full, in advance."

"As you wish Mr Doherty. Kindly furnish me with your account details and it will be done."

With their business concluded, Doherty shook the Arab's hand and the man left.

CHAPTER ONE

Plastic fantastic

"Hon', would you mind dropping the kids at mum's on your way to work? I'm running late for an appointment to get my nails sorted. I'll take the Beemer, it'll be easier to park," Natasha said, her face flushed from rushing about.

"Of course love, no problem. Are they ready to go?"

"Yes, all ready, don't forget David's car seat, and Monica's booster. You left them in the garage when you had the seats down."

Neil remembered, she was right, he'd used the family car to drop some rubbish at the tip. He would have to put the back seats back up too.

"Got to rush love, catch you soon." She pecked him on the cheek and darted out of the front door, BMW keys in hand.

Neil observed his wife as she gently wheel-spun on the gravel of the drive; hard to fathom what she'd been through, what she'd survived. Just two years before, Natasha's psychotic ex-boyfriend had kidnapped her, abducted her to Ireland into slavery, then subjected her to a lifestyle of drugs and prostitution, destroying in the process the little life growing inside of her and her body's ability to reproduce. Mentally, she had made an almost full recovery; the only thing missing from their relationship was the physical side. Those scars would take longer to heal. Neil could feel the recoil of tension through her skin whenever he touched her and, fearing rejection, he had stopped trying. Therapy had helped at first, but now it just seemed like so much 'jaw jaw'. Only time could heal these wounds. His love for her was so strong; he would wait forever if that's how long it took.

The children were sitting at the dining room table working their way through a small bag of Jelly Tots each. Neil decided to leave them there while he went out to the garage to sort out the car.

His sensitive nose registered the faint smell as he entered the garage; it was somehow out of place. As he righted the back seats, his subconscious continued scanning an invisible database, trying to place the familiar aroma without success.

David's child seat was a formidable brand, with quick release straps joined to the seatbelt floor mounts. Neil remembered to click the redundant middle belts together to avoid the incessant 'nanny' complaining of the seat belt warning system. Conversely, Monica's booster seat didn't trigger the pressure activated system at all, a small manufacturing oversight which would prove a life saver.

He returned to the dining room and gathered up his charges, and not before time as little David was about to attempt a daring raid on his sister's sweetie bag!

"Hey, hey Master Curland, less of that, you'll end up in a life of crime! Now c'mon you two, let's be making tracks to Nannie's. No doubt she'll have you loaded up with sugar and E numbers the moment my back's turned," he laughed.

He strapped the children into the sumptuous rear seat of the Range Rover and turned his attention to the garage door. The motor clicked and whirred as he pressed the button to raise the door. With it fully elevated, he looked down at the dashboard, the nagging voice in his head still quizzing him over the peculiar smell as he pushed the ignition key home. *Pears,* he thought. *Acetone?* He was thinking of Natasha's false nails, *did she use acetone to remove them?* He turned the key from park to the first click, the ignition lights burned brightly, briefly then extinguished.

ALMONDS! The thought from his subconscious was like a warning shout from his past. He weighed up his options in a heartbeat; it had to be the seatbelt circuit, it was the terrorist's circuit of choice; less chance of the wrong passenger triggering the charge. The Land Rover oversight on the rear seatbelt circuit could provide the time he needed to get them clear. Turning in his seat, he said to Monica, "Honey, unfasten your seatbelt, unbuckle your brother, then take him out of the car. Run as fast as you can down to the paddock and hide, Daddy will come and look for you."

"Like hide and seek Daddy?" the little girl replied.

"Exactly Hon'. You and David go hide, fast as you can, don't come back until you hear me calling that I give up!"

"You'll never find us Daddy!"

"I know that, you're a clever girl, now off you go, hurry!"

Neil held his breath as the little girl released the harnesses, the circuit failed to trigger, and the two innocent children jumped out of the car, ran through the open doorway, and away from the garage. He gave them ample time to be well clear of the vicinity before attempting to follow. He knew the bomb would have a backup timer; his life was now in the lap of the gods. He needed the children clear before he attempted any escape.

Leaving the ignition as it was, he reached into the glove box and produced a Swiss army knife he kept there for emergencies. Withdrawing the sharpest blade, he cut through the belt and gingerly opened the door.

He was running flat out as soon as his feet touched the floor of the garage, sheer terror adding fuel to his muscles and propelling him towards the paddock faster than he'd ever moved before.

The blast lifted the Range Rover up and through the roof of the garage. Simultaneously, the shockwave expanded through the roomy four car garage before ripping through the open garage door, giving Neil time to cover about 20 feet from the opening before the blast picked him up and threw him into the air landing him softly into the bushes which lined the drive. He looked back at the garage, the house was engulfed in an enormous dust cloud but there was no sound at all. The pressure in his ears was unbearable and he pressed his fingers into them to relieve it. Without fully comprehending what had happened, he stared in shock at his bloodied fingers as the sounds of the blast's aftermath slowly penetrated his stupor.

The smoke and flames set off the sophisticated sprinkler system, and the fire alarm wailed out its tortured cry. *The children!* Neil thought, and ran down the garden towards the paddock.

The children were standing at the entrance to the stables, staring back towards the remains of their family home in shock. Neil stooped down and gathered them into his arms as the magnitude of what they had just survived sank in!

CHAPTER TWO

Flashback

The woman must have been about fifteen years her senior. Standing as she was between the fire escape and the rusty remains of the alley gate, she prevented Natasha's escape.

Dire thoughts were creeping into Natasha's mind, she could feel the darkness closing in on her, she felt the nightmare was about to start all over again.

"Are you Natasha?" the older woman questioned.

"Yes," she replied, her voice sounding remote to her, disconnected.

"Natasha, I'm so sorry to have startled you this way. I must speak with you. It's a matter of life and death. I am Anna Bergkamp. I am the wife of Isa Hashim Al-Kooheji."

Natasha's heart began to slow, the muscles in her neck slowly released the stranglehold they had on her throat, allowing her to breathe, refreshing the oxygen supply to her brain. "You nearly made me pass out!" Nervous laughter overcame her power of speech, leaving her alternately sobbing and retching.

"I am so sorry; it was not my intention to frighten you. We have been looking for you for days. I need to speak with you. We need to talk. It's my husband Isa, he is trying to kill me. I think he may be trying to kill us both!"

Bombshell dropped, the older woman just stopped, waiting for the enormity of what she had said to sink in.

“Izzy. Why? What earthly reason could he have to want us dead? Anyway, surely you mean ex-husband?” Natasha questioned.

“It’s a long story. I don’t know why he should see you as a threat but I know why he is after me. Firstly, I am still his wife, we were never divorced. I know that an attempt has been made on my life. I think attempts may have been made on your life too.”

Natasha was understandably confused; she hadn’t even thought about Izzy since she’d left him. She considered that part of her life over and forgotten. “I have no idea what you’re talking about, I’ve had no contact with Isa for years.”

“I know what’s happened to you, what you’ve been through. Are you so certain that Isa was not involved?”

Natasha thought about Brian, about the living hell he had put her through. The final seconds before she’d snuffed out his existence. “No, that had nothing to do with Isa, that was all to do with before we even met!”

“Are you so sure?” the woman asked.

Suddenly, a flashback ripped open the fabric of Natasha’s fragile psyche, she was propelled back to the fateful day she was abducted. Clearly, she could recall the day on the riverbank, with the 20/20 vision of hindsight, she could see the face of the woman who had enticed her there. It was a memory her brain had long suppressed, and the force of the revelation caused her to almost lose her balance. She caught hold of the fire escape to steady herself. “No! No!” She screamed, “No! It can’t be! It has to be over.” The older woman put her arms around her, pulled her into an awkward embrace in an attempt to give her strength.

Natasha was now sobbing uncontrollably. “Eve,” she sobbed, “it was Eve. Oh God, Izzy was behind it all along!” Retching uncontrollably now, Natasha was violently sick onto the pavement.

“Come Natasha, let us find somewhere quiet to talk. It is imperative that I tell you what I know, I may not get another opportunity.”

Anna guided a confused Natasha into a quiet tea shop, run by the Women’s Institute, just off the main street where it was quiet and subdued, unlike the bustling coffee shops in the precinct; a place they could talk and not be overheard.

With dainty cups of weak tea set on the table in front of them, and the elderly lady serving them twisting the knob on her hearing aid to the max just to hear whether or not they required sugar, they were assured the place was a good choice.

“So you were never divorced from Isa the whole time he was with me?”

“That is so. I left Isa when his behaviour became too intolerable. He married me to provide him with an heir, a light skinned Western son. A move he felt would buy him political credibility with his American allies. Unfortunately for him, and, with hindsight, fortuitous for me, I was barren and could not conceive."

"But you did give birth to Izzy's son; Mahmood is your son."

Anna gave Natasha a grave look. "Mahmood was not my son, he was Isa's son but not conceived with me."

"I don't understand, so whose child is Mahmood? Who and where is *his* mother?" She stared into Anna's face, uncomprehending.

"Mahmood lived with his mother and with his father. Isa and Mahmood shared the same mother!"

The weight of her answer sank in with Natasha. "Oh good God! Isa and his mother?"

"Yes, Natasha, with his own mother. Isa's father Hashim was a bad man, an evil man. He dominated the family, only married Isa's mother to humiliate her because she was a beautiful, proud woman. He got her father in some sort of trouble, and then took his youngest daughter as settlement. By the time Isa was a teenager his father had started courting a young woman from a wealthy family."

"So what led to Izzy having sex with his mother?"

"I don't know. I think by this time the old man must have hated them both. He forced the boy to commit the act."

"Forced him to rape his own mother?"

"I believe so."

"I am so confused by all you're telling me. Why didn't Izzy go to the police?"

"In an Islamic state Natasha, the boy's word against his father's would have been a waste of breath and his poor mother would possibly have been stoned to death."

"Not in Bahrain, they're not a bunch of savages in Bahrain?"

"Natasha my dear, you are quite naïve of the ways of the Middle East. Isa's mother is from Pakistan, from a remote primitive village. Without a husband she would be forced to seek refuge with her people. Her fate would have been stoning or suicide."

"Oh my God, this is all too much. Why are you telling me all this? You're making me a target!" Natasha suddenly appeared frail, vulnerable.

"I am sorry Natasha. I am sorry to burden you with all this trouble, but knowledge is power, and you were a target long before I shared with you what I know."

"I don't understand. Where is the father then? How come the old woman didn't get stoned?"

"Because Isa, the teenage boy, killed his father and took over as the patriarch, in league with Jalil, his younger brother. They killed him to protect the mother and their own inheritance. Now Isa wishes to kill me, because I know, and because he knows that I know!"

"I don't follow. I didn't have a clue until you just told me. Why would Isa want *me* dead? I had no idea."

"You must search yourself for the answer to that question, I am considered a 'loose end' which is why Isa wishes me 'tied off'. Just what he feels you may have on him is for you to discover."

"How do you know all this? How come you have all this information but are still alive to tell the tale?" Natasha questioned.

"I moved home to Holland. I am not a wealthy woman Natasha. I have no family and have lived all my life on the move, on barges, houseboats, lodged with friends, a settee here a caravan there. I have not been an easy target for Isa and I don't intend to become one."

"So how did you find out that he was after you?"

"My guardian angel, my little sister, in soul if not in blood, Aalia. We kept in touch through the Dutch consulate. It was Aalia who first confided in me about Mahmood and she who reached out to me when Isa conspired to have me killed."

"Oh Aalia. I do so miss her, how is she? Is she well?" Natasha inquired.

Anna's head tilted forward slightly, a tear welled in the corner of her heavily made up eye and set off on its journey down her cheek. She grasped Natasha's hands. "Aalia, my little Persian flower, I'm afraid she is dead, just as I would be had it not been for her timely forewarning."

"Why? How?" Natasha sobbed.

"I am so sorry Natasha, Mahmood, Aalia, her husband and children, the whole family were killed in a freak boating accident in Sharm El-Sheik, a trip organised by Jalil's elder brother, Isa."

"No, it can't be; Izzy could not harm his brother, kill his own son?"

"He could and he did, Natasha."

"How can you possibly know all this?" Natasha questioned.

"It was my very good fortune to be tracked down and contacted by a member of the Israeli secret police, the Mossad. They advised me against informing the Dutch authorities. Mossad believe that the Americans have interests which involve Isa, that he is protected by the Western powers. It isn't safe to speak to any of our own security forces as the CIA either control them or are at least monitoring them."

"This is all too ridiculous to be true. I can't believe that this man could be capable of all this, wiping out his whole family? He would have to be a monster."

"Isa is most certainly a monster, a callous, calculating monster," she continued. "Adiel Zeev is the name of my contact. He is a captain in the Mossad. It was he that organised my safe passage here to speak with you. He will be in touch with you himself presently, but wanted you to hear from me first."

"What does he want from me?" Natasha asked.

"I don't know Natasha, but I can tell you that this man has kept me from harm since we met, and I trust him, I suggest you do too."

"I don't know, I really don't know. I'm so confused."

"Natasha, take my advice: talk to this man and no other. Trust no one. It is my sincere belief that we cannot survive if Isa continues to live!"

As she drove towards home, Natasha's mind was turning over and over, processing the information, splicing it with what she remembered from her abduction. Suddenly, the pieces of the puzzle fell into place. *It was the rape, it had to be!* Mahmood, Izzy's son, had raped her; that was the 'loose end' which he needed to tie off. Why she had to die.

CHAPTER THREE

A problem shared

As Natasha approached the house, her attention was diverted to her nails; in all the excitement she'd forgotten about her appointment. She shook her head, surprised at the way her subconscious remembered the banal when she had matters of such importance on her mind.

As she approached the village, she was distracted by the flashing police lights. As she drew closer to the stone walls which marked the start of the Curland family estate, her worst fears were realised: the activity centred around their home.

Yellow police tape and the presence of a burly police officer prevented her from entering the gate. She noticed that the officer was armed.

"I'm sorry Madam, I'm afraid I cannot allow you inside the grounds. Would you mind stating your business?" he requested, with a hint of impatience.

"I'm Natasha Curland, this is my home! What's happened? My husband, my children, are they all right?"

The policeman could hear the anxiety in Natasha's voice, see the panic in her eyes. He moved quickly to reassure her.

"There are no casualties ma'am, Your husband and children are just fine. Give me a moment, I will get someone to come out and escort you inside."

The policeman spoke briefly on the radio, then beckoned to Natasha. "If I can just see some identification ma'am, an officer will be with us presently to escort you into the incident room."

Natasha, still in a state of shock, showed the officer her driving licence. A young female officer soon arrived at the gate and walked Natasha towards the white marquee which had hastily been erected on the lawn, down near the paddock, some 100 yards from the house.

"My husband and children are OK, you're sure?"

"Yes ma'am, quite sure, your husband and children are having a cup of tea in the incident room. They are a little shocked but the ambulance crew have checked them over and they are quite unhurt."

"Unhurt? Unhurt from what?" Natasha was clearly becoming quite anxious.

"There's been an explosion ma'am, quite a substantial one, we don't know what caused it but your family are lucky to be alive."

Natasha caught sight of Neil in the tent and ran towards him. Tears streamed from her eyes as they locked together in an embrace. Natasha knelt down and scooped up little David in one arm whilst wrapping her free arm around Monica.

Neil knelt beside her and whispered, "It was a bomb Natasha, a bloody huge bomb! It would have killed all three of us!"

"It was meant for me Neil, the bomb was meant for me!"

"What?" Neil exclaimed. "Why? How do you know it was meant for you?"

"Oh God Neil, I have so much to tell you. It was Isa, the man I left you for, the man that took me to Bahrain. It's Isa that wants me dead. It was always him!"

"What do you mean, it was always him?"

"Brian," Natasha whispered, making sure she didn't share her information with anyone but Neil. "Brian was being paid by Isa Al-Kooheji to kill me!"

CHAPTER FOUR

Tribal colours

Brodie pulled off the turnpike and onto the back roads which would take him and his wife Tarina home through the mountains. The weekend had been a blast. Partying with some old outlaw buddies down on the Mexican border. They had some five hundred miles to cover, but their bright red Harley-Davidson FLSTF Fat Boy trike was running like a dream as always. The sheer reliability of the machine allowed Brodie to relax, to let his thoughts meander back to life before the fateful day that Brian Dix burst into his life, running roughshod over everything he held dear, ruining the lives of those he cared for most, and leaving him a cripple.

The trike, and this new life, were also a part of the Brian Dix legacy. If not for Brian, Brodie would not have met his friend and business partner, Neil Curland. Neil and his wife Natasha had also suffered dearly at the hands of Brian Dix and it was this common enemy which had forged the solid friendship between them that had become Brodie's deliverance.

Between Fort Davis and Fort Stockton, Brodie encountered an eighteen wheeler, the driver frantically changing down through the gears to cope with the impending ascent. Brodie flicked the Kliktronic button on his left bar and the trike seamlessly selected a lower gear, allowing them to effortlessly power past the struggling behemoth.

Once clear of the obstacle, Brodie again drifted into the rhythm of the ride and allowed his mind to wander back into a nostalgic past.

The president of a notorious outlaw bike club, Brodie had been a man to fear and respect in equal measures, but it was a mantle which didn't always suit him. Joining an outlaw gang was a life commitment, especially a club with ties to a terrorist organisation, running protection and extortion rackets for the Provisional IRA. You died in your colours or you were thrown out and endured the humiliation of losing the cut, removing all club ink and being ostracised from your friends, your brothers, your family.

Brodie loved his club with a passion, loved his brothers, but he had a secret side; he loved a woman from outside of the lifestyle, a woman who wanted a different way of life from that offered by the outlaw creed. Brodie had kept her secret and Tarina loved him enough to be the mistress to his lawful wedded wife: the club.

Brian Dix changed everything. When he destroyed his life, crippled his body, the club stood by his decision to step down and walk away. They re-wrote the rule book out of respect for the great man, and allowed him to retire with full honours, sort of a chairman emeritus.

With his duties to the club absolved, Brodie was able to marry Tarina and take up Neil's offer of a legitimate business venture, and with Neil providing the venture capital from his highly successful 'Copper Road Choppers' business empire, 'Rhino Trikes' was launched, so named after Brodie's armour plated ability to survive onslaught against all odds.

The business had grown beyond their wildest dreams. Now with his beloved Tarina by his side and the continuing respect and friendship of his former 'brothers in arms', Brodie's life was sweeter than honey. He owed it all to the day fate led Neil Curland to his door.

CHAPTER FIVE

Reach out

"Warren, it's Neil."

"Howdy Neil, how the hell are you?" With typical Texan exuberance, Warren continued without giving Neil an opportunity to answer. "Hey Neil, that was a wise call investing in those computer graphics guys, we made a small fortune, didn't we just?"

"We did Warren, we did. Warren, I hate to be the bearer of bad news but we're in big trouble again."

"We? Who's the we Neil, you and me, or you and my favourite gal?" he asked.

"Well, it appears that Natasha's life is in danger again. There's been an attempt on our lives. They planted a huge bomb in the family car, Warren, wired through the seatbelt circuit, and backed up by a timer apparently. It nearly blew me and the kids to kingdom come. The MO had the hallmarks of an IRA hit."

"Oh Jesus Neil. Life was just settling back to fat and sassy. What have you got so far?"

"We'll need to get together for a pow-wow at some point Warren, there's so much to tell. In a nutshell: the guy Natasha was with in Bahrain, the one whose son raped and beat her, turns out that he is trying to kill her. He's made contact with IRA mercenaries, terrorists for hire. He's taken out a hit on Natasha."

"Jesus Neil, why's that crazy bullbat trying to kill our gal?"

"He's trying to guarantee silence Warren, we think it's connected with his son's crime, not too sure of the whats and whys but it's connected with a secret our man's keen to keep."

"A secret worth killing for? Just how big is this secret?"

"It would appear that our Arab indulged an Oedipus complex which resulted in his handicapped son."

"Hell, Neil, incestuous mother fucker." Warren exclaimed.

"Quite, there's much more too Warren. It turns out that our Mr Kooheji was the driving force behind Brian Dix too."

"Jesus Neil, he's on a first-name basis with the bottom of the deck."

"Could you have a poke around Warren, maybe knock up a few of your pet agents, politicians and the like, see what they've got on this character, who his friends are, who his enemies are?"

"Sure thing Neil, you got it. Can you fax me over everything you know so I've something to start with? Maybe get a crime report over or at least a crime number so my people can find out what your people know."

"Consider it on the way Warren. I need to speak to Goose and Brodie. Brodie has history with the IRA, he may have some ideas."

"Give me a few days to poke around Neil, then we should get together, maybe get all the players together in a safe place to discuss what we've found and what we do about it."

"Will do Warren. If I haven't heard from you in a few days, I'll give you a shout."

"Tell Natasha to hang tough Neil, you tell her that we're all rooting for her."

"I will Warren. You're a real friend you know. Natasha worships you."

"With everything that gal's been through, Neil, I reckon she has a red carpet ceremony waiting for her at the pearly gates."

"You know my religious leanings Warren, but whoever's right, let's hope that's a long way off yet."

"Amen to that Neil."

Neil rang Goose immediately after his conversation with Warren.

"Hey Neil, how goes it?" his best friend asked.

Neil brought Goose up to speed on recent events.

"Jesus Neil, the shit never stops hitting your poor wife does it?"

"This is it Goose, the final showdown. Natasha can't take anymore. This is more than any one person should ever have to face. This bastard needs to go down and go down hard."

"I'm going to clear my diary Neil. I've got a few ideas, need to put my thinking cap on, but I reckon we should organise a safe, secure place to meet up where we can plan. Leave it with me, I'll ring around and call in a few favours."

After replacing the receiver, Neil placed a call to Brodie, who immediately suggested he reach out to a high ranking former contact of his within the Provisional Irish Republican Army to see if he could at least confirm or deny their involvement.

CHAPTER SIX

Outreach

"Mr Doherty? It's Brodie. Thank you for taking my call."

"Think nothing of it Mr Brodie, we have a long history of cooperation, it would be disloyal of me to refuse a hearing to an old friend."

"It's regarding a good friend of mine Mr Doherty, a valued friend whose life I believe is in considerable danger."

"Oh, to whom do you refer Mr Brodie? If I might be so bold as to ask."

Brodie's voice dropped to hushed tones, almost a whisper, "Natasha Curland, the wife of my good friend and business partner, Neil Curland."

"Ah, I thought that may be the party you were referring to." Doherty paused a while and considered his next words carefully. "Now Brodie, can I not persuade you to look out for number one and let this matter resolve itself?"

"I'm afraid not Mr Doherty. You see, these people have come to mean a great deal to me and to hurt them is to hurt me."

"Have you ever been to Dublin Mr Brodie? 'Tis a beautiful city to be sure. We should meet, talk face to face, you should come and visit, as my guest."

"Thank you Mr Doherty, I will make arrangements to pay you a visit."

“No need Mr Brodie, I’ll make all the arrangements, you just wait for my call.”

“Even better, until then Mr Doherty.”

“I’ll look forward to finally meeting you in person Mr Brodie.”

Brodie’s recent medical history, a consequence of which was the need to fly around the world to visit the best consultants and surgeons money could buy, meant that his travel documents were all up to date.

Brodie decided not to inform Neil of his plans, best to see if he could achieve anything before giving false hope.

A week had passed since the conversation with Doherty. Brodie was up, shaved and ready to face a normal day at the workshop. Tarina had already left for her job at the nearby hospital. Brodie had given her as much information as he dared regarding his impending trip so that she would not panic if he suddenly disappeared without explanation.

As he fumbled with the key in the lock of his front door, he was startled by the two shady figures flanking him. Turning quickly, he recognised one of the characters immediately as a contact in the IRA fundraising charity ‘Nor-Relief’. They had done business before in the past. “Tommy, how the hell are you man? it’s been a lifetime.”

“I’m good Brodie, so I am. This here’s Sean, he’ll be seeing you all the way to Dublin, I’m just along for the ride and to introduce you two lads so there's no misunderstandings. We're to put you straight on a plane as ye' are Brodie, no cases no nothing, so if we can get ourselves off now we'll have our jobs done all the sooner."

"I need my medication, there's stuff I need to carry for the leg." Brodie tapped his prosthetic limb to emphasise.

"Your passport is all you can take Brodie. Bring a prescription, anything you need will be provided for you in Dublin."

The pair accompanied Brodie back into the house where he picked up his passport and shoved it into his pocket.

"I'm real sorry Brodie, but yer' to be sedated all the way to Dublin for yer' own safety. Will yer' go down willingly or do I have to get mean?" Tommy showed Brodie the Taser gun.

"Just get it done Tommy, I'll go willingly."

"Good lad, yer' know it makes sense." Sean produced a syringe full of a clear liquid while Tommy, still brandishing the Taser, held his distance.

After a few moments, the sedative hit its mark and Brodie had to hastily lie down on the couch before he fell down.

Within minutes, Tommy had made a quick call and a US Army ambulance, complete with two soldiers in hospital whites, arrived at the door and they bundled an unconscious Brodie onto a hospital gurney.

With military precision, Brodie was expedited to a USAF air base and on to a waiting medi-vac flight. Within a few hours he was leaving the United States and en-route to Ireland without a solitary question asked, such was the reach of the Provisional IRA.

"Mr Brodie. I am so pleased to finally meet you in person."

"Not really the friendly meeting I was expecting Mr Doherty."

Brodie was sitting in a crude NHS style wheelchair; his prosthetic leg had been removed and was nowhere in the near vicinity.

"Can I please have my leg back Mr Doherty? It is making me very uncomfortable sitting here like this."

"All in good time Mr Brodie, you sitting there makes us able to have an initial conversation without the need for other distractions."

Brodie looked around the room he had just been wheeled into, there were no windows to be seen, the room was air conditioned and comfortable, but Brodie sensed it could be used for more sinister covert means if the need were justified.

"Mr Doherty," Brodie began.

"Please Brodie, call me Kieren, we're all good friends now."

"Kieren," he started over.

"Now what shall I call you Mr Brodie, now that we're all on cosy first name terms? Brodie, Mr

Brodie, it's all so formal, why don't I already know your Christian name?"

Brodie looked uncomfortable for a moment, then offered, "I ain't got a Christian name, I'm just Brodie, always has been."

"You must have a Christian name Brodie, what does it say on your passport?"

Doherty held Brodie's passport up to the artificial light and scrutinised it. "How very odd, it says Christian name 'Blank', am I to take it you were Christened 'Blank Brodie'?"

Brodie's face took on a stoic grimace. "Story is, my mom, she was raped when she was a young girl. Being a good Catholic girl, she couldn't go having no abortion, but she didn't want no rapist's kid neither. Brodie was the name of some young beau she was sweet on so she gave me that as a name. Anyway, she couldn't get the monster child out of her quick enough by all accounts, already decided to give me up as a ward of the church. When she filled out the birth certificate they said you gotta put something in as a Christian name, my mom said this ain't no Christian birth so they can leave it blank. Well, seems they insisted she put something in, so she wrote Blank."

Doherty, who was captivated by this little piece of Brodie trivia said, "So she never relented and you've gone by the name Brodie ever since?"

"She left me at the hospital and ran off, three weeks later they fished her out of the Brazos River. Kids' homes and foster homes give me a few names, nothing really stuck, just Brodie."

"Well, I can't call you Blank, so Brodie it is then. So down to business Brodie. What do you want from me?"

"You have a hit out on Natasha Curland. I'd like to know why you want her dead and what I have to do to convince you to let her live."

"Well, I must say, I respect your candour Brodie, right to the point. In return, I'm not going to waste your time with the 'he said, she said' nonsense; I'm going to give you the straight answers you seek."

"Thank you."

"The information I am going to give you is for your ears only. If any word gets back to the authorities then our friendship is terminated, and I mean terminated."

Brodie nodded an affirmative.

"Mrs Curland is not an enemy of the army and as such, we have no reason or purpose to want her dead, however, our former acquaintance, Mr Brian Dix, entered into an arrangement with a third party to carry out a termination on the young Mrs Curland, which we are now honour bound to fulfil. So do you see my dilemma here Brodie?"

"You're the Boss; can't you just call off the hit?"

"Call off the hit? No I'm afraid that I cannot. Even in the unlikely event of my death, the hit would still take place. The army has many heads you see Brodie, you cut off one, another one is ready to take its place. The army is changing Brodie. Since the peace talks, the politicos and the foot soldiers are starting to see our futures separating, along the lines of those that seek a peaceful solution, and those that see no future for themselves in a united Ireland. What does a soldier do when there's no war to fight? We are a huge organisation Brodie, with a reach which would astound you. Now, if we lose the cause which binds us, we will need a new cause to rally behind."

"Surely you can just lay down your arms and go home if the cause is won?" Brodie questioned.

"Go home? These are men of violence we are talking about Brodie, men of the gun and the bomb; what are they to do in a peaceful Ireland? Well the situation is this: the army is already starting to fragment into smaller cells, these cells think of themselves as the 'real' IRA, they consider the politicos, their peace talks and talks of a ceasefire to be selling us down the street. To your problem in hand Brodie, a cell has been given the task to carry out the termination of your friend, this cell is now off the radar until the task has been completed. No one from the organisation can contact this cell now, and they won't resurface until the task is completed."

"So nobody can call off the hit then," Brodie said.

"I didn't say that. There's always a way. Each cell works to certain protocols my friend. The person who can call off the hit is the client who arranged the hit in the first instance."

"So you're saying it's impossible to cancel the hit, so I can't save my friend's life?"

"What I am saying is that you can't stop the hit from here, you must go to the source, the client, he has a code and a protocol. With that, you can stop the hit."

"How the hell do I find out who the client is to stop the hit?"

"Well, you could start by asking me."

"Could it possibly be that simple?"

"Brodie, I am not a mercenary and the army is not a gun for hire. We are principled men fighting a legitimate cause. We made a genuine mistake with Brian Dix, I made a genuine mistake, and we have both paid the price. I personally am a man of peace; I would like myself and the army painlessly extracted from this whole situation, you just might be my salvation. Now come along, I will re-unite you with your missing leg, and then one of my subordinates will take you on a whistlestop tour of the sights of Dublin. I will see to it that you have a name to take back to the USA with you, somewhere you can start."

"That's mighty kind of you Kieren."

"Don't mention it Brodie, I am only sorry you didn't manage to terminate Brian Dix before he did so much harm. He killed a lot of US nationals, that's not good for the cause stateside, not good at all."

"It was Natasha that put a stop to him."

"Well good for her! I sincerely hope you manage to save the plucky lady Brodie, I really do."

"Can you give me an idea when the next attempt on her life might be?"

"That depends on how close they are to her now. I would imagine, with the expected increased security precautions, for sure it'll be a month or two before the cell will have gathered the necessary intelligence to act. If by then the client has not delivered the protocol to cancel, the hit, it'll be carried out. The only other way to prevent the hit is to completely destroy the cell."

"I figure that would be a long shot," Brodie replied.

"I'm inclined to agree with you on that. My men are highly trained and highly motivated."

"Thank you again for your help Kieren, I sure do hope it will lead to Natasha's salvation. Poor gal sure has seen her share of winters."

"There's a little fly in the ointment though to be sure my friend."

Brodie looked puzzled. "What'd you mean by that?"

"Well, you see Brodie, that little bomb incident on the mainland, the one that nearly killed your friend and his wee kiddies?"

"Uh huh."

"Well you see, 'twasn't ours."

"You're kidding me?"

"I swear to God Brodie. It had our marks all over it, so it did, but it wasn't us. Your man is playing some sort of a double bluff so he is. You're going to have your work cut out to stop this going down I can tell you."

“Christ almighty.”

“Aye, you could make a start by praying to him for guidance to be sure.”

“Truth be told, I don’t know where to start.”

“Start with the name I give you. He’s the lad that made contact with us, he has to be somewhere in the inner circle. Good luck to you Brodie, I fear you’re going to need it.”

CHAPTER SEVEN

Anna

Anna Bergkamp alighted the Olau Line ferry at the Rotterdam port. The trip to England had been risky. She had followed the advice and the route supplied by her captain from the Israeli Mossad, nevertheless, she knew that her every visible move was potentially fatal. The trip to England had been necessary. Natasha Curland was wealthy; she and her husband were high profile. Surely with her wealth and social position, she would not be so simple to eliminate. Perhaps with their power and influence, and the help from her Mossad contact, they would be able to turn the tables on Isa Hashim Al-Kooheji.

Back on Dutch soil, she would once again be able to blend into the undergrowth. Anna had been quite an active member of the eighties 'New Age traveller' movement, thus she was able to fall back on a comprehensive network of Bohemian friends, all similarly 'unplugged' from society as she.

Her passport safely stowed, Anna knew to buy all tickets and travel warrants from here on in strictly cash, no paper trail. The carefully laid plan was for her to get a train across Holland towards the German border. She had some friends living off the land near Roermond, they would ask no questions and with the German border patrols and the British Air Force stationed so close by, it would make the task of tracking her down as difficult as possible. In an emergency, the British forces could be relied upon to help a member of the Mossad with few complicated questions asked. She had a forty minute wait for her train, so decided to eat before the journey. As she walked towards the café at the terminal, a commuter train arrived at the station. The commuters all seemed to have the same thing in mind as Anna, and the seats in the small café were soon swallowed up.

The vending machines seemed a better bet and Anna was soon engrossed in the search for coins at the bottom of her purse. Some sort of scuffle momentarily distracted her and a young man fell or was pushed into her, knocking the wind from her lungs. As he apologised profusely in some foreign language, Anna felt a sharp ache in her chest as if she had been punched hard in the ribs. She held the side of the vending machine for support. The pain was increasing, she tried to cry out but the pain was too severe, crushing the air from her chest. Anna felt the breath sucked from her lungs as she fell to the floor. The station became very dark and cold as she slipped into unconsciousness.

The young man casually stowed the passport and purse he had 'dipped' from the woman during the scuffle stage of the exercise before wiping any residual prints from the handle of the stiletto switch blade with a tissue. After wiping the blood from his hands, he casually dropped the weapon and cloth into the concrete culvert before seamlessly disappearing into the bustling commuter crowd.

CHAPTER EIGHT

Warren

Following his conversation with Neil, Warren rang a friend of his. Samuel Frobisher was an FBI agent of some repute. He had been involved in the Watergate investigations, and the resulting resignation of President Nixon saw Sam catapulted up the ranks within the agency. If there was a whisper on the grapevine, you could bet that Sam had an ear to it.

"Sam, it's Warren Bateson. I need your help again, do you mind if I get straight to the point?"

"Well, hello to you too Warren. We're both busy men, please do. Fire away," the agent replied.

"It's with regards to my friends the Curlands again; there's been another attempt on their lives."

"I thought we'd put all that to bed?"

"So did we Sam, so did we."

"So what have we got? Was the attack here?" he asked.

"No, it was at their home; a bomb. All the hallmarks of an IRA hit, or so the British think anyway."

"You want to know what we think?" Sam anticipated.

"You're the best place I know of to start Sam," Warren replied.

"Leave it with me, I'll knock on some doors, see what I can find."

“Thanks Sam, just don’t dig up more snakes than you can kill.”

Sam laughed at his friend’s colourful turn of phrase. “You’re a card Warren. I’ll see what I can do without stirring the hornets too much.”

A couple of days passed before Sam had something concrete to report.

“Warren? It’s Sam. Listen, this business with the Curlands, I’ve done some poking around, I’ve gotta tell you, this is a whole can of worms. I’ve found out stuff I’d sooner not have known. We’d better meet up.”

“You free this afternoon Sam?” Warren asked.

“Yeah Warren, I’ll make myself free. We need to get this on the table soonest so we can decide the best thing to do.”

“Hey, calm down Sam, you’re scaring me!” Warren advised.

“This is some scary stuff my friend,” he replied.

“Well let us put on our sitting britches and chaw the rag,” Warren replied in his inimitable Texan way.

This time, Warren’s humour failed to raise a smile. “I’ll come to you Warren OK?”

“OK Sam. See you soon.”

It was a little after three in the afternoon that the two men sat down in the privacy of Warren’s New York office.

"So what do you have for me Sam?" Warren asked, starting the ball rolling.

"It's got all the hallmarks of a terrorist bombing Warren, the British are looking to the IRA."

"What about you Sam, where are you looking?"

"She's not a legitimate IRA target, Warren, that must be obvious to anyone. The IRA would not mount such an audacious attack just to avenge the killing of a mercenary, a man who wasn't even a soldier to the cause."

"You're confirming what I already know; can you tell me something I don't know?"

"You're a perceptive man Warren; you should've joined the Bureau yourself."

"When you've read as many detective story scripts as I have Sam, some of it's bound to stick."

"OK my friend, I'm going to give you what I know."

"Fire away."

"What I've discovered Warren is a thread, tied to a piece of string, tied to a rope which is tied to a cable."

"I don't follow my friend."

"The Irish have been contracted to assassinate your friend Natasha Curland. She lived for a time in the Middle East, Bahrain and later Saudi Arabia to be precise."

"Yes, I was aware of that."

“Well, it appears that she was paid a large amount of money to go away, and to keep her mouth shut about something, something which would prove embarrassing for an important individual, a gentleman who is becoming something of a rising star in Middle Eastern politics. For whatever reason, this gentleman has decided to make doubly sure that his secret remains safe.”

“Good God almighty!”

“Moreover, it would appear that this same individual was the force behind Brian Dix and his clumsy attempts at taking Ms Curland out before.”

“How the hell did you discover this Sam?”

“The agency hides its biggest secrets out in the open Warren; they just don’t expect anyone to look.”

“With a heavy heart, Warren picked up the receiver and rang the private number of Dan Ruthers, his CIA contact. He hadn’t had much contact with him since Natasha’s abduction. “Howdy Dan, it’s Warren Bateson, I’m afraid I need your help again.”

“Warren, long time no speak. What can I do for you my friend?”

“Can we meet up Dan? I need to talk to you regarding a grave matter. I think we need a ‘face to face’.”

“Sure thing Warren, get your people to pencil you in some free time and we’ll do lunch.”

"I can do better than that, you just give me a day and a time, I'll be there."

"Hell, Warren, it sure must be important if you don't have to schedule, how's Wednesday afternoon look for you?"

"It's a matter of life and death. Wednesday will do just fine Dan. Time and place?"

"I'll get us some reservations someplace close and cosy where we can talk discretely. I'm guessing this matter will require discretion?"

"I guess so Dan. Thank you for giving me a hearing."

"Hey, think nothin' of it Warren, a friend in need and all that. I'll ring you when I have a there and then."

Warren rang to persuade Sam to accompany him on a trip to the capital to meet with Dan Ruthers.

"I don't know Warren," Sam protested. "This stuff is top drawer, are you sure this guy can be trusted?"

"Sam, I've known Dan Ruthers since he was half as big as a minute. He's one of my most trusted friends."

"I hope you're right, the biggest scandals start small and I fear we may be right at the beginning of this one! Gotta be real careful who we trust, you hear what I'm saying?" Sam cautioned.

"I hear you Sam, but I'm telling you, Dan's one of the good guys."

"OK Warren, I'm with you. I'll put a dossier together of what we've discovered so far, we can let your friend have a look-see."

They decided to take the Amtrak down to the capital a day early, get a good night's sleep before their meeting with Dan. His friend could knock back the scotch, and enjoyed the company of a drinking partner. Warren knew he was a difficult man to refuse, especially when you were the one asking the favour.

Acting on the CIA man's suggestion, Warren booked himself and Sam rooms at the hotel they would be lunching in. Dan had ordered a table for three thirty PM so an afternoon in the company of Mr Jim Beam and Mr Jack Daniels was clearly on the cards.

Dressed casually, Warren was a stark contrast to his friend Dan who appeared in a suit of plain black, sporting the regulation mirror shades; he couldn't have looked more CIA if he'd been wearing the logo across his back.

He offered his right hand in a formal handshake. Warren, now more accustomed to the tactile nature of his genial 'biker' friends, pulled the smaller man into a hearty embrace.

"Dan the man, how the hell are you? How's that growing family of yours?"

Initially surprised by the intimacy, Dan soon returned the gesture and patted Warren on the shoulder. "Great, Warren, just great. Grandkids are coming in thick and fast now! Tell truth, I'm looking forward to my retirement soon, so's I can spend a bit more time with them, and you? How's my best girl Nell, she still keeping the great man's feet on solid ground?"

"She is Dan; my rock as ever, girls are good too, though we never seem to see them these days, got their own families and careers to occupy them I guess."

"You want to get down to business before we eat Warren? After the meal I intend to drink you under the table, so if you've serious issues to discuss, best we start now."

Warren looked over to the bar and gestured for Sam to join them. "I hope you don't mind, I invited my friend Sam to join us. He's a pretty shrewd FBI agent, and he's uncovered some important intelligence which I think you need to hear."

"Hey Warren, the more the merrier and the bigger your bar bill my friend," Dan sniggered.

Sam joined them at the table, and shook hands with Dan as the introductions were made.

"It's about my unfortunate friend Natasha again I'm afraid, Dan. It seems we only cut off the snake's tail with that messy business back along, the head is still mighty determined to kill her," Warren began.

"Yea, I figured as much Warren, I did a little digging after we spoke, I understand there's been a pretty serious attempt on her life, nearly took out her whole family by all accounts."

"I'll let Sam talk you through what he's managed to uncover, then we'll see if it rings any alarm bells with you. I'd try to bring you up to speed but you know what I'm like; my tongue would get caught in my eyeteeth and I wouldn't see what I was saying."

The two strangers grinned at each other in response to Warren's babbling, then Sam showed Dan the dossier and filled him in on what he'd been able to uncover.

When Sam had finished his delivery, Warren asked, "Where do we stand on all this Dan?"

"Well that's the thing Warren, the US has a vested interest in this Middle Eastern gentleman's endeavours. He is what you might call a 'friend of the state'."

"So what can I do to help my friend, Dan?"

"Nothing Warren. You have no cards to play. You've put all of us at considerable risk just by poking around the way you have. There's no one here in the agency that will help you. I can only tell you that if you walk away from this now, you will be safe and your life will continue on as before. If you dig around this anymore, speak to your friends in Congress, or be seen to be involved in any way, they will crush you, and that goes for your friend too."

"Dan, are you for real? We've been friends for years, I know your family, your kids grew up with mine, are you really threatening me?"

"Forgive me Warren, I'm trying my best to protect a good friend, and myself. This goes a very long way. The sums of money, power and influence involved are greater than even you can imagine; billions of dollars. When sums like that are flowing, it's easy for a lot of lives to be swept away by the current; I'm trying to protect you from becoming a victim. If I have to threaten you to do that, I will."

Warren's demeanour softened slightly. "I understand Dan, it's just taken me a little by surprise. I don't see how I can just walk away from this though, this woman means a hell of a lot to me, you know that."

"I do know that, but my loyalty is to you big guy, I know what you're up against here and I'll do all in my power to protect you even if it means I have to protect you from yourself."

Warren and Sam shot furtive glances at one another. This was an unexpected turn of events, one that would have to be handled cautiously. For now, Warren decided to keep Dan onside and continue with the friendly reunion, he and Sam could carry out the autopsy later, in private.

"Thanks Dan, you are a true friend."

"Yes I am Warren, now come on, let's get ordering, I've got a raging thirst on after all that talking."

Sam excused himself from the table to return his papers to the room safe. "Won't be a tick guys. Order me a steak medium."

Dan waved his finger in the air. A waiter soon scurried over and the first of many trays of bourbon soon followed.

Sam soon returned to the table. After the meal Dan switched taste to Tennessee whiskey, and a further couple of trays were devoured. Sam was looking the worse for wear. Warren, whose considerable size gave him an advantage in the constitution stakes, excused himself from the table to help Sam up to his room.

"Just you be sure to come back down, d'yuh hear? I ain't sitting down here with just Jack and Jim fer company, d'yuh hear? Nothin' worse than a lonely drunk," Dan slurred.

By the time he had Sam safely tucked into bed, Warren was feeling the room spinning. He felt his legs may give way at any second. Forgetting his promise to Dan, he made for the lift and his own room, absent-mindedly tucking Sam's key into his pocket as he left the room.

Inside his own room, Warren felt his throat was constricting, making breathing difficult and laboured. He wrenched open the mini bar and quickly devoured a bottle of Perrier water from inside the door shelf. The room began to slowly spin. He slumped to the floor beside the bed and passed out.

Hours later, Warren woke up. He was in bed. The room was still spinning and his head felt like he'd been kicked by an ornery mule.

As his senses slowly woke up, he became aware of the musky smell of the room, he could sense that he hadn't spent the night alone. His torso felt sticky, almost greasy to the touch. He felt under the covers, felt his genitals. An unfamiliar feeling made him throw back the covers in shock. His entire groin area was crusted with dried blood. In shock, he staggered to the bathroom, feeling suddenly overpowered by the need to vomit. Turning the hot and cold taps on full pelt, he cupped the water in his hands and splashed his face intermittently from the stream of both faucets.

As his head began to clear, logic and reason began to function once again and he began to wash his genitals clean with the flannel, fully expecting to find some sort of injury to his person to explain the considerable quantity of dried blood.

Preoccupied with his self-examination, he didn't notice the mirror steaming up from the vapour rising from the hot faucet. Confused but satisfied that he was wound free, his attention was caught by an out of place reflection in the distorted steam covered surface of the mirror. Wiping the glass with the flannel, his mind at first refused to acknowledge what it registered. He slowly turned, hoping that the image was nothing more than a strange mirage.

Lying in the bathtub, half submerged in crimson coloured water lay the body of a girl. She couldn't have been much more than thirteen or fourteen years of age. She was naked, and she was quite dead.

The retching began deep down in the pit of his stomach. It was all he could do to reach the toilet bowl before the contents of his guts were deposited into the white porcelain receptacle.

"Oh dear God, what is happening to me?" he called out, half cry, half whisper. His innate sense of right and wrong meant that his next action was second nature; he reached for the phone to alert the emergency services.

Propped up against the receiver, demanding his immediate attention was a brown paper envelope bearing the simple inscription, 'open me'. Inside the envelope were a number of full colour photos, crisp, well lit and in focus, there was no mistaking that the naked man in the photos was himself, there was also no mistaking what he was doing, and to whom he appeared to be doing it. The girl looked different in life, smaller, her youthful skin looked much darker, Hispanic or possibly Latino. The photos were quite graphic in nature, one implied that Warren was having penetrative sex with the girl; another showed her allegedly performing fellatio on him.

After the initial shock wore off, Warren examined the photos more closely, none of them showed his facial expressions, although it was clear to see who it was, it was unclear as to whether the man was actually consciously performing or whether the whole thing was staged.

On the back of one of the photos was written, 'Ring ext 201'.

Warren quickly dressed, then picked up the receiver to place the call. As he sat on the chair by the phone, he felt the key in his pocket. "Oh Jesus Christ, Sam."

Warren slipped out of his room and took the elevator to the relevant floor. He hurriedly ran along the corridor to Sam's room. Letting himself in, the room was in darkness. It was deathly silent; Warren could only hear his own breathing, his own heartbeat. "Sam? Sam?" He called out, hoping for the best and fearing the worst.

He switched on the light and crossed the room to the bed.

Sam was lying on his back under the covers, eyes and mouth open but seeing nothing. In the corners of his mouth were traces of dried saliva and blood. Warren touched his face, he was stone cold.

"Oh God no Sam. I'm so sorry," he cried.

Thinking on his feet, Warren went over to the closet where the room safe was. The safe key was on the room key. Warren turned the lock, the dossier was still there. He stuffed it inside his jacket and inserted the key into the inside lock. Shutting the door behind him, he returned to his own room, picked up the brown envelope, and rang the number written on it.

"Warren?"

"Dan, you son of a bitch, what have you done?"

"It's you that's done something Warren, haven't you seen?"

"That girl Dan, so young, why?"

"Walk away Warren, just walk away. Keep your mouth shut and this all goes away."

"Dan, you bastard, this won't work, you drugged me, there'll be traces in my system, there are experts who can tell those photos are staged. I'm going to have a dozen agents here as soon as I hang up this phone, I'll hang you out to dry, expose you for the double crossing bastard you are."

"Listen to me Warren, that corpse in there has a belly full of your DNA, you will have a hard time talking your way around the circumstantial evidence. What's going to happen if you call anyone is that you're going to be in the city jail by nightfall. By tomorrow, you'll be found dead, hung by the neck from your bed sheets; you won't even have a chance to call your hot- shot lawyers. Sure, there'll be charges to answer, a few cops will be reprimanded for failing to follow protocol, but you'll be dead, another high profile murdering paedophile dead. Is that what you want your fans, your family, to think? Is that the legacy you want to leave Nell?"

"Dan, I can't believe it, we were friends, I thought we were real friends?"

"Warren, this scenario was my idea, I set it all up. I had to beg them to let me try to get you to back off, this was the one scenario which left you breathing, do you understand?"

"What about Sam? He knows what you've done; he'll put two and two together," Warren said, his acting as convincing as his best ever performance.

"Sam won't be putting anything together Warren, not now, not ever," Dan growled.

"You've killed him? You bastard Dan, Sam has a wife and children."

"He has a widow and orphaned children. Nell will be a widow too if you don't let this drop Warren."

"Dan, I talked Sam into coming here, I told him he could trust you," Warren reasoned, close to tears.

"Yeah, and that got him killed Warren. *You* got him killed."

"Don't put this on to me Dan, this is about you. It's about greed. You know me well enough to know that I would sooner have sacrificed my own life than to cost Sam and that poor gal in the bathtub theirs!"

"I'm not in it for money Warren, I'm afraid I sold my soul to the Devil a long time ago. I'm in it, and I can't get out, just the same as you are now. This is it Warren, walk away, I make all this go away and when the people have got what they want, all record of this sorry state of affairs is expunged and you and I get to enjoy our retirement with our families. This'll all just be a bad memory."

"And Natasha?"

"Not my concern Warren. I hope she gets lucky and finds herself another Prince Charming to save her. As long as it ain't you or me, then it ain't my concern."

Warren's next question sealed the deal, as soon as he uttered it Dan thought that he had him.

"Who was she Dan?"

"She was nobody, a two bit runaway junkie street whore who'd sell her ass for the price of the next fix. She wouldn't have seen her next birthday Warren, you can be sure of that."

"Did I touch her?"

"No Warren, you had no real physical contact with her, you've nothing to be ashamed about or to concern yourself with on that score."

"Then how?"

"I don't want to get too gruesome, let's just say, there's a sample of your man juice inside her and some on ice for the crime report if you don't cooperate. You will cooperate though won't you Warren?"

"I will."

"Goodbye Warren. Don't attempt to contact Neil and Natasha Curland. If they contact you, you are to say nothing, just say that you can't help. You're being watched Warren, every move you make, every call you place. Don't try to be smart, just go home; go home to your wife. Make some movies, live your life."

Warren took one last long look at the poor wretch in the bathtub before gathering his things together in his overnight case and picking up the room key. Just as he turned to leave, he looked back at the photos on the bed, he thought to leave them for Ruthers' clean-up crew to dispose of, but thinking better of it, he gathered them up and stowed them in the pocket of his sports jacket, with the dossier he'd taken from Sam's safe.

As he left the room, a subconscious thought came to Warren with the clarity of an epiphany. Suddenly he knew exactly what to do, even if he didn't know why.

He rode the elevator down to the first floor. From there, he took the stairs to the underground parking garage. Security lights and cameras were employed covering the vehicle entrances and exits, other than that the garage was dim, devoid of too much natural light and away from prying eyes. Scouting around quickly, he found a car in a corner slot with the hood still warm; a good indication that the car had arrived recently, and logically, wouldn't be moving away again too soon. He stowed his overnight bag between the concrete wall and the radiator grill and made his way to the street exit of the garage. Keeping to the pedestrian walk ways, he was pretty sure he'd stayed out of the coverage of the security cameras. Once outside, he ran across the busy intersection to a hotel on the other side of the block. Once inside, he casually strolled over to the reception desk and asked the receptionist for a postage stamp and an envelope. The purchase concluded, Warren sat down in the lobby to collect his thoughts. After a brief moment of contemplation he returned to the reception desk and requested a Beverly Hills telephone book, a number of stamps and a medium sized padded mailer bag. Searching quickly, he found the phone number and address of 'Fizzy Door Productions', a company he and Neil had invested in back before Natasha was kidnapped. After writing a brief summary of the last twenty four hours' events on the back of one of the incriminating prints, he inserted the photos and the dossier into the envelope. Sealing it up, he wrote 'For the attention of Neil Curland' on the front and placed the entirety into the padded bag. On the front of this he wrote the address of 'Fizzy Door Productions', and slipped a note inside, telling them to wait for further instructions before forwarding the sealed envelope to Neil.

"Excuse me Miss," Warren said to the receptionist, "would you have any idea how many stamps I need to send this package to Beverly Hills?"

"I'll be glad to weigh it and put it through our franking machine for you if you like Mr Bateson," she replied.

"I'd just as soon post it myself if you could just tell me how much postage to put on it," Warren replied, cursing his notoriety.

With the package sporting a little more than enough stamps, Warren left the hotel lobby, made for the first mail box en-route and deposited it into the safe hands of Uncle Sam's postal service. For the first time in the last twenty four hours, Warren felt as though he had a little control over events, and it felt good.

Slipping back into the parking garage, Warren retrieved his overnight bag, climbed the stairs back up to the first floor and rode the elevator back down to the ground floor lobby.

As he stepped out of the elevator in the lobby, he was met, just as he had suspected, by an agent, dressed as a VIP limo driver who told him he was instructed to take him to the airport terminal where he was to take a direct flight back to Austin and await further instructions.

At the terminal, Warren could normally expect the full hospitality of the VIP suite and a hassle free trip through airport security. This time however, things were decidedly abnormal.

Two homeland security agents singled Warren out and approached him with the stereotypical, "Could you come with us please sir?"

"What's going on?" Warren asked.

"Could you please come with us sir?" they reiterated, trying to remain discrete.

"What's going on?" Warren enquired, his voice rising in volume. "What are you doing? Do you know who I am? I'm Warren Bateson, I'm a goddamn important person. Who the hell do you think you are, manhandling me?"

Warren was now playing to the audience, making sure he had at least a dozen VIP witnesses should proceedings turn sour.

He was separated from his overnight bag and sat down in a small interview room where he was asked to turn out his pockets before surrendering to a more thorough search.

When the search failed to reveal a thing out of place, the more senior of the homeland security officers asked, "Sir, where are the documents?"

Warren allowed himself the satisfaction of a slight grin and answered, "I don't know what you're talking about."

Warren was soon escorted on to his flight back to Austin.

He hadn't been home more than an hour when the phone rang. It was Neil.

"Hi Neil." Warren sounded subdued, distant.

"Hi Warren, do you have anything for me?"

"Sorry Neil, I've got nothing," Warren remarked coldly. "Nobody has anything on your man Neil. Sorry I couldn't help."

"Are you OK Warren, is everything OK?" Neil asked, concerned.

The Texan replied, "I'm fine Neil. I'm just a little bummed about that investment you talked me into; I lost a packet. You tell Natasha that I'll be praying for her. I know you'll be praying for her too. I've gotta go now buddy, I'll catch up with you sometime. Speak again soon." Warren put the phone down.

Neil was somewhat perplexed, but he knew without a shadow of a doubt that Warren was telling him he'd been compromised and that his own life was possibly at risk.

CHAPTER NINE

Adiel Zeev

With the main house still bomb damaged, the Curlands were temporarily living in the granny annex.

The policeman on detail at the gate rang through to the cottage. "Mr Curland, we have a gentleman here by the name of Adiel Zeev. He claims to have an appointment to speak to you and your wife."

"Are you sure he's who he says he is?" Neil questioned.

"Yes Mr Curland, his security credentials are impeccable," the policeman confirmed.

"OK, send him on in."

Adiel introduced himself to Neil and Natasha and was invited in to sit down.

"You heard what happened?" Natasha asked.

"Well no," Adiel confessed, "I was coming to see you anyway, I just found out about the bomb at the gate."

"How is Anna? Did she get home OK?" Natasha asked.

"I'm afraid she did not Natasha. I received word from our agents in Holland that Anna's body has just been identified as a 'Jane Doe' victim of a mugging at the train station in Rotterdam."

"Oh God no," Natasha cried.

“I’m so sorry Natasha,” Neil commiserated, pulling her to him.

“Was it quick?” she asked, once over the initial shock.

“Mercifully, yes,” Adiel answered. “It was a clinical assassination; stabbed through the heart. She died very quickly.”

“Oh God, this is all so awful,” she sobbed.

“We must protect you now at all costs Natasha,” Adiel said. “Whatever it is that Al-Kooheji fears, it is now down to you and you alone to expose.”

“Don’t you think we’re safe here?” Neil asked. “We have around the clock police protection.”

“Neil,” Adiel answered, trying not to sound patronising, “I could have overpowered your ‘police protection’ with a sharp stick. We need to move you to somewhere safe, and we need to do it now.”

“What are you suggesting?” Natasha asked.

“We need to get you out of the country. We can tell your ‘protection’ that we’re taking the children somewhere safe,” the Mossad Captain said.

“We’re only under police protection Adiel,” Neil said, “not protective custody. It shouldn’t be too difficult to slip away.”

“Do you have anywhere we could go, where people wouldn’t think to look for you?” Adiel asked.

“No, but I’ve got a man working on it,” Neil answered. “I’ll give Goose a ring, fill him in on the developments and see what he suggests.”

Goose was just about to call him when the phone rang. Neil quickly brought him up to speed with Anna's death.

"I've got a place sorted Neil. Call me from a payphone and I will give you the details. I suggest that we get all the interested parties to this safe-house without delay."

Within forty-eight hours, they were on a flight to Marseilles.

CHAPTER TEN

Safe house

The Israeli Captain sat at the desk surrounded by Goose, Neil, Natasha, Brodie and Jimbo, Goose's best friend from England. To the left of Goose sat a man who Neil didn't recognise. From their body language, the stranger was someone that Goose knew and trusted well. The cabin was a sumptuous affair, on loan to Goose from an underworld associate he had performed a service for in the capacity of his successful private detective agency. Built during a period of extreme underworld tension, the cabin was a bolt hole, lost, far from reality perched on the top of a berm, high above the Verdon River in a region of France between Provence and the high Alps. Surrounded as it was by tall pine trees, it commanded excellent views of the escarpment and the approach road, itself a natural defence, negotiable by four wheel drive vehicle only. Down river, some years before, the huge glacial gorge its low lying valleys and the ancient farming communities had been flooded to create massive hydroelectricity plants to feed the demand for electricity to the economically booming French Riviera resorts some forty miles to the south. The area had not yet recovered and thus was a beautiful empty wilderness. It was somewhere they could all feel safe for a time.

Neil had elected to keep Natasha close as she was without a doubt the 'primary' target. It was a tough decision to separate once again from the children, but both Natasha and Neil had been through enough to know that they were safer as far away from them as possible. To minimise the risk of the children being taken as a lure to locate Natasha, they had been spirited away in the middle of the night with Natasha's mum as their guardian and the company of a highly trained ex SAS bodyguard (courtesy of Goose) and were now enjoying the hospitality of Neil's reclusive tax exile brother in Australia.

Before getting down to business Goose made the introductions, leaving until last the man seated to his left. "With the exception of Mr Zeev, we all know each other pretty well so I'll just bring you all up to speed with the other mystery guest here: this is my good friend Jack Dare. Jack and I go way back, which I know will surprise all of you who think you know me well. Jack is what you might call our 'ace in the hole'. He is ex US Navy Seal and to top that, he was the Seals' CIA liaison officer. Jack was party to some pretty bad shit at the hands of the agency, so let's just say he owes them no favours. He is a loyal friend and his loyalty cannot be bought, on that you have my word."

Jimbo raised an eyebrow but uttered not a word. Most of his best friend's RAF career was shrouded in mystery.

"Adiel's credentials check out. He lost a brother at the Munich Olympic affair, Anna Bergkamp convinced Natasha that he was a man to be trusted, he's clearly not in league with the CIA and I've not known a Jew to be in bed with the Arabs so, on the face of it, I say we trust him too. So Adiel, what can you tell us?"

"Well briefly, I don't know how much you all understand about politics and religion in the Middle East, so I will start by briefly summarising how I see it and how my experience tells me it functions. The Arab nations are predominantly Muslim in faith. Moderate Muslims would argue that they are all the same and that the division is of man and not the word of Allah. However, all politics in the region follow religious lines. The Muslim faith divides into two basic factions, Sunni and Shiite."

Jimbo's massive frame shook as he stifled a giggle at the word Shiite. Goose shot him a disapproving scowl.

"Sunni Muslims make up the vast majority in the greater Muslim world. Shiites make up the majority in the more influential and strategically important countries, particularly Iran. In broad terms, the Sunni controlled countries have historically been 'friended' by the US, with the Shiite countries leaning towards the Soviet Union. The US and its corporate puppet masters have been trying to impose their own brand of democracy on the region for decades but it cannot work, as the vote will always split along religious lines. Add into this cauldron of hatred and mistrust the tension caused by the recent secret 'cold war' between the US and USSR in Afghanistan and then inject the majority of the world's oil into the region."

"Where do we come into all this?" Goose interrupted.

"What you are caught up in is what the Americans refer to as a 'shit storm'," Adiel replied. "You see, we, the Israeli Government, rely heavily on the US to support us. Without our super-power ally, we would not be able to exist in the region, surrounded as we are by our enemies."

"Israel holds nuclear armaments, you seem to have done okay at throwing your weight around in the past," interjected Neil.

"It is true, we are a wealthy state with well equipped, well trained forces, but we are isolated and our enemies are not. Iran, Iraq, Syria and Libya all refuse to acknowledge our right to exist, not to mention our immediate enemies: Palestine, Lebanon and Yemen. Even those that grudgingly accept us like Pakistan, Egypt and Saudi Arabia would sooner we did not exist. It is our close ties with the US that keep us safe, Nevertheless, sometimes we do not agree on a certain course of action. This my friends is one of those times."

"I still don't see for the life of me why a bunch of unimportant minnows like us are even showing up as tiny blips on this giant radar screen," Neil enquired.

"Well Neil, some of this is fact and some is logical guesswork. Where I see your two circles interject is Isa Hashim Al-Kooheji. This is a man the Israeli forces have had our eye on for some time. To the outside world, this man is a wealthy Bahraini businessman, an oil tycoon, an obscenely rich Sunni Muslim from a respectable family. He makes regular trips around the world, furthering his business empire and funding new opportunities as a venture capitalist. His friends range from presidents to princes, quite the man about town and without doubt a finer upstanding pillar of the community you would be unlikely to find. Wrong! Al-Kooheji is the financial head of the fastest growing terrorist network the world has ever seen, not only does he pump his own considerable wealth into various terrorist excursions, he was also the gateway the US used to channel funds to the Mujahidin fighting against the Russians during the Afghanistan conflict."

Now Jimbo was the one to butt in. "And we're going to take on these big boys; this rag taggle of knobs you see in this room? We're going to take on international terrorists and the might of the most powerful countries on the planet?"

"Yes," was Adiel's short answer.

"OK, let's get on with it then," Jimbo replied. "Not like we haven't been here before is it boys?"

A subdued rumble of laughter filled the room followed by a number of macho remarks.

Adiel rapped his fist on the desk to quiet the room and bring back their attention to the task in hand. "If I can elaborate, we have something which Isa Al-Kooheji wants: Natasha. Something in the past she shared with him."

Now it was Brodie's turn to interrupt. "Sorry *Ariel*, but if it's all the same to you, could we just refer to him as Aykay? You're the only sorry son of a bitch in this room with a tongue hairy enough to get around that little Isa Hashim Al-Kahoolieoohly moniker. It's doing a number on my head just thinking it."

"As you wish, for now we will refer to him as Aykay. However, I suggest you all try to familiarise yourselves with the basics of the language as we will without a doubt be travelling to the Middle East in the near future. By the way Mr *Bodie*, my name is Adiel, I am not the little mermaid." The Mossad Captain paused awhile to allow the chatter and sniggering to subside.

"Touché Mr Zeev," Brodie remarked, smiling.

Adiel continued, "Before her untimely demise, I learned much about Mr Al-Koo', uh, Aykay from Anna Bergkamp. It was clear to me that Anna was a victim of his 'clean sweep' policy. You see she knew that he and his mother had conceived the boy Mahmood. The brother and his wife also knew. The brother Jalil also shared the secret of the father's death at Isa's hands. They all had to go in order for Isa to be the pure Muslim man the Americans need him to be."

"He killed his own son?"

"Yes Neil, the boy was a big secret waiting to be discovered. Put simply, Mahmood would have had just too much DNA from his maternal family. If the rumour had got out, the boy would have been there as proof. He was cremated and scattered within a day of his death, as required by the Muslim faith. No record of his DNA or blood type remains. That secret is safe. For Anna and Natasha to remain such a risk to him, something, somewhere must remain that could potentially tie Isa to the boy. That, my friends, is what we must discover if we are to save Natasha and bring about the fall of Mr Aykay!"

Now it was Natasha's turn to bring something to the table. "He raped me." The room fell into a surprised silence. Neil held on to Natasha's hand, hoping to channel all his strength and support into her. “Mahmood raped and beat me, put me in the hospital. That was why Isa paid me off. He paid me to drop all charges against his son. It wasn’t his son or his family’s name he was protecting; it was the boy’s DNA. No wonder he was willing to pay such a high price.”

CHAPTER ELEVEN

Natasha's burden

The room fell into awkward silence as the assembled friends digested what Natasha had revealed. It was Adiel who broke the silence. "Well gentlemen, I think that gives us the smoking gun, now we must find the 'magic bullet'!"

Natasha addressed the room once more. "Guys, can I just say, I really appreciate what you are all doing to try and keep me alive, and all you've done in the past. You're all very special friends, I don't want you to think that I am not aware of all you've done for me, and all that you're doing, but this happened to me a lifetime ago, it wasn't pleasant and it was nothing compared to what's happened since, so I would appreciate it if you could swallow down your macho instincts of revulsion and pity and let's just get on with the deal in hand. I don't know about the rest of you, but I'd just as soon get this over so we can all go on with living the rest of our lives!"

The room fell into total silence, Jack, the new guy, was the first to react. He stood to his feet and began a slow hand clap. Before long, all the men in the room were on their feet, giving Natasha a rapturous applause.

Neil too got to his feet and hugged Natasha to him. "Wow, where did that come from?"

"If I live or die Neil, I'm not going to be the victim anymore."

Adiel brought the meeting back to order. “So, we have an attack and rape, I’m assuming that swabs, photographs, samples will have been taken, so somewhere there will have been a crime report. Do you remember much about the first few hours after you arrived at the hospital Natasha?”

“Not a great deal, I was unconscious or in shock for much of the time. Isa was at my bedside when I came to fully, but I do remember being examined and they were certainly aware that I had suffered a sexual assault. I can remember them removing my night clothes and bagging them, I can also recall other unpleasant examinations, an internal, and scrapings from under my fingernails.”

“Do you recall at any time divulging the name of your attacker to anyone?” Adiel asked.

“I don’t know if I spoke to the police at the hospital. Like I said, I was pretty traumatised and in shock. I had been raped, beaten and strangled half to death, I wasn’t feeling all that trusting of my Arab hosts at that moment in time.”

“So, do we know if Mahmood’s name was ever connected with the assault?” Adiel asked.

“Aykay would have had the crime report quashed, you can bet your last nickel on that,” Brodie remarked. “So that can’t be the ‘magic bullet’ we’re after can it?”

“No, we are missing something, of that I am sure. We are missing something which has caused our Mr Aykay to risk everything in order to prevent his ex-wife and ex-girlfriend from exposing him.”

"The consulate," Natasha stated with a firm certainty in her voice. "I had a visit from the Ambassador's staff while I was recuperating, I told them everything. They took a copy of everything."

"That has to be it," Goose interrupted. "I'm no expert on international protocol, but I'm willing to bet that the consulate handed a copy of the whole kit and caboodle over to Interpol, or CID or some government agency to be loaded up to some secret database. Probably find they have a sample somewhere on ice with that bastard's genetic signature written all over it."

"That confuses me further," Adiel confessed. "If the British had something on file which could potentially damage Aykay, why hasn't he found it? The British are so far up the Americans' asses it's hard to see where one ends and the other begins."

"I'm Italian," Natasha answered.

"What?" Adiel questioned aghast.

"I am an Italian, I have dual nationality. It wasn't British. It was the Italian consulate."

"Did Isa know that?" Adiel asked.

"I don't think he did, I didn't travel on my Italian passport; I didn't even have it with me. Monica is on my British passport. He never asked, I never told him."

"Why did you not call the British Consulate?" Adiel asked.

"I don't really know, I guess I just didn't want all that connected to my British identity. I can't properly explain, it's as if I'm two different people sometimes."

"That's it Natasha," Adiel declared. "That's it. Don't you see? Isa cannot obtain the crime report; that is why he is going to such risks to cover his tracks. We must find out what the Italians have, we must obtain it before Isa does, for all our sakes."

CHAPTER TWELVE

Alabaster

Neil and Natasha lay in bed together in the sumptuous guest annexe of the cabin. This was no ordinary cabin in the woods. It was more a Swiss chateau built in a style which sacrificed little comfort to security but instead merged the two seamlessly in a symbiotic style which only the opulence and paranoia of the criminal mind could create. They were as safe and as comfortable as was possible, given the circumstances.

“Jesus Natasha,” Neil whispered. “I realised tonight that all of this, Brian, the rape, the shit going down now, it's all my fault, all because of the way I made you behave, the things I made you do. I thought it was all down to Brian; just a mental ex-boyfriend of yours, nothing to do with me, but it turns out that it was, is, all my fault. Can you ever forgive me?”

“Things are what they are Neil, you're not to blame for any of this and neither am I. We've both made mistakes and we've paid a high price for them. We didn't set out to hurt anybody and as far as I'm aware, we didn't. Now I'm not willing to waste a further second of my time feeling sorry for myself and I'd appreciate it if you didn't either.”

“I was so proud of you tonight. All that stuff you had to re-live, you seemed so strong, so confident. A little like the old you, you know, before everything.”

“I don't want you to be proud of me Neil, just make love to me, the way you used to,” she replied.

Taken a little by surprise, especially after the evening's revelations, Neil began to softly kiss the nape of her neck, to softly stroke the skin of her arms, ever so gently touching the side of her breasts as he caressed her in long sweeping motions from her wrists, back up to the soft creamy coloured skin of her shoulders.

Abruptly Natasha grabbed hold of his hand and thrust it roughly between her legs. "Don't treat me like a china doll Neil. I want you to fuck me!"

Natasha was back!

CHAPTER THIRTEEN

Zealots

Goose, Jack and Adiel remained seated in the room after the others had retired for the night. The drinks cabinet had been raided and each of the men sat with a generous sized glass of fifteen-year-old single malt in his hand.

Goose focused his attention on the Mossad Captain. "So Adiel, what's it all about? I'm sure Jack has an inkling of what's up, but me? I'm in the dark. When I was 'wired in' it was all about fighting when we had to and keeping one step ahead of the Ruskies the rest of the time. What's with all this 'New World order'?"

"Well Goose, 'New World order' is a pretty good way to describe what the Americans have planned." Adiel took a deep breath and settled back into the sumptuous leather chair. "Since the fall of the Soviet Union, the US has had to take stock of where it's at. Winning the arms race and the space race exacted a high price on the US super economy. Keeping the American dream 'pink and rosy' has left the economy near to flat-lining, the indigenous oil reserves are declining fast and America now has to import crude from the Middle East in huge quantities to make up the shortfall; Russia, in contrast has huge oil and natural gas reserves."

Jack interrupted, "So Adiel, you think the US is planning on taking over the Middle East? That's a bit optimistic even for the US."

"Not taking over the Middle East, but yes, I believe that the US thinks itself capable of controlling the Middle East, thereby controlling the oil."

"And this is where Isa Al-Kooheji comes in?" Goose interjected. "He is the Prince who is to unite the clans and lead Scotland to victory?"

Adiel allowed himself a little smirk at the analogy. "Yes Goose, eloquently put. The Americans have deals, trysts, arrangements and understandings with many of the Sheiks, Dictators, Kings, Warlords and Presidents in the region. Just as they think they have the snake by the tail, they get bitten again. I believe the Americans think that by controlling and uniting the terrorist factions in the region, they can lead an uprising; an 'Arab spring' so to speak, overthrowing all the heads of state, and uniting the region, creating a sort of democratic United States of Arabia, under the overall control and influence of course of the man who made it all possible: Mr Isa Hashim Al-Kooheji."

"And you doubt that such a plan can work?" Jack questioned.

"I know that such a plan is doomed to catastrophic failure and that the fallout would be enormous. Israel, isolated as we are in the region, would be destroyed. I am avowed to prevent that from happening."

"Why are you so sure the plan would fail? If as you say, the Americans are so convinced it's the right thing to do?" Goose asked.

"Just look at the overriding success the Americans have had at imposing their will on others in the past Goose: Vietnam, Korea, South America, and more recently Mogadishu. The Americans are a stoic ally, they are well equipped and fight best when their backs are against the wall or they are fighting for the underdog against an obvious aggressor. The American psyche thinks in five year terms of office. Their enemies think in lifetimes, generations. How many reliable native intelligence operatives do you think the Americans have managed to recruit in the Middle East? I'll answer that for you: none. The Americans rely on us, Israel, to provide them with local agents, they have been unable to recruit a solitary indigenous operative in the Middle East. You know why? They offer money to individuals to gather information, vast sums of money, the intelligence is poor, often misleading, but still they think they can buy loyalty. The money ends up back on the streets of Lebanon, Palestine and in the slums of Pakistan, funding weapons, and the radicalisation of young men, funding organisations sworn to destroy America, Israel and everything they stand for. They do not and never will understand how different these people are to the enemies they have faced in the past."

"Mogadishu's a little below the belt; we were there as a peacekeeping force not an army of occupation," Jack snapped. As the only American in the room, there was more than a hint of cynicism in his voice. "So how do you see it then Adiel?"

"I am sorry Jack. I do not wish to cause insult or to belittle the memory of the brave men who fought and fell in Mogadishu, but it illustrates that your country doesn't always have its finger on the pulse. I believe in Israel Jack. I believe that the Jews deserve to have a home, but in truth, I am something of an atheist; an evolutionist. I believe the problem lies with religion. You see, I believe that religion has a purpose in evolution, unlike all other creatures; man has a need to understand the meaning of life, has to cling to the belief that he has a divine purpose other than just standing on a fast spinning rock for eighty or so years before ceasing to exist. Procreation, that's what we're here for, all the other creatures on the planet seem to be OK with this, just not man. Man has evolved an enormous capacity for thought, we have invented fantastical things to preserve life, drugs to prevent illness, seatbelts, air bags and anti-lock brakes to protect us from accidental death, yet the single biggest cause of death is still war, and the biggest single cause of war is still religion."

"But the US is religious, the Bible belt and the South are pretty damn fiercely Christian!" Jack corrected.

"Forgive me Jack, but they are not. Religion in the West is manipulating and exploitative, overrun with the same corporate greed as most Western organisations. The slogan, 'In God we trust' was only adopted as your national motto during the 'cold war' when it was decided to combine religion and democracy against the godless Communists. This is the problem, the West compares its own institutions with those in the Middle East; there is no comparison, Religion in the East is pure, primitive with, in my opinion, the Darwinian purpose of repression and population control."

"That's some pretty radical theorising Adiel, especially from a Jew," Goose concluded, his tone conveying that the use of the word 'Jew' was not meant as an insult.

"Well Goose, my theories aside, the Muslim faith is as I have explained it - pure and primitive. There will be no reconciling Sunni and Shiite; there will be no uniting of the Arab nations behind one leader, only bloodshed and suffering along ethnic lines. If the Americans were to succeed in their plan to create an Arab super state, it would ultimately be a Caliphate, run by a Caliph; a mortal with the belief that he and only he was the rightful successor to Mohamed; an Islamic State, and depending on which sect was ultimately victorious. The Shiite or Sunni minority in each state would be suppressed by ethnic cleansing. Women would be slaves, with no place and no voice. Israel would be wiped out and America and the West would find themselves engaged in a war, a war on two fronts; one against highly motivated fanatical terrorist groups and the other with a Caliphate; an Islamic super state in possession of nuclear weapons and with the finger on the button just itching to press it. Such a war, gentlemen, would have nothing 'cold' about it, nothing at all."

The men finished off their drinks and said their good nights. Jack and Goose were billeted on the top floor of the chateau and parted company with Adiel on the stairs. Goose waited until they were on the top landing to ask, "So what do *you* think Jack? Do you think Adiel is right or have we hooked up with a nut job?"

"I hate to admit it Goose, but a lot of what he mentioned was flagging up things in my memory. He did join a lot of dots for me with what he was saying."

"I was afraid you'd say that. Looks like we're about to fly into a shit storm on a paper glider."

"Fucking 'Nam all over again! God bless the US of A!" Jack hissed in a loud whisper.

"I'm going to slice my buttocks off myself, stop the bastards from handing me my ass!" Goose added.

CHAPTER FOURTEEN

Course of action

After breakfast, the group assembled once more in the sumptuous conference room. Again, Adiel addressed the group. "Gentlemen," he politely glanced towards Natasha and added, "and lady. We need to achieve two goals: to prevent any further attempts on Natasha's life and to recover the evidence we need to prevent Aykay's plans from progressing. My first priority is to retrieve whatever evidence the Italian authorities may be holding, regarding the assault on Natasha. To achieve this goal, it is my suggestion that I travel with Natasha immediately to Rome, I'm guessing that SCIP headquarters is as good a place as any to start knocking on doors."

"SCIP?" Neil questioned.

"Interpol. The Italians have their own intelligence agency; the SISMI, I could contact them through official channels but I think as there was no risk to the state from this crime, in all likelihood it will have been passed to SCIP rather than SISMI."

Adiel was busy scribbling his own secure version of shorthand into a notebook. "I will engage the services of a criminal lawyer in Rome and we will work quickly to obtain whatever evidence they may have, we will tell them it is for a civil prosecution, which should be enough. We may need a court order in which case, it may be better to circumvent the whole procedure."

"Circumvent?" Neil questioned.

"The Italian authorities are notoriously corrupt. If we engage a good criminal lawyer from the area, he will know when we must follow procedure and when we must apply a little grease to the wheels. In any circumstance, we must obtain *any* evidence before our Mr, uh, Aykay is alerted."

"So what do you want us to do while you travel to Italy, come with you?" Neil asked.

"Well I see no sense in you flying out to Saudi without me as none of you speak Arabic. Myself and Natasha will take the trip, I speak no Italian and I will doubtless need her to sign papers, the rest of you may as well remain here until our return."

"There are a number of Alpine passes between here and Italy," Natasha said, "where there are no border checks. The border guards knock off around four then it operates on a sort of 'honour' system. You're not supposed to use them at night but the locals use them as rat runs between France and Italy all the time."

"That's perfect, the less times we have to show our documents the better," Adiel replied.

Neil stared at Natasha, mouth slightly agape.

"What?" she questioned, slightly irritated.

"Sometimes, I don't think I know you at all," Neil remarked, the grin on his face showing the remark was jovial.

"Hey, I'm Eyetalian, get the fock over it. What the hell are you, some kind of a focking 'wise' guy?" she replied in a perfect 'Hell's Kitchen' accent, cheeks puffed out like Marlon Brando in 'The Godfather'.

"Oy yoy yoy!" Adiel exclaimed. "You sound just like my ex-wife, the Balabusta."

"I was doing a Marlon Brando!" Natasha replied, just a little of that old trademark pout showing through.

The spontaneous laughter which followed was something of a welcome relief after the serious planning they'd concluded.

"I'll be coming with you," Neil remarked, after order had been restored. Clearly this was not negotiable.

"As you wish Neil," Adiel answered.

Brodie, who'd, sat pretty much silently for most of the proceedings, now leant forward to speak. "We can get our asses over to Saudi, I've got some sound connections over in the Middle East who will get us over the language barrier and keep us from attracting too much attention."Now it was Neil's turn to act surprised. "You have connections in Saudi Arabia?"

"Sure thing Neil, you don't think we got outlaw bikers in the desert?" Brodie replied.

"I never really thought about it. I kind of thought it was all flip-flops and Toyota Hi-luxes truth be told."

"No Neil, us and our rivals, we been there since the eighties. Sammy, the Prez of the opposition, expanded his club's influence abroad, we followed suit. Lot of our merchandise comes in from that direction." He touched his nose to describe discretion advised.

"Where there's muck, there's brass," Jimbo added.

"What the heck do they ride, camels?" Neil asked.

"They got their share of WWII Harleys, lots of Russian stuff, Beemers, little dirt bikes. The boys get around you know," Brodie replied. "Got a sound bunch of boys up in Riyadh that I'm sure will make us welcome. It's a couple hundred miles from the Gulf but it's a sight closer than we are now. Get us acclimatised before the rest of you rock up."

"I don't think that your biker friends will welcome the presence of a Jew among them Brodie!" Adiel cautioned.

"Hell, these boys are bikers; as long as the coke's pure and the pussy's warm," Brodie joked.

"Again, you see how you Americans do not understand the mind of an Arab man. To bring a Jew into the midst of your friends, no matter how strong your biker bond, would be an unforgivable insult. Besides, any plan which would provide a favourable outcome for Israel would be viewed with suspicion and distrust by your Arab connections."

"Well Brodie," Jack added. "I suppose it won't hurt to keep your mates in the dark about the little 'world domination' plot; just bring them in on the plan to kill Natasha. That's all we really know for sure anyway, the rest's just supposition."

"I guess so, if Adiel really thinks they'll react that strongly," Brodie said. "I will say though, I've known my Arab friend Aarif for years and I would vouch that he's way too laid back for all that."

"Trust me on this Brodie," Adiel said. "Mr Has...uh, Aykay is a Sunni Muslim, the majority of Saudis are Sunni Muslims; they will not depose him on the word of a Zionist."

"Well, we'll just have to keep you and the Arabs apart then wont we Adiel," Neil interjected impatiently. "Gents, I respectfully suggest that we are trying to catch a bull that has not yet bolted. We are about here," Neil held his hands about 4 inches apart, "and you guys are panicking about something we *might* encounter here." This time his hands were held about 3 feet apart. "Let's just get there first; we can cross certain bridges when we encounter them."

"OK Neil," Adiel concurred, adding, "I suggest we cut all telephone ties once we leave this place. Cell phones are *'streng verbot'* off limits. Don't even turn your cell phones on unless it's a dire emergency. It would be advisable to switch off cellular phones and leave them here; they are instantly traceable and very possibly monitored."

"Right, so just how do we keep in touch? Mail will be way too slow and putting cryptic messages in the local newspapers will take us till we're old and grey," Goose added.

"When you touch down in Riyadh, travel as quickly as you can to the Holiday Inn, and book a room for two weeks under the name Mr and Mrs Bennett. This can be our contact and rendezvous point." Adiel turned to Brodie. "Make sure your Arab friends do not visit this place, it will be a safe house for us to meet up and communicate." He turned back to Goose. "Pay for the room up front and in cash. Leave a message with your contact address for Mrs Bennett at the desk."

"You've done this before," Neil remarked.

"Won't we need a passport?" Goose enquired.

Adiel fumbled through the contents of his briefcase. "Here, Mr Bennett's passport." He handed the document to Goose who opened it up and examined the photo.

"He does look a bit like me," Goose remarked.

"You all look alike to them, they won't scrutinise it too carefully," Adiel replied.

Goose closed up the passport and stowed it in his pocket.

"Mr and Mrs Bennett's room will be our safe house and our point of contact should we be separated. Natasha will be Mrs Bennett and you, Goose, will be her husband."

"Charming, do I get 'husband's privileges'?" Goose enquired.

"You'll get the pointy end of a pineapple jammed down your Jap's eye," Neil replied.

Goose winced.

Natasha put her arm around Goose's shoulder and said, "We're going through some marital difficulties at the moment, me and Mr Bennett, he's presently sleeping in the bathtub."

"Bugger!" Goose exclaimed.

CHAPTER FIFTEEN

Jet set

"Boys," Goose commanded, "can we make a stop on route to the airport? I need to get myself some hot weather gear. I was expecting bloody snow in the Alps, all I've got is what I'm wearing: winter gear. I didn't realise how bloody hot it got here in summer."

"Bugger Goose," Jimbo exclaimed. "It's the South of France; the clue is in the name mate."

"My client said the bloody cabin was in the Alps, I thought fucking snow covered peaks and frozen rivers. I've got boots, scarves, the lot," Goose retorted.

"Shit mate, for a smart fella, you can be a bit thick," Jimbo laughed.

"Well if we can stop over somewhere, I'll get meself some sunnies, shorts, and all that bollocks. Best we get some bloody sunscreen for you too Jimbo, you don't look like you've seen any sun in a while."

"I'm bloody English, sunshine comes in liquid form. You Yank imports, always whinging about the weather."

Goose turned to Jack and joked, "Jimbo's the only geezer I know who likes the rain."

"Nothing wrong with rain, cleans the 'Farmer Palmer' shit off the roads, keeps the space cadets at home watching 'Grandstand' and leaves the road free for me and my Harley. 'Win-win I say!" Jimbo snorted.

"Oy, scuse si por favour," Goose said, attempting to attract the taxi driver's attention.

"Goose, you're such an embarrassment; the driver's French," Jimbo scolded.

"I don't speak bloody French, I speak Spanish," Goose snapped back.

"There's logic in that, I just don't see it," Jack commented.

The driver laughed and said, "I speak a little English, what can I do for you?"

"Awesome," Goose replied. "I need like a supermarket, department store, somewhere I can pick up some cheap clothes quickly."

"There are some shops in Draguignan. I will stop there, it is on route," the driver replied.

Half an hour later, the driver pulled into a busy shopping centre car park in the town. Goose quickly exited the taxi. Jack followed, also deciding to do a little last minute shopping before the trip to Saudi Arabia. Jimbo and Brodie chose to stay put in the taxi to reassure the driver that he wasn't being hustled.

Goose ran around the shops, choosing clothes based on type rather than style. Dress to impress was not a phrase which meant anything to him. So close to Cannes, the nation's capital of style, Goose could have been on a faraway planet for all the effect it had on him.

Jack was already sat in the front seat of the taxi when a breathless Goose thumped down into the back seat next to an impatient Jimbo. Wearing a brand new ensemble of shorts, linen shirt, sunglasses, sun hat and a smart new set of summer shoes he looked every bit the Japanese tourist. Clutched in both hands were bags of his own clothes which he'd been wearing prior to the purchases.

Jimbo looked down at his friend's new shoes. “Ummm, canvas shoes Goose, really?”

“What?”

“Canvas shoes and no socks with your body odour problems?” Jimbo elaborated.

“Oh piss off you cunt!”

“Goddamn it you two, why don't you just have angry sex and relieve the tension?” Jack exclaimed.

The trip continued in silence for the next half an hour before Jimbo chimed up again with, “I don't know if it's just me, but it *is* getting a bit niffy back here.”

“Oh bollocks, me dogs *are* barking a bit,” Goose admitted. “Sorry boys. I'll get some talcum on 'em as soon as I can.”

“Bin the fucking things, and while you're at it, bin off your bloody smelly feet too!” Jimbo exclaimed.

“You two are mates aren't you?” Jack questioned.

“No we're bloody not,” Goose replied. “He's a bloody fat retard.”

Jimbo responded with a loud fart of the long, reverberating variety.

“Oh bloody nice, and me stuck here in the back,” Goose responded.

“Controlled, proportional, retaliatory response to an unprovoked chemical and verbal attack,” Jimbo assured him.

The remainder of the trip was bathed in silence.

CHAPTER SIXTEEN

Mountain air

"So, where do we find these 'rat runs' between France and Italy then?" Neil addressed the question to Natasha.

"Ah, well," she replied. "See, I know the runs exist, but I haven't a clue where they are. I assume some of the minor routes across the mountains."

"Well we can't just keep trying each one, it takes hours just to reach the mountain passes and we'll attract the wrong kind of attention if we keep turning around at the border," Adiel said. "We need to find out which passes are unmanned, any suggestions?"

"I suggest we take a leaf out of Brodie's book," Neil replied. "I'll make some phone calls, find out what biker clubs stalk the border areas. If there's a covert way of getting drugs between France and Italy, they're the boy's who'll know about it."

"Calls to England will be risky," Adiel warned.

"It's a risk we'll have to take otherwise we might just as well take the toll roads and show our passports. That would be the quickest way," Neil said.

"Make the call then, I suppose it's the lesser risk," Adiel conceded.

Neil made the call to a contact in the UK. The man was a client of Neil's, his brother worked in Neil's custom shop. He was a member of an outlaw motorcycle club, and as luck would have it, he owed Neil a favour.

Neil replaced the receiver at the end of the call. “Right, I’ve got a name and a town. We need to nip over to Riez, it’s not far from here. A local back patch club organise a yearly rock concert there. They have a café they hang out at. If we’re lucky, our man may be about.” Neil turned his attention to Natasha. “You stay here with Adiel honey, no need for us all to go.”

“Sod that Neil, I’m coming. You may need an Italian speaker,” Natasha replied. “Adiel, can you speak French? You may as well come too.”

“Oui Madame,” the Captain replied.

The café was not hard to find, the line of low rider Harleys parked in a row outside was a dead give-away. Part concealed between a couple of French plated Harleys was a scruffy, wellused Arlen Ness Triumph chop from the seventies. Neil’s face erupted into a smile; this was the man he’d been told to seek out.

The three of them entered the café. Unlike the biker clubs back in the UK, the French café was quite inconspicuous. Apart from the flyers advertising rock groups and venues it was no different to any of the other establishments dotted around the town square. Most of the seats were occupied by bikers and civilians, mingling in a relaxed and unintimidating atmosphere.

Neil walked straight up to the biggest, badass biker at the bar and, placing both hands on the bar face down, he said, “I’m looking for Moss, the owner of the rigid Triumph out front, is he here?”

The brick shithouse moved with lightning speed, and before Neil knew it, there was a long blade butterfly knife sticking out of the top of the bar, between two of his fingers. Neil didn't flinch.

"Who wants to fucking know?" the brick shithouse spat in his best TV tutored English.

"Neil Curland, a friend; that is a friend of Sid Garvey from Moss's club back in England."

A face appeared from around the corner of the bar. Attached to the suntanned leather face was an equally bronzed body, swathed in faded, threadbare jeans, "How is Sid?" Moss enquired. "I miss me old brother."

"He's well Moss, sends you his very best," Neil replied. Moss looked at the knife between Neil's fingers and spoke a few words of reassurance to the man-mountain in French. The man withdrew his knife.

"You're a brave man to keep your cool when Tueur kicks off, Neil," Moss observed.

Neil replied in a whisper, "Nothing to do with brave, the bugger moved so fast I was rooted to the spot in fear. Only part of me that reacted was my sphincter; I think I may have touched cloth."

The gnarly, weather-worn face of the biker broke out into a broad grin. "What can I help you with Neil?"

"We need to get into Italy, through the back door."

"When do you need to go?"

"Now, or soonest."

"We can go over tonight. You got bikes?" Moss asked.

"No, we're in a car," Neil replied.

"No can do man, no crossings by car. There's a gorge see, footbridge will take bikes, not cars. You got money man?"

"We have money," Neil said.

"Well we're sorted then, you give me three thousand Francs, I organise bikes for the crossing. We go tonight. I'll get two bikes, your squeeze can ride shotgun."

Natasha winced. Neil shot her a glance which said *'let it go'*.

"What's your preference?" Moss asked.

"Harleys," Neil replied. "Sportsters. We have a fair distance to travel once we're in Italy, better have something that can munch up the miles."

"I was thinking of a couple of dirt bikes, Harleys at such short notice are going to cost nearer ten thousand Francs, you want good ones, more like fifteen thousand Francs."

"What do you suggest then?"

Moss looked contemplative for a moment. "Might be able to get you the Sporties, one of our blokes brings 'em in from the States, he might have a couple knocking about. Otherwise, I've got a mate who runs a bike hire place, you could buy a couple of Beemers from him cheap, sell 'em back to him if you pass back through. That'd be the best bet, all insured and legal like, just in case you get stopped."

“Whatever you can get, we’re in your hands,” Neil replied.

Neil handed Moss a large wad of cash.

“Wow, you must really need to slip into Italy, 'ay,” Moss exclaimed.

“Well,” Neil replied, “Sid said you’re a man to be trusted.”

Moss handed back a substantial part of the wad. “Down the road on the left, there’s a bike shop, go and get yourself some bike gear; helmets and leathers. Get some waterproofs too. It don’t often rain here, but when it does, it fucking pours.”

“Cheers mate, you’re a diamond,” Neil replied.

“Be here at seven tonight, we’ll give you a guide and an escort over the mountains.”

“What do I owe you?” Neil enquired.

“Nothing mate, I’m going anyway. Need to score some blow, we’ve got a few farms over there,” Moss confided.

“How does that work then, why not here?” Neil asked, curious.

“French are totally anal about grass, the Eyeties couldn’t care less, and if they did, there’d always be someone you could chuck a bung to, keep out of trouble.”

“Well thanks again Moss, we’ll shoot off and get some stuff, see you back here at seven,” Neil said.

“Not a second sooner,” Moss laughed.

CHAPTER SEVENTEEN

Surveillance

The convoy of bikes took off just after seven thirty that night. At the head of the column rode Moss with his long, low hard-tail chop. In the middle of the group rode Neil and Natasha on a tidy BMW R100R, behind them, Adiel on a similar steed kept close formation with the other bikes. It took around two hours by road to reach the pass at the remote village of Sainte Veran, just beyond which the road ended and the route continued along a dirt track. A few miles on, a flimsy arched footbridge spanned a gorge with a drop of several hundred feet. Natasha stayed calm as they carefully picked their way one at a time across the fragile bridge, electing to stay on the bike and get the ordeal over quickly. With all the bikes across, the last biker riding tail end, Charlie, strode over to have a chin wag with Moss. When they had finished their brief exchange, Moss walked over to Neil and gestured for him to take off his helmet.

"Neil, we've got a bit of a problem," he announced.

"What do you mean?" Neil asked.

"We've had a tail on us, kept an even distance behind us right up until we left the tarmac. We posted a sentry to leave a few minutes behind the convoy, just to check for tails, seems the guy was stopped talking on a two way radio when my man passed him."

"What do you reckon it means?" Neil asked.

"Don't know. Could be for us; rivals, another M/C, maybe even the law, or it could be for you. I don't know what you're running from or what you're up against, so I don't know how to read it. What do you think?"

Neil looked over to Adiel who'd been party to the disclosure. He nodded agreement.

"I think we can assume it's us Moss," Neil replied.

"How bad is this threat?" Moss asked.

"The worst, professional assassins, maybe even terrorists," Neil admitted honestly.

"Shit," Moss exclaimed. "I'll have to let the boys know, give them the chance to turn back."

Moss had words with the others while Adiel and the Curlands waited to see if they would face this perceived threat alone.

Moss strode back after a few minutes. "Who?" he asked Neil.

"The target? Me," Natasha butted in. "Who? God knows, the IRA, Middle Eastern terrorists, we're not sure."

"Shit," Moss exclaimed. "Sid's gonna owe me big time for this. We'd better press on, we've a head start 'cause you can't follow us in a motor, but we have to guess that whoever was on the other end of that walkie-talkie is gonna know where we're coming down the mountain. Keep her in the middle of the group and stay alert."

"What about your boys?" Neil asked.

"You're with us, under our protection. Nobody leaves."

Once again, Neil was in awe of the unspoken biker code.

CHAPTER EIGHTEEN

First blood

The track deteriorated into what could best be described as a goat trail. Progress was painfully slow as they carefully climbed to a little over two thousand feet in altitude towards the peak of Col de Sainte Veran, high above the cloud line. Abruptly the track began a rapid descent down from the rocky face of the mountain, crossing from France into Italy on the way. Neil was grateful that Moss had failed to secure a pair of Harleys for this trip as the Beemers were far more suited to this terrain. Moss himself was riding perhaps the most uncomfortable and unsuitable bike possible, nevertheless, he made the track look easy. The pack stopped to re-group shortly before a particularly difficult and dangerous part of the descent.

"Jesus Moss, I pity you poor bastards having to come back up here. This is like mountaineering on a bloody bike," Neil exclaimed.

"I'm not coming back this way mate; we'll have one of the prospects on a dirt bike mule our shit back. We'll come back by road. There's a decent tarmac road a few clicks from here. It's not quite as discreet as this way but it's a sight more comfortable. We'll be joining the tarmac when we come off the mountain, I'll show you where it goes, in case you want to come back that way."

"Cheers mate," Neil answered.

The trail eventually levelled out at a crystal clear river, obviously the destination the footpath was designed to lead to. There was no obvious continuation of the path to be seen.

“Where do we go now?” Neil asked, pulling alongside Moss.

“We do a little cross country now Neil, make sure we keep our routes secret,” Moss answered before setting off into the bed of the river.

The bikes pitched and bounced along the shallow river bed for a couple of miles before climbing the bank and continuing along the polished rock face, following an invisible trail. Eventually, a line of telegraph poles could just be made out in the distance. Moss brought the Triumph to a standstill and gestured the pack to group in around him.

“OK Neil, we have to make for Pontechianale to pick up the Strada. This is as far as we can get off road. I reckon if we’re facing trouble, it’ll be somewhere between there and Costigliole Saluzzo. After Saluzzo, there are a number of alternative routes you could take. If I was going to hit you, it’d be just beyond Pontechianale,” Moss stated.

“That’s reassuring,” Neil replied.

“Forewarned is forearmed hey? This is the road you want. Left takes you back into France; right takes you deeper into Italy,” Moss concluded. “Shall we?”

“Lead on Macduff,” Neil said.

The village of Pontechianale was a picture postcard ancient Italian village, set deep in the Alpine valley and squeezed by an enormous Hydro-electric damn. The road through the village was narrow with myriad twists and turns. With the lake on the right and the mountain to the left, the village itself was not the perfect place for an ambush, giving only one avenue of escape. Beyond Pontechianale was a different matter.

In the middle of the village, Moss brought the convoy to a stop and made his way across to Neil. "Well, the sun's well and truly gone down now so at least we've darkness on our side. I've had an idea Neil. We should park up half the bikes here in the village; double up on all the machines where they have pillion seats."

Neil looked confused and questioned, "How will that help us?"

"Well, I figure, if they're gunning for your lady, they're going to be looking for a pillion rider, if we double up on all the bikes, we could cause a bit of confusion."

"You think like a soldier Moss," Adiel added.

"Yea, that's right, in another lifetime mate, before the army shafted me." Neil leant forward, a question on his lips. "Another time hey mate? When we're not in deep shit!" he cut Neil off before he'd even spoken a word. "Between here and Saluzzo, there's a section of narrow road with dense woodland along both sides. The road is narrow and sunken between the trees; the woods are peppered with tracks. If our enemy has local knowledge, that's where we'll be most vulnerable. I suggest we crack on through that region as fast as we dare to roll."

The poor condition of the tarmac, submerged in snow for several months of the year, was slowing the progress of the convoy. The two Beemers could cope, but Moss and some of the other chopper pilots were suffering and a hasty tractor pace was the best they could manage.

The pick-up truck came at speed out of nowhere. Tail end Charlie, one of the prospects on one of only two dirt bikes, was rear ended and quickly disappeared under the axles of the speeding truck. By the time the vehicle had ploughed the back four bikes off the road, it had lost sufficient momentum that the remainder of the convoy were able to dissipate into the woodland on either side of the track. Neil and Adiel rode blindly into the dense woodland with Adiel in the lead. Adiel's passenger screamed at him to stop and he deftly skidded the bike sideways to a controlled stop. The pillion passenger gestured to Neil to keep going. Neil powered on deeper into the forest before bringing his mount to a skidding, sliding halt, catapulting himself and Natasha down a shallow bank and into a mountain stream. For a few seconds, there was blissful silence as the echoes of the motorcycle engines died away. Abruptly, the night sky lit up with muzzle flashes as small arms fire erupted from both sides of the road.

"Neil, what the fuck's happening?" Natasha screamed in terror.

"Keep quiet for fuck's sake, stay down, I'll see what's going on." Neil scrambled back up the bank in the darkness.

"Adiel! Adiel!" he called out in a hoarse whisper. "Adiel, where the fuck are you?"

The Mossad Captain was suddenly visible, lit up by gun muzzle flashes from the biker whom until recently had been riding pillion. He rolled over to the bank and threw himself over to the relative safety of the stream.

"Harah," Adiel exclaimed. "Shit!"

"What the fuck is going on Adiel?"

"Some ben zona ran a fucking truck into the back of the convoy. Moss's men are armed to the fucking teeth. All hell has broken loose!"

"Are they after Natasha, Adiel?"

"I don't know, I don't know. I don't think so; I think we're caught up in a turf war."

A scream from Natasha turned the two men around in shock.

With surprisingly quick reactions, Adiel's pillion rider swung the bars of Neil's bike around and flicked on the headlight switch. Lit up like a beacon a dark figure wearing unusual headgear was momentarily stunned by the piercing bright light. As the man hurriedly ripped the hardware from his head, Natasha dropped out of his grasp and splashed down into the stream. That was all the break the pillion rider needed; a dull 'thud', emanated twice from the muzzle of his weapon and Natasha's assailant fell backwards into the stream, away from her.

Adiel ran forward and examined the fallen man, pulling the headgear from under his prostrate form. By the light of the motorbike, he examined the hardware. "Oy gevalt, Neil. This is for us, this is

Fercokt. Night vision goggles, and not old stuff either. This is American military hardware!"

"This is another assassination attempt then. Jesus Adiel, how are they on to us so quickly?" Neil asked, moving forward to help Natasha back to her feet.

"Our enemies are resourceful and determined Neil," Adiel answered. "We must gather the information we need, and then we must go on the attack. That is the only way we can defeat this enemy; attack it, go for the throat. I fear that to survive this, we will need to kill Mr Isa Hashim Al-Kooheji."

The sound of a diesel truck accelerating away in the direction of Saluzzo indicated that at least this engagement had been won by the unexpected discipline and superior firepower of the bikers.

A scream of anger and frustration rent through the sudden peace of the night. "Give me a fucking gun, I'll kill the miserable bastard myself." Natasha flung herself at the corpse bleeding out into the stream. Snatching the tiny pistol from his rapidly cooling hand, she brought the butt down repeatedly on the man's inert face.

Neil ran to her and put his arms around her chest, hugging her to him from behind. Desperate sobs wracked her body in spasms.

"I don't understand Neil, I just don't understand. Why are so many people risking their own lives to protect mine? Why am I so special?"

"We're bikers, Natasha, ex-soldiers. You're part of my world; you're part of their world now. It's just how it is. We protect the people we love, at any cost!"

"I don't deserve it Neil," she cried. "I don't want any more people to get hurt saving me. I'm not worth it."

"Well we obviously don't agree," Neil said.

Moss ran into the clearing following the bike light and the screaming. "Neil, Neil, come on, we need to get going, we've got to get clear of Saluzzo while your man is still on the run. After that, we've got options."

On automatic pilot, the men and a soaked through, terrified Natasha mounted up and rode back out onto the tarmac.

The scene back down the road was carnage with mangled bikes, spilled oil, bodies and spilled blood strewn about on the tarmac and the verge.

Moss sent most of the remaining bikers back to retrieve the bikes they'd left behind with instructions to get back into France and split up. He, Tueur and one other man would take over the task of escorting their three charges to the comparative safety which lay beyond the bottleneck of Saluzzo.

"All in the valley of Death rode the six hundred," Neil muttered, quoting from Tennyson's *'The Charge of the Light Brigade'.*

"What was that Neil?" Adiel asked.

"Nothing Adiel. British folly. Hopefully not about to be repeated, you know, like Custer's last stand?"

"Bighorn? Yes, I see your point."

Moss interrupted, “Yea well, this time we were the fucking Russian artillery and Chief Crazy Horse. Let’s stop gassing like old washer women and press home the advantage.” With that he gunned his old Triumph in the direction of Saluzzo. The reduced convoy fell in behind.

CHAPTER NINETEEN

Camembert

Goose, Jack, Jimbo and Brodie reached the airport in Nice, paid off the taxi driver and started towards the departure lounge.

Goose held up the queue at check-in while he packed his winter clothes into his suitcase, only then could the three men check their baggage.

Wearing a scruffy pair of paratrooper's boots round his neck like some refugee city kid off to spend the duration of the war in the countryside, Goose shuffled through the gate.

"Nice," Jimbo remarked.

"Oh get off my back big guy; I can't fit them in my case cause *my* case is bulging full of equipment, so I'm taking them on as hand luggage all right?" Goose protested, now seriously miffed and determined to defend his corner.

The plane was delayed on the tarmac while an item of luggage with no corresponding passenger was located and removed. Despite the running of the air conditioning, temperature in the cabin was a little uncomfortable. Jimbo, staring down at Goose's feet, was adding to the nervous man's discomfort.

"Right, as soon as the seatbelt sign goes out, I'm going to the loo and I'll wash my feet and dump these bloody things in the waste bin," Goose snorted, gesturing towards his shoes.

Jimbo was doubled up in hysterics from the success of his campaign of torment.

True to his word, as soon as the flight began its eight hour journey to Riyadh, Goose got up and headed for the toilet. By the time he returned to his seat, Jimbo, Jack and Brodie were mercifully fast asleep.

The trip passed without further drama and the four men soon found themselves outside Riyadh airport hailing a cab.

With their luggage stowed in the boot of the aging Mercedes, Jimbo got his first glimpse of Goose's attire and began to laugh out loud. Goose was wearing a white linen shirt, bright orange shorts and para-boots.

The front seat of the cab was occupied by a family member of the driver hitching a free ride for himself and his goat, causing the four men, one cursing quietly, one smiling discretely, one biting his lip, and one crying with laughter, to squash themselves into the back seats. Jack instructed the driver to take them to the Holiday inn.

They hadn't travelled more than a few miles when Jimbo exclaimed, "There's two unwashed rag-heads and a goat in this cab, but still *all* I can smell is your smelly fucking feet you bloody hippy."

Goose flew into a nuclear rage. "It's not my fucking feet, I scrubbed my feet with soap and paper towels until they bled, I threw those bloody canvas shoes that cost me fifty Francs in the bin, I'm wearing bloody para-boots and shorts in seventy degree heat, looking like a total div and still you're on my case." His voice went up an octave. "IT'S

NOT MY BLOODY FEET." To prove his case, he stuck a boot under Jimbo's nose.

"Hmm, they don't smell too bad," Jimbo admitted. "Where the hell *is* that horrible cheesy smell coming from then?"

"Well, it's not me guys," Brodie exclaimed, tapping his knuckles against his prosthetic leg. "Plastic don't sweat."

They turned to Jack who had an enormous carrier bag from the supermarket on his lap.

"What's in the carrier bag Jack?" Goose asked politely.

"What this you mean?" Jack said, lifting the bag slightly. "Just some French cheese I bought back at the supermarket."

Jimbo was now laughing with such force that tears were cascading down his cheeks.

"I like French cheese," Jack added, matter of factly.

CHAPTER TWENTY

Iron horse

Mr Bennett booked a suite at the Holiday Inn as arranged. The false passport was accepted without question, and the room paid up for two weeks, in cash and in advance. The four men decided to take the opportunity to use the hotel facilities to catch some shut eye and freshen up.

After seeing off the 'jet lag' Brodie hastened to make contact with his Saudi brethren. For added security, they made the call to arrange the meet from a payphone in the street.

"Well boys," Brodie laughed, "looks like we need to find a four wheel drive taxi. I've just spoken to my 'good old boy' Aarif. Seems the boys are based out in the desert, a place called Almuzayri. I don't know if there will be any roads heading out there."

"The rag-heads would drive across the desert in a milk float if they had to. Any cab will take us, trust me, I've done a stint in the Middle East," Goose scoffed.

"He's not wrong," Jack chimed in. "I was once sentenced to a posting in the Middle East with the agency. The rag-heads could drive a train across the sand without rails. It's spooky; they just seem to know what each grain of sand is going to do next. We would just sink without trace."

Goose stared at jack with a look of distaste. "Don't think agreeing with me is going to get you forgiven, Jack. You my friend are firmly in my bad books."

Jack screwed his face up and bit down hard on his tongue, an attack of the giggles threatening to push his friend into an even darker mood.

"You're never wearing boots in this heat mate," Jimbo laughed, "where's those smart shoes you had on in the plane?"

"Don't, please don't," Jack said, laughing so hard his sides were threatening to split.

Goose scowled at both men, then turning his attention to the task in hand, he wrote the address they would be heading out to on a piece of paper, sealed it in an envelope and asked the receptionist to make sure it was passed on to Mrs Bennett when she arrived.

A taxi was hailed, once again the ubiquitous beige coloured Mercedes model, windscreen decorated with so many pelmets, carpet remnants and junk that the driver was left with a letter box sized slot of opaque sand-blasted glass to see out of. Nevertheless, with the grace of Allah, and the blessings of Mohammed *peace be upon him,* the driver deposited the intrepid travellers at their requested destination.

The place was more of a small fortified village than a series of sole dwellings. Cut into the side of a sandstone outcrop on two sides, the houses were modest but of thick solid construction, single story but with expansive flat roofs used for al fresco eating. The front approach to the village was walled with local sandstone cut from the surrounding cliffs.

A narrow archway made surreptitious infiltration all but impossible. The biker commune, like their kind anywhere in the world, had fashioned for themselves a veritable fortress.

The four travellers were welcomed into the village like long lost family.

"Aarif, how goes it you old Allah botherer?" Brodie asked.

Breaking into a broad smile, the Arab answered, "Brodie! Ila jaheem ma'ik. Go to hell infidel!"

The two men embraced with fond familiarity.

After a short round of introductions, Brodie and Aarif had a little catch up.

"How's it been Brodie? I haven't seen you since Uni," the Arab asked.

"Shh, Aarif. I don't let on that I'm an educated man, doesn't hold with the outlaw image," Brodie cautioned.

"Don't sweat it Brodie," Goose advised. "We suspected you were a big faggoty phony."

"Got my engineers degree, just like my man here, lifetime ago, hey Aarif?"

"Had us some good times though Brodie. American pussy still the sweetest?" the Arab asked.

"Sweeter than stolen honey," Brodie replied.

"Got anything brewing Aarif? I'm so dry the Baptists are sprinkling, the Muslims are spitting, and the Catholics are giving rain checks!"

"Texas moonshine and home grown blow on the house boys," Aarif answered.

"Allah be bloody praised," exclaimed Goose. "And I thought you boys were gonna be boring."

"Didn't I tell you my man's a fucking biker? Bikers are the universal brethren; nothing comes above that," Brodie laughed.

"A-fucking-men to that," Goose added, grabbing a pitcher of home-made whiskey.

"Allahu Akbar," exclaimed the Arab.

"Fucking 'a'," chimed in Jimbo, burying his snout in a pitcher of moonshine.

Like Native Americans around a camp fire, the Arabs had a communal gathering spot in the middle of a dust bowl at the centre of the compound. An impressive sandstone table took centre stage with an interesting assortment of van and car seats dealing with the matter of comfort.

Jimbo settled himself in to a large van seat. "I thought you A-rabs liked to squat on your heals on carpets Aarif?" he exclaimed rudely.

"Only for the tourists my friend or when we play extras in Aladdin. Most of the time we sit on chairs, and we wipe our arses with toilet paper too!" the Arab answered.

"Touché mate," Goose sniggered, making bunny ears with his fingers over his best friend's head.

"Ow," Goose exclaimed, swatting a large angry yellow jacket from his arm. "Jesus Aarif, a fucking great wasp has just stabbed me in the arm." Goose was examining an angry welt rapidly growing on his arm. "You don't have wasps in the piggin' desert?"

"We most certainly do Goose, you'd better suck out the poison, I'll get you something to calm the sting." Aarif disappeared into one of the doorway holes cut into the sandstone wall, returning quickly with a weighty spliff. He handed Goose the reefer and cut a fat leaf from a nearby plant.

"Dr Aarif, I love your herbal remedies, if only we could persuade the National Health Service to dispense your product," Goose laughed.

"Here," Aarif replied, handing Goose the aloe vera leaf. "Squeeze out the milk onto the sting."

"I had a real wasp problem in me garden once," Jimbo commented. "Had a hippy bird at the time, she told me to blow up a brown paper bag and stick it in the tree, next to me patio, she said the wasps would think there was a colony there already and leave me alone." A long pause ensued.

Goose couldn't contain himself and broke the silence with, "So? Did it work?"

Jimbo looked contemplative and said, "A wasp came along, had a look at the bag, burst out laughing, then came back later with a load of his mates and took the piss!"

"Oh, you're such an anus Jimbo," Goose replied, miffed. "Why do I always fall for it?"

"Because you just ain't too smart, smelly," Jimbo replied. "Have you missed me Honey? I've missed you!" Jimbo embraced his smaller buddy in a half headlock half hug.

"Gerrof you big soft wanker," Goose protested, but the carefully concealed smile on his face showed that despite all the torment and stick he took from Jimbo, he too was happy to be back in the company of his best friend. America had been too quiet without Jimbo.

CHAPTER TWENTY-ONE

Light Brigade

The small convoy of bikes pressed on at breakneck speed in the direction of Saluzzo. After covering only a few miles, they could see the pick-up truck lights still ablaze, half on the road and half in the verge. Moss gestured for the bikers to stop. They killed their engines and looked to Moss for their next move.

"What do you think he's up to now?" Neil asked Moss in a hoarse whisper.

"Well he's not stopped to pick flowers that's a given," Moss replied before barking a command to Tueur in French. "We don't have time to fuck about, Tueur will cover me, I'm going to find out what's going on."

"Be careful, it might be another ambush," Adiel whispered.

"No shit Sherlock, you don't say! Well it's a nice night to die. If it kicks off again, get way back into the woods; back down into the stream. You can get round behind him using the stream bed as cover. It runs parallel to the road all the way to Saluzzo. Get behind him and slot him, make sure you double tap the bastard."

Neil alone understood the terminology. He looked on Moss with new found respect; the man was ex Special Air Service.

Moss rode head-on towards the pick-up truck, bringing his bike to a sliding, rear brake only stop alongside the passenger door and levelling his pistol almost in the same instant. The driver was slumped forwards, face into the steering wheel. Moss wrenched the car door open, bathing the inside with light from the interior lamp, and simultaneously fired a round into the man's leg. The leg twitched with the impact, but the man did not react. Moss reached in to check his vitals but thought better of it when his hand slipped in the puddle of fresh blood on the vinyl seats. The man had obviously been shot in the fire-fight and had since bled out.

Moss fired his bike up and returned to where the others were waiting.

"You OK?" Neil enquired.

"Yeah, our man's pegged it. We must have slotted the cunt earlier. Shocked the fuckers didn't it when we lit the place up? They weren't expecting that," Moss laughed.

"We owe you big time Moss," Neil said, sincerely.

"Yeah yeah. Just get a crack on, get past Saluzzo and then take a bunch of detours. This place is pretty much out of the way, but you can bet your arse that the border guards and the Carabinieri will be running around like headless chickens before long. I better get back and help clear my boys off the road. Good luck to you all. Come back and see us when you've sorted out your shit."

"We will Moss," Neil said. "We will. I can't thank you enough Moss, you saved our asses."

"Yeah well, you let old Sid know that I've still got it!"

"I'll do that mate, with pleasure."

Adiel, Natasha and Neil rode on in the direction of Saluzzo. Moss fired up the old Triumph and started back the way they had come. Way off in the distance, the familiar wail of police sirens could just be heard faintly.

CHAPTER TWENTY-TWO

Mission improbable

The information Moss had given them was accurate. At Costigliole Saluzzo there were a number of routes the riders could take; presuming that their enemies had no idea what their plans were, the odds would improve from here on.

Neil on the lead bike decided to take them on the less direct route, taking the road to Genoa, followed by the meandering coast road all the way to Rome. As the sun began to rise, the steady reassuring thump thump of the boxer twin engine soon relaxed Neil to the point that he was able to escape a little into the ride and enjoy the beautiful Italian coastline. He remembered Natasha, still wearing the stream soaked leathers, and squeezed her knee reassuringly. She too was relaxing a little with the therapeutic warming effect of the strengthening rays coupled with the majesty of the hitherto forgotten, enchanting beauty of her native land. She squeezed her thighs against Neil and wrapped her arms tightly around his waist.

Just outside Savona, Neil's Beemer coughed and missed a beat, a timely reminder that the last fuel stop had been in France. Switching over to reserve, Neil signalled to Adiel by tapping the tank and running a finger around his throat. Adiel on the lighter bike was obviously not so desperate, but understood and gave Neil a thumbs up.

They coasted onto the forecourt of the next garage. Natasha hopped off the back of the bike as Neil undid the fuel cap.

“I’m going to see if there’s a hand dryer in the ladies, Neil, see if I can’t dry out a bit,” she said, striding off in the direction of the loos.

“OK, but don’t take too long. I want to put as much distance between ourselves and last night’s events as possible.”

Adiel tapped the last residual fuel from the nozzle and replaced it in the side of the pump. “I assume that our assailants will be thinking we are running towards England unless someone has been indiscreet, so our journey should now be uninterrupted until we reach Rome. Once we start asking questions, we will have to be on a higher state of security than we have been so far. I think that your wife is of fragile mind. This could present us with issues. We will have to work hard to keep her safe. Are you ready for that?”

“Ready for it? Adiel, you don’t know the half of it. I’ve only ever slept with one eye open since Natasha and I met. You want me to ratchet it up a gear? You got it. From now on, we’d better sleep in shifts; make sure one of us is alert at all times,” Neil replied.

Both Adiel and Neil had filled their tanks and paid for their fuel. Natasha had still not returned from the loo.

Concerned, Neil rushed over to the ladies. Barging a determined fat lady out of the way, he shouldered the door open to reveal a sobbing Natasha crouched on the floor in front of the toilet, retching the contents of her stomach into the bowl.

"Come on now Honey," Neil reassured her. "We'll get through this I swear."

"Why me Neil? Why is this happening to me?"

Neil wrapped his arms around her trembling form and said, "I don't know Honey, he's a bad man, and bad men make bad things happen."

"I just want to go home. I haven't seen my kids in weeks. I want to go home and cuddle the children. I want to go home Neil, can't I just go home?"

"We can't go home Honey, if we do, the bad man will destroy everything we love. We have to make a stand now. You have to make a stand. I need you to be stronger than you've ever been. Lord knows you've found the strength in the past; you've got to find it again and fight back. This time it's a fight to the finish Natasha and we have to win."

She straightened up and wiped away the tears with a piece of tissue she had squashed between her fingers. "You're right Neil. It's time for a showdown. If that bastard won't give us back our lives, we'll take it back."

"That's the spirit Hon, you tell 'em."

"And Neil," she added, "stop being such a patronising git!"

Neil's face contorted into a grin as the two of them burst into spontaneous laughter and hugged each other.

Back on the forecourt, Neil put his arm on Adiel's shoulder and said, "She'll be fine."

They strapped on their helmets and Neil switched the BMW's tap back to 'on' before firing the bikes up and heading back out onto the highway in the direction of Rome.

CHAPTER TWENTY-THREE

Triple X

Breakfast consisted of goat and some stuff which none of the Westerners' pallets could identify.

"Uh, what is this exactly Aarif?" Goose asked politely.

"It is good? Eat," the Arab replied. Jimbo was tucking into his second plateful, watching Goose delicately propelling his food around the dish with a wedge of hard crusty bread. "Eat it, don't play with it, you spoilt powder puff. It's lush," he exclaimed. "If you don't want it, hand it on over."

Brodie polished of the last of his meal and asked, "So Aarif, did you manage to score us some transport? Some bikes?"

"Of course Brodie. I even managed to get a trike for you, seeing as how you cannot ride a solo machine anymore," the Arab replied.

"Nice one Aarif. I thought that might have been a tall order for you out in the desert like this. Can we take a look?"

"Of course," Aarif said, stepping up from the table. "Come with me." Addressing the rest of the travellers, he said, "The rest of you might as well come along too, choose which bikes you want to use."

They walked across to the far side of the compound wall; there was a crescent shaped opening in the cliff face, leading into a dark, spacious cave. With all the bikers inside the cave,

Aarif fired up a small generator and the place was soon basking in artificial light. Right at the front was a small machine covered with a tarpaulin; the Arab pulled off the cover and made a traditional 'tah dah' to accompany the reveal. Sitting before them, resplendent in all its three wheeled glory was a faded Ariel three tricycle from the sixties; possibly the smallest and silliest tricycle ever made.

Brodie looked at the machine in horror. "You don't really expect me to ride this?"

Aarif looked upset. "I shall be offended if you do not at least try the machine my friend; I have gone to considerable trouble to acquire it for you."

Brodie looked around him at the assembled throng, each man willing him to sit down on the comedy machine. He let out a long sigh and sat on the Ariel's miniscule seat. With his imposing bulk, he looked like the archetypal circus gorilla sat on a tot's trike.

The cave erupted into laughter as Brodie tried unsuccessfully to put both his prosthetic and his real leg onto the peddles without kicking himself in the face.

"Nice one Aarif," Brodie exclaimed. "No doubt in the far off distant past, I did something to deserve this."

"If you did, I don't remember. No, I just couldn't resist seeing you sitting on that trike. Fortunately for you, the engine doesn't work, so I can't make you ride it around the camp."

Aarif approached another machine; this one was covered with a considerably bigger tarpaulin. Brodie snatched the cover off himself to deny his friend the reveal. This time the concealed vehicle was of a more serious nature; a Russian Ural 650cc with a sidecar. The sidecar wheel was also driven, making the outfit a formidable two wheel drive.

“Now that’s more like it Aarif,” Brodie said, nodding his approval.

“It has both brakes on the bars, the clutch is operated by pressing and holding the gear shift down. It even has a reverse gear and somewhere to stow your Kalashnikov.”

“They think of everything, them Commies don’t they?” Brodie laughed.

CHAPTER TWENTY-FOUR

Legal tender

The route Neil had chosen was arduous albeit scenic and beautiful. It took a hard day's riding through the mountainous terrain to see the trio reach the outskirts of the capital. They decided to overnight in the resort of Moai beach to the West of Rome, giving them the opportunity to travel the short distance into the centre of the city fresh and well rested. They booked the rooms for a week, giving them a base to return to and somewhere discrete to research and plan their next moves.

Lying in bed, Natasha said, “I'm really worried about Warren, Neil. What did he say to you that made you think he's in trouble?”

Neil contemplated how his conversation with Warren had gone. “Well, he told me to pray for you for a start. I knew something was wrong then; Warren knows I'm an atheist. The other odd thing he did was chew me out about losing money on a business venture that I allegedly recommended. That was weird because all our mutual concerns have been very profitable, besides, the only investment I've ever advised him about was a CGI firm we both had a flutter on, and that's been mega successful.”

“Well that's it Neil,” Natasha said. “It's bloody obvious; he said pray for me when he knows you're not religious and cussed you for losing him money on that firm. He's giving you a clue. Can you call them?”

"Who?" Neil was a little travel weary; it was taking the edge off his usually sharp wits.

"The CGI firm," Natasha shouted impatiently. "What were they called?"

"Oh crap, I remember they worked out of a suite in Beverly Hills, hang on... Fuzzy door, no, I've got it. It was Fizzy Door Productions."

"Ring them Neil," Natasha insisted.

"What? It's the middle of the night."

"It's not, it's late afternoon in Beverly Hills Neil, try them now, it's important."

The phone was picked up at the first ring. A male voice answered.

"Hi, this is Neil Curland, A friend of Warren Bateson. Can I speak with Karl or James please?"

"Hi Neil, it's Karl, I've been expecting your call."

"Karl, I have no idea why I'm contacting you so as you were expecting my call, perhaps you can enlighten me?"

"I have a package for you, from Warren. Look Neil, I have to confess I'm a bit of an animal when it comes to opening mail. I ripped the package open and tipped the contents onto my desk, seems I ripped right through a sealed envelope inside; an envelope meant for you," Karl said.

"What did the envelope contain Karl?"

"I can't say over the phone Neil, but I can say Warren is in serious trouble, as are you."

"Karl, get a pen, I'll give you the address where I am now, can you seal up the envelope and Fed-Ex it to me immediately?"

"Can do Neil. If there is anything we can do to help Neil, just make the call."

"Thanks Karl, I really appreciate that. For now, if you could just forward that envelope and don't discuss this with anyone."

"Don't you worry about that Neil. I've seen what this package contains, it's pretty toxic."

Neil gave Karl the address of the hotel and hung up the phone. Turning to Natasha, he said, "Warren is in big trouble and so are we."

At breakfast Neil briefed Adiel on the previous night's developments, and they discussed how best to proceed with the tasks facing them.

"Until we receive the package from the US we'd best go on with our plans. I suggest we first engage the services of an Italian lawyer who will be conversant with the ways of the local officialdom," Adiel declared.

"We should have got Goose to get a recommendation from his mob clients. I'm way out of my comfort zone here guys so feel free to take the lead if either of you has an idea," Neil confessed.

"Well, we can't contact Goose now so we will have to, how is it you say, 'wing it'," Adiel replied.

Natasha looked up from her third espresso, her breakfast of croissant and rolls remained untouched. “There’s a phone book for Rome at the front desk,” she said. “I’ll go and ask to borrow it; we can scout through and ring around. At the end of the day, we will have to stick a pin in the page and ring one. I don’t know what else to suggest.”

“How is the ready cash situation holding up Neil?” Adiel asked.

“No shortage Adiel. I have about sixty gazillion Italian Lira, which is about five hundred quids worth, seventy thousand French Francs, and just short of twenty grand in Sterling. Around thirty grand Sterling in total, oh and I’ve a big wedge of US Dollars too, about fifteen thousand,” Neil answered.

“Good. We’ll avoid the banks for the time being, Dollars are better currency for what we need to do anyway, we’ll keep the Lira for buying meals, drinks and such like, oh and the hotel bills.”

“We might as well go back up to our room and phone around, Neil,” Natasha suggested. “There’s nothing to be gained by riding around until we know where we’re going.”

“Makes sense,” Neil replied. “I’ll get a pot of coffee sent up to our room and we’ll get started.”

“No more coffee for me Neil,” Natasha said. “I’m feeling a little off colour.”

Neil strolled over to the bar to organise the coffees. On his return, he was staring at numerous bags of sweets and peanuts in his hands.

"What gives, Natasha?" he asked, puzzled. "I just paid for the coffees and the woman gave me all this instead of change. I didn't ask for sweets and peanuts did I?"

Natasha laughed, "Don't worry darling, you're not going doolally, your change would have been pocketful of shrapnel. They often give sweeties instead of change. It's normal practice here."

"That gives a new slant to impulse buying. I didn't even know I had the impulse to buy some sweets," Neil replied. "I suppose when you have sex with a whore, she gives you a blow job as change?"

"Charge everything to the room and we'll pay up when we leave," Natasha laughed.

"They'll do that with us paying cash?" Neil replied.

"They'll do that. Only in England do you have to pay for everything in advance, here, we're more trusting; bar bills, hotels, everything you settle when you've finished."

"I'm more comfortable paying for my drinks before I'm drunk!" Neil added, soberly.

"Uncouth people you English, uncouth and mistrusting," Natasha chided.

"Hey, mind how you talk woman, your children are English."

"Part English," Natasha hastened to correct him. "And we both know which part," she added, holding her nose.

It was the first time Neil had seen Natasha relaxed and smiling in days. He wished he could make it last.

"Oh and Neil?" she said.

"What?" he replied.

"No whores charged to the room please. That's my job."

"In that case, how much change would I get from anal?" Neil joked.

Natasha slapped him playfully around the head. "Cheeky!"

Adiel butted in. "Enough narrishkeit you guys, time to mach shnell; get the ball rolling in our favour."

"What's with the German phrases Adiel?" Neil asked.

"Yiddish Neil. It's a habit we Jews have when we've spent time around the *Gentiles.* Jews in English speaking countries tend to mix in a few Yiddish phrases here and there. It's a little Aramaic, a little Hebrew but mostly German. The languages evolved together. You could say the Germans speak a little Yiddish. Do you speak German?"

"I do Adiel, I spent a lot of my life there; man and boy."

Adiel looked wistful and paused for a second. "My mother was German; a German Jew. As a child she survived the Holocaust; survived Birkenau."

"Auschwitz? Jesus, I'm sorry to hear that Adiel. Glad she survived, but sorry for what she must have gone through," Neil answered.

"She survived," Adiel continued, "by making herself useful; collecting up the discarded shoes for the German war effort."

"We had a lot of old Germans working on the bases. I managed to get some of them talking about the war; enlightening stuff. They all knew what was going on, but it takes a brave man to stand up against a bully, especially when the bully is the state," Neil said.

"Genocide and bullying aren't quite on an equal scale Neil," Adiel said. "Six million reasons to stand up to the bullies."

"The whole world bears some of the guilt for what happened Adiel; we missed opportunities before and during the war years," Neil said.

"Guilt. You know that's an odd emotion Neil," Adiel mused. "Do you know that my mother was ridden with guilt most of her life for surviving that hell hole when so many didn't?"

"I spent a lot of time talking with these old guys; those that would discuss it. We must sit down some time and have a proper chat. I'd like to share with you their thoughts, if that's something you could bear to hear," Neil added.

The topic was obviously a caustic but fascinating subject for Adiel, one he wasn't quite in the humour to probe further.

“We will Neil, for now I think we should concentrate on our next move: finding a lawyer.”

Natasha marked a forward slash against the first name she found listed under lawyers. Dialling the number, Natasha attuned seamlessly to her native Italian language, and asked the receptionist if the firm handled civil proceedings, they did. She asked to speak to one of the partners and was put on hold.

“This is going to take a while,” she commented to no one in particular.

When the relevant body picked up the other end, Natasha briefly outlined the story they had agreed to use in their initial contact; they wanted a brief that could easily negotiate between the Judiciary, the police and Interpol. They were gearing up to open civil proceedings against a foreign national in a foreign land, and needed to obtain certain documents and items of evidence currently archived within the Interpol closed cases database, that there may be historical physical evidence to be obtained, that time was of the essence and that they would pay for his services in cash.

The lawyer's reply was somewhat discourteous. Natasha turned the slash into a cross with her pen and moved on to the next name. This time, after delivering her practised speech, the reply was somewhat more promising.

“I think I understand where you are coming from,” he said. “I take it that this matter is of the utmost discretion and could possibly involve an element of danger?” the perceptive lawyer asked.

"It is and it could," Natasha replied. "We would be willing to pay well and in cash for your services, however."

The lawyer laughed, "I am not the adventurous sort my friend. This practice would not be able to help with the services you require. However, I do know someone who specialises in exactly the kind of work you are offering."

"Can you let me have his name and a contact number?"

He laughed again. "He is a she: Alessandra Armenti."

He proceeded to furnish Natasha with the office phone number for Alessandra.

"Be sure to mention me to her. Tell her Adriano sent you."

"Will she know who I mean?" Natasha asked.

"I hope so, she is my twin sister," Adriano replied.

Alessandra agreed to speak with Natasha and a meeting was arranged for the following day at her offices in the centre of Rome.

CHAPTER TWENTY-FIVE

Shifting sands

"Can we take the bikes out for a turn Aarif?" Goose asked. "Of course my friend, we can go for a little excursion across the dunes, give you a chance to familiarise yourselves with your mounts. Have you ridden on sand before?"

"Yeah, some," Goose replied. "A bit, sand quarry and what not."

"The dunes are a bit special, the sand is powder dry, more like a fluid than a solid."

"I'm not a pleb Aarif. I have lived by the coast most of me life, and I've made a few sandcastles you know."

"If you're looking for a little humility Aarif, you've come to the wrong place," Jimbo laughed. "Goose has to make a complete cunt of himself before he'll learn anything."

Goose looked at Jimbo, he was physically shaking with anger. "You fat, fucking, fat, tossing, bastard, wanking, fucking, fat turd. Fuck off!"

"Don't mince your words Goose. Tell me how you really feel," Jimbo replied with a patronising laugh.

"OK, you fat fuck. For the record I can ride a bike on sand. I don't need any help or advice, I've ridden on sand before, I've ridden a trials bike in a sand race before, so I am supremely confident that I can and will cut the mustard. You, my well fed friend, may encounter a few problems, and I will laugh until I throw up this morning's goat, OK?"

Aarif led the small group out of the compound and into the open desert. After a few miles, they encountered their first proper dune.

Goose was riding behind Jimbo who was sat back on his dirt bike as if he were at home in a comfy armchair watching Countdown on the goggle-box. A rude awakening was in the offing and Goose couldn't wait to rip the piss afterwards.

Brodie launched the Ural combo into the massive dune; with its two wheel drive the steep climb out the other side was a doddle.

The necessary stance of a trial rider is the attack stance; standing on the pegs, leant forward, elbows bent, loading the front wheel. The rider gives the bike big beans, allowing the bike to power over the terrain, creating its own route, Jimbo in stark contrast was riding cautiously, with all his weight over the rear wheel causing the front wheel to flop about like a priest who'd been at the communion wine. The outcome was inevitable. After a particularly dramatic wobble, he grabbed a handful of front brake, the wheel washed out entirely and Jimbo pitched forward face first into the sand.

Goose could hardly contain himself. "Serves you right you fucker, revenge is sweet!" he yelled, screwing back the throttle and spinning a stream of loose sand in Jimbo's face, adding insult to injury as he roared past him and on up the dune at full throttle. Goose was still laughing out loud with self-satisfaction as he ripped out of the top of the slope and encountered the slip face of the dune. To the unenlightened, this is the back slope of the dune; something akin to a cliff face.

Brodie, who had gingerly crested the top of the slope before pitching the combo over the slip face in a controlled descent, was impressed at the way Goose flew through the air, rear wheel at eight o'clock front wheel at one, like a real pro. The illusion lasted all of a few seconds before Goose, by now screaming like a baby, let go of the handlebars and slowly he and the bike parted company briefly before being rudely reacquainted at the bottom of the dune as a flailing Goose landed squarely on the clutch lever of the prostrated bike, anus first.

A wobbling, over-cautious Jimbo was the first to arrive at the scene to witness a screaming Goose, crawling on his knees clutching his backside.

"Oh Jesus, I think I've done myself a mischief," he whimpered between cries.

"What have you done you wally?" his sympathetic friend asked.

"The clutch lever's gone right through my shorts and up my ring. I think I've disembowelled myself," Goose cried.

"Better let Daddy have a look," Jimbo said, showing genuine concern for once.

"Quickly then," he said, observing Brodie almost falling off the combo with laughter. "Have a look before the others get here."

Goose pulled his shorts down and Jimbo took up position, hands on his buttocks, peering into Goose's 'man cave'.

"Oh shit!" Jimbo exclaimed.

"What?" Goose replied, terrified.

"No, I mean, there's shit. You've crapped yourself."

"Am I OK? Is my arse OK?" Goose snapped angrily.

"Were you an anal virgin?" Jimbo asked.

"What? Yes of course I'm a bloody anal virgin, what's that supposed to mean?

"Were mate, you *were* an anal virgin; past tense mate; you've been de-flowered."

Just then, Aarif, Jack and the others rounded the dune to be confronted by Goose lying on the sand, arse in the air with Jimbo holding his ass cheeks apart and Brodie watching, trying hard not to piss himself any further.

"You Christians are something else," Aarif said without even a hint of humour in his voice. "That's what we have goats for."

Jimbo slapped Goose hard across the arse cheeks and said, "Pull your bloody pants up you nonce, there's nothing down there a wet wipe and some Germolene won't put right." He added, "Can we please get on now; I'm supposed to be learning how to ride a bike on sand dunes."

Goose pulled his bike back to the upright position and gingerly hoisted his sore body back into the saddle.

“Tell you what buddy,” Jimbo laughed, “let’s just follow Aarif shall we? Let him teach us how to ride on sand!”

If a scowl could kill, Jimbo would be a dead man.

CHAPTER TWENTY-SIX

Allies

The first meeting with Alessandra was promising. A fluent English speaker, she seemed on the face of it to be exactly what they were looking for; what she didn't know, someone in her acquaintance would know and she was willing to use any means at her disposal to find things out. After the initial introduction, the trio decided to come clean and tell Alessandra the full story. She would need to know everything if she were to help. She listened intently as Natasha told the story, with input from Neil and Adiel to fill in any blanks.

"So what you need to do is find out if there is any information or evidence, and if there is, who is in possession of it. Correct?" she asked.

"That's right," Natasha agreed.

"OK. I know where to start. I have a friend in Interpol, he can contact the Embassy in Bahrain, find out what the procedure is in such a case, who would have gathered the evidence and who, if anyone, would be likely to have it in cold storage," Alessandra said.

"I would advise against any direct contact with Bahrain," Adiel interjected. "The moment you contact Bahrain, we must consider our security compromised. I suggest you work backwards, get your friend to check his own agency first, only contact Bahrain as a last resort. We must look on all Government agencies as hostile until we know otherwise."

"It's going to be hard to search without turning over any stones," Alessandra replied. "But I'll do as you suggest and ask my friend to start with his own files. Rape of a foreign national is considered a 'crime against humanity' which puts it firmly at Interpol's door. We'll knock on it and see where that leads us."

It was two days before Alessandra called the hotel and asked to speak with Natasha.

"Hi Alessandra, do you have anything?" Natasha asked.

"I do Natasha, I will be with you in one hour, I don't want to talk over the phone."

"OK, we'll see you at the hotel in an hour then," Natasha answered.

On Alessandra's suggestion, they met in the lobby, and then crossed the street to a secluded restaurant where they could talk without fear of being overheard or observed.

"Hi Alessandra, what have you got for us?" Neil asked.

"Well Neil, my contact came through well for us. There was indeed a crime report filed by the Embassy in Bahrain in the name of Natasha Caraccio on the dates you gave me. The file, and it would seem some physical evidence gathered at the time, is in the Interpol cold cases storage facility here in Rome."

“Well that’s fabulous news,” Neil replied. “How soon can we get hold of everything and get our asses away to somewhere safer?”

“The files are no problem; we can get a copy of everything they hold. It won’t be cheap. How do you say? There are palms to be greased,” she answered.

“Not a problem,” Neil assured her. “Just get hold of everything; I’ll make sure any palms which need greasing get it in spades.”

“The actual evidence is something else,” Alessandra cautioned. “That cannot be copied; we must go through the courts. A judge must sign a court order for anything physical to be released.”

“So, can we apply for a court order?” Natasha asked.

“No, not directly. A judge will not sign a court order releasing the physical evidence to any parties other than another court, a Government agency, or an officially recognised testing facility,” Alessandra stated.

“What about the clinic back in Austin, couldn’t we get them to request the evidence?” Natasha asked.

“God no!” Neil exclaimed. “We daren’t contact anyone in the States. We already have a can of worms to take care of in Warren’s back yard. We are temporarily out of friends Stateside I’m afraid.” Neil turned back to the lawyer. “Is there any other way to do this Alessandra, any way at all?”

“Of course Neil. This is Italy. We can buy a requisition from a testing facility, and then pay a judge not to scrutinise it too carefully. All we need is lots of money."

"Let's do it then," Natasha replied.

Upon their return to the hotel that night, a package with a US postmark was waiting at the front desk. The trio sat down in the deserted lounge. Neil carefully tore open the large envelope.

Natasha picked up the photographs, looked at them uncomprehendingly, then the colour literally drained from her face as she dropped the pictures on to the table and rushed to the toilet, the bile rising in her throat. Neil was reading the note written on the back of one of the photos while Adiel studied the dossier.

"Oy Vey! Oy Vey!" Adiel exclaimed. "This is mishegas, crazy, insane. Why me lord, why am I the shlimazel again?"

A little colour had returned to Natasha's face when she returned. Neil read out the note on the back of the photo in his hand.

"Oh God, poor Warren," Natasha cried. "Everyone who cares for me is roped into my awful past."

"This is much bigger than you and your friends Natasha," Adiel commiserated. "This dossier confirms what I had suspected. All this death and destruction is down to a group of greedy industrialists, their pet politicians, and their desire to control the Middle Eastern oil fields. We, my friends, are a tiny obstacle standing in their way."

CHAPTER TWENTY-SEVEN

Inquisition

With large sums of money greasing the wheels, it's surprising just how quickly those wheels can turn. Within a matter of days, Alessandra had acquired the necessary paperwork to release the evidence. All that remained was a final meeting with her clients and her friend from Interpol to hand over what they had.

Alessandra lived a modest existence in a spacious first floor apartment in Rome. She was an adventurer and had no need for luxurious home furnishings and the like, preferring always to be in transit. Her work often called for her to live out of suitcases and hotel rooms and as such, her apartment seldom played host to visitors. The sudden staccato drum beat of footsteps on the fire escape immediately set alarm bells ringing in her head and she ran for the hallway door, pausing only momentarily to hit the off button on the answer machine as she passed; it was an established signal to anyone that mattered that something was wrong.

As she wrenched open the front door, a heavy-set figure ran headlong into her, winding her and pushing her backwards into the arms of the assailant who'd come in from the fire escape. Before she could regain her breath, a cloth soaked in chloroform was pressed over her mouth and she lost consciousness.

As the mist slowly receded, Alessandra was aware that her mouth was gagged and taped. She was restrained, laid out on her own brass bedstead, spread-eagled and naked.

There were two men: Italians. The smaller of the two spoke to her. “Good evening Miss Armenti, my name is Rocco Montisi, I will be your torturer for this evening. We require information from you, and it is possible that extracting this information will kill you. That, my dear, will be your decision.” He could see the terror in Alessandra’s eyes, it excited him. “What you will do when you feel the first wave of pain is lie to me. You will tell me a pack of lies, anything to stop the pain. I don’t know the truth so I must judge the moment when you are no longer capable of lying but are still coherent enough to make sense. The whole technique of extracting information has changed in recent times.” He continued, “The Americans have discovered a technique they call ‘water-boarding’. It eliminates the need for blood, pain and needless suffering. Apparently, they get the same results within minutes as it takes hours to extract by ‘traditional’ methods. Now, I like to think of myself as an artisan, keeping the old ways, the old skills alive. I could have come here tonight with a whole bag of interesting devices of persuasion, but you know what? I much prefer to just improvise with what I find lying around. Now if you were a man, I would be inclined to take this harmless steam iron,” he picked up the iron and pumped the steam plunger a few times, causing the utensil to give off a plume of steam. “I would place this innocent household item on your genitals and then I would wait until I was convinced you were ready to talk to me before I would remove the gag and allow you to scream." He walked across to the bed and ran his hand up her ribs, along the side of her breast and up to her neck. Alessandra's body convulsed with revulsion at his touch, stretching the restraints as she arched her back in an effort to put distance between her vulnerable skin and his repulsive fingers.

"However, you are of the gentler sex," he continued, "and have no ugly protuberances for me to work on." He turned the thermostat on the iron down to cool and placed it on the bedside locker, close to hand. He then bent down beside the bed and picked something up off the floor. She couldn't see what he had, but she could see the electric cord which hung from behind his back. The sight filled her with renewed terror. Alessandra prayed for a miracle.

"As I said before, I am a man who has a gift for improvisation. Rifling through your drawers, I found this interesting item." He held the curling tongs out in clear sight before making arcs in the air with them as if they were a lightsaber. The tongs had been plugged in for some time; Alessandra recognised the smell of hot ceramic which emanated from them. They were an expensive, top of the range model. Always short of time, Alessandra had bought the ceramic element type capable of reaching a temperature of 230 degrees centigrade; they would tightly curl her hair in just seconds.

On the night stand, he'd placed a bottle of cooking oil. With his right hand, he picked up the oil and poured it over the tongs. Instantly plumes of white smoke rose from them before a small flame burst into existence, extinguishing itself moments later as the fuel was consumed.

"That's hot!" he giggled out loud, like a child tormenting a spider. "Now, I want you to relax my dear, try to think of positively everything you can tell me about Natasha Curland, and why she is here." Withdrawing a gum shield from his pocket, he pulled the gag off and replaced it with the shield before taping her mouth back up. "Just so you don't bite off your own tongue," he explained.

He poured the remainder of the oil between Alessandra's legs, and then without further dialogue, he callously thrust the glowing tongs inside her until only the handle could be seen. Plumes of white smoke soon filled the room.

Alessandra's body arched back at an unnatural angle as the nerves deep within her pelvis screamed their message of intolerable pain to her brain, prompting a rush of adrenaline to every muscle and fibre in her body. Her eyes bulged from the exertion, flushed red as the tiny capillary vessels burst from the overload.

"I'm going to count up to one hundred now, slowly, and then I will remove your gag. If you tell me all that I want to know, your suffering will be at an end, if not, I will find somewhere to put the iron then my associate and I will go outside for a cigarette break and leave you in here to enjoy your smoke alone." He chuckled a little at his own macabre joke.

CHAPTER TWENTY-EIGHT

Revelation

Alessandra's Interpol friend stood at the front desk at the hotel. The receptionist directed him towards the bar where the trio were seated.

He walked over and introduced himself in a lazy American English accent. "Hi, I'm Ludo Vincelli, Alessandra's friend." He spoke first to Neil. "Where is Alessandra? She should be here."

"I don't know," Neil replied. "She should have been here some time ago; she was supposed to introduce us."

"Something is wrong." Ludo glanced at the screen of his cellular phone. "Che cazzo. No signal. I must use the phone!" He rushed over to the reception and barked something in Italian. The receptionist quickly responded by handing him the desk phone. He dialled a number then shaking his head, slammed the receiver down. Neil had already reached the reception desk when Ludo handed him an attaché case and said, "Take this and leave quickly, something is wrong. I must get round to Alessandra's quickly. Leave! Leave now!"

As they ran up the stairs to their rooms, Ludo barked some further command to the receptionist.

"What did he say?" Neil asked Natasha.

"He told her to ring the police," she answered. "He gave her Alessandra's address, told her to get the police over there."

"Oh my God, the poor girl!" Adiel said.

The trio had barely strapped their luggage to the bikes when they heard the screech of tortured tyres on hot tarmac as their relentless persecutors arrived at the front entrance of the hotel. The hotel had been a fortuitous choice, with frontage onto the main seafront thoroughfare, the underground garage, built to house all manner of launch vehicles and boats, opened out via a short steep ramp directly onto the sandy beach at the rear and hidden from view by other buildings. The three fugitives were able to leave unnoticed and took off down the beach towards the road and escape.

CHAPTER TWENTY-NINE

Back draft

It took less than ten minutes for the Polizia to reach Alessandra's home. They had received little information from the hotel receptionist and knew only that a possible crime had been, or was in the process of being committed.

The inexperienced officer, the first man on the scene, was running a list of possible scenarios through his mind; a domestic dispute, possibly a robbery. He was met in the foyer of the tenement by an occupant from one of the ground floor apartments. The man informed him that there had been muffled screams and more recently smoke and a strong burning smell. He indicated that he'd just got off the phone to the fire department.

The lone officer cautiously withdrew his Beretta pistol from its holster and nervously slid the safety catch off, making the weapon live. The door of the apartment was closed but unlocked, he turned the handle and pushed the door forward before agilely stepping to the side, putting the wall between himself and the interior of the dwelling. As he spun around the door stop, his training caused him to crouch down with his side arm pointing straight ahead, covering his face, ready to fire into a potentially hostile situation. As the door opened it created a back draft from the open fire escape door. The officer was hit full force by the pungent white smoke, which filled his nostrils and stung his eyes. Instinctively, he threw himself back out onto the landing. As the smoke diffused, he found himself laughing at his overreaction; the smell was that of burnt cooking, chances are that this was nothing more than a domestic dispute after all.

With the plumes of smoke dissipating into the corridor by the draft, he once again entered the apartment, this time with a little more confidence. Instinct told him that he was in no imminent danger and he headed first into the room which looked like the kitchen in search of the source of the smoke. Finding the kitchen empty and inert, he noticed a peal of smoke feeding up from the bottom of the bedroom door. Peculiarly, the smell was still not the acrid smell of burning plastics or furniture; it was more like the smell of an abandoned barbecue. Once again, training kicked in and he felt the door and wall for hot spots before venturing further. Finding no sign of heat, he took one final precaution and closed the fire escape and front door to minimise the influx of oxygen, just in case a silent inferno lay behind the door, waiting for a back draft to fuel it with essential oxygen. Mirroring his previous entrance to the apartment, he slipped the door open only a crack and waited behind the wall to see what would happen. Smoke billowed out into the void as before, but when it wasn't followed by a violent vacuum of air, he knew his hunch was right; there would be no flash of combustion.

Satisfied that the apartment didn't present him with an immediate danger to his life, he opened the doors again to give fresh air a chance to circulate and clear the room of smoke before venturing into the room to neutralise whatever was causing the fog and overpowering odour. As he stepped into the room, the drapes were pulled, necessitating him finding the light switch before any of his questions would be answered. Feeling along the wall, he found the offending article and flicked it down. For a second, the smoke still clouded his sight. As his eyes adjusted to the artificial light, he caught his first glimpse of the naked woman bound to the bed. At first, he simply couldn't comprehend what he was seeing, the smoke was rising mainly from a bubbling and hissing steam iron which was duct taped to her chest, where her left breast would have been. A lesser plume of smoke was emanating from between her legs. The officer's stomach heaved and he was violently sick.

CHAPTER THIRTY

Miracle of birth

By the time Ludo reached Alessandra's apartment, the paramedics were on the scene as were the Guardia di Finanza, a special division of the Italian Police who were responsible for organised crime. Ludo's voice was heavy with emotion as he spoke to the police officer who had first responded to the emergency call.

"Was she dead when you got here?"

"I don't know. There was so much smoke. I didn't know what to expect, I was on my own. I should have gone straight in and found her, but I didn't know what to expect, so I hesitated. God I hope she was already dead. I pray that I didn't prolong her suffering."

Ludo put a reassuring arm around the man's shoulder. "I'm sure she was." Ludo had already worked out that anything up to an hour could have passed since she had missed their appointment. It had been two hours since he had spoken to her last; theoretically, she could have switched off the answerphone any time after that.

"What made you call in the Guardia di Finanza and not the Carabinieri?" Ludo asked.

"She had a heating element inside her and a clothes iron taped to her chest. I've read of Cosa Nostra assassins doing that to their victims. It boils the heart. I thought it was just fiction though."

The colour drained from Ludo's face. This was the first he had heard about how Alessandra had died. As an Interpol officer he wanted to find out as much as possible about what had happened before subjecting himself to the intense scrutiny of another department by offering up what he knew.

He showed his badge at the bedroom door and passed through into the chamber he'd occasionally had the good fortune to be invited into. Tears welled up in his eyes as he realised that the hope of one day permanently sharing this inner sanctum with the beautiful, gregarious free spirit who had inhabited it were now an impossible dream. The room was now a crime scene and the final resting place of a mutilated, lifeless corpse.

"Wish they'd removed this while it was still hot," the paramedic remarked, working around the iron with a stethoscope whilst trying to extract the obstruction from the congealed tissue and fluids which held it fast. "I'm going to leave this for the coroner to remove, I'm satisfied there's no heartbeat." He held Alessandra's wrist for a moment before shouting, "Jesus Christ! I have a faint pulse." He barked into his handheld radio to his colleagues in the unit out in the street, "Code blue, I repeat, code blue." He frantically cut away the plate of the steam iron with a scalpel until it was free of the destroyed tissue. He threw the innocuous weapon across the room. With the iron removed he could see the charred ribs exposed, could see into where the sac containing the cooked, necrotised heart should be. Instead, he could see a portion of damaged lung and extensive seared tissue in the thoracic cavity, but no heart. Instinct kicked in and he felt inside the thoracic cavity to the right. "Oh sweet Jesus, there it is: dextrocardia. Her heart's on the right side and it's still beating!"

Suddenly the apartment was no longer a murder scene but an emergency room. Alessandra was alive!

CHAPTER THIRTY-ONE

Recruits

At the end of the resort thoroughfare there was a section of beach and scrub, generally used by surfers as a car park. Adiel and Neil deftly piloted the bikes through the scrub, over the soft dunes and back onto the highway, making pursuit unlikely, if not impossible. They rode hard for the next hour, back towards France, putting some miles between themselves and their pursuers. They pulled off the highway and onto a quiet dirt road which headed back towards the sea. Bringing the bikes to a halt in a dense fir tree coppice, they climbed off the bikes and removed their helmets.

"Jesus, that was a close call," Neil admitted. "We need a better strategy Adiel, before we get caught with our pants down."

Natasha jumped off the back of Neil's bike. "Oh my God. What do you think happened to Alessandra?"

"I hate to think what has happened," Adiel answered. "But we must find out. If she's been hurt or killed then we are compromised; we must assume that our enemies know everything that we have achieved. The stakes will now be very high."

"We'd better find a phone, ring Alessandra's brother, and find out what he knows," Natasha suggested.

"Not a good idea," Neil interjected. "If he even knows anything yet, he's not in the loop with our situation. In all likelihood, he will have us down as suspects."

"The Interpol guy then," Adiel said. "Can anyone remember his name?"

"Ludo Vincelli," Natasha said.

"Right," Neil said. "Let's find a phone and call Interpol in Rome, see if we can get a message to Ludo."

The trio came upon a small, innocuous bistro-cum-diner. The clientele were mostly truckers and farmers. The phone booth sat discretely behind the corner of the building, perfect for keeping a low profile but with a good field of vision for security.

The Interpol agents operated 'off the radar' in Rome; it took Natasha some time and some awkward questions to track down their suite of offices. Eventually, she was put through to the section in which Ludo worked. His name was instantly recognised but he wasn't available. Natasha took a chance and told the agent that Ludo was working on a case which she was involved in.

"What is your name Madame?" the agent asked.

"Natasha Curland," she replied, then excused and corrected herself. "Natasha Carraccio."

"Miss Carraccio," the agent replied. "Officer Vincelli has left instructions for you to ring him as soon as possible."

"Well where is he?" she asked.

"He is at the New Sant' Eugenio here in Rome."

"What's the New Sant' Euginio?" Natasha asked.

"It's a specialist burns unit, a hospital. Ludo has a friend that's been admitted with grave injuries. He is keeping a vigil at her bedside."

Natasha choked back the tears, thanked the agent for the information and hung up the receiver.

"What is it?" Neil asked.

"Oh God, poor Alessandra," she exclaimed. "She's in hospital, a burns unit. She's badly hurt."

"Well at least she's alive," Adiel said. "Perhaps we have not been as exposed as we thought?"

"I must talk to Ludo," Natasha said, picking up the phone and dialling directory enquiries.

After a few minutes, she acquired the number of the clinic and placed the call. It was a further ten minutes before the officer was tracked down and brought to the phone.

"Hello? This is Ludo Vincelli," he snapped into the mouthpiece.

"Ludo? It's Natasha Carraccio. What happened to Alessandra? How is she?"

"Thank the stars you got away. She is gravely ill Natasha. They burned her horrifically. They burned her inside and out. She may not survive."

"I'm so sorry Ludo. What can we do?" Natasha asked.

"There is nothing Alessandra needs from us now except our prayers and revenge," Ludo said, his voice filled with anger. "I will help you now. Anything

I can do to help you bring down the people responsible for this, I will do it, do you understand me?"

"Yes Ludo, I do. We will be glad to accept your help, God knows we need it," Natasha told him. "Ludo, do you think Alessandra was interrogated? Was she tortured? Do you think she would have told them what she knew? I'm so sorry to ask, but we need to know what they know."

"They will know everything that she knew Natasha, of that there can be no doubt."

The magnitude of what he implied did not escape Natasha. Alessandra had been tortured to beyond human endurance; it was a place Natasha knew well. She felt the bile rising again, threatening to cut the conversation short.

Ludo snapped her out of her macabre reverie. "Take down my cell phone number. Don't call me at the office. I'm going to stick around here for a while, until Alessandra's out of the woods, if it's God's will that she survives at all. I'll see what I can do for you on the official front. If I draw a blank I'm coming with you to confront these bastards first hand."

Natasha knew how passionately Italians felt about revenge. She knew that Ludo could prove a formidable ally. She scribbled the number down and hung up the phone.

CHAPTER THIRTY-TWO

Progress

"We've been here for days now and all we've done is ride bikes, eat goat and get stoned," Goose complained. "Now whilst that might be some people's idea of heaven, we are supposed to be gathering intel on the evil bastard who's trying to top our best mate's lady. I for one am beginning to think it's time we shook a tail feather and tried to achieve something."

"You're right Goose," Brodie agreed. "I'll speak to Aarif and see if we can take a ride over to Bahrain, knock a few doors and ask a few questions."

Goose called a pow-wow in the centre of the compound where the Westerners sat down alongside their local brethren and guides to discuss a reconnaissance mission into Bahrain.

"Right guys, the place we need to recce is in Bahrain; a place called Tubli." As Goose spoke, Aarif quietly translated to a few of the Arabs who spoke no English. "According to Natasha, the place is a fuck-off big palace, so shouldn't be difficult to spot. She described it as a pretty opulent fortress with only one way in and out. My plan is to take a look-see before asking a lot of questions. Now we have a logistical problem; Bahrain Island is thirty miles in length and 11 miles wide. There's a big ass American base to the south and a major airport in the middle which we need to keep our distance from. Riding over the causeway like a bunch of 'ton up' boys is going to attract a lot of attention so I suggest we ride to Dammam and dump the bikes; at least, us infidels should, you 'rag heads' can ride on over, you won't look out of place. There's a million and a quarter souls living on the island; a hell of a lot of foreigners too, so we shouldn't stick out once we get there, I'm just worried that foreigners amongst a group on bikes might ring alarm bells. Anyway, we'll follow on by Johnny cab and meet up in Tubli." Goose paused to see if anyone wanted to jump in. When the break was met with silence, he continued, "Aarif, you've got the idea about what we need to know; I want to know who's in the palace, who comes and goes, whether they order out, who delivers the groceries, messengers, whores, laundry women, stray dogs. If it visits the palace, I want a note of when, where and if possible, who. First we need to build up a picture of Mr Aykay's life, then we need to find the chink in his armour so that we can look for some leverage.

"Thanks to Brodie, we have a name to kick off with: Yazan Rahimi. Now I expect that this geezer is more of a legal beagle, but don't underestimate the bastard, he's more than comfortable with organising the sponsored murder of innocents and has successfully ordered a remote killing at least once to our knowledge."

Goose gestured for the group to saddle up the bikes. "Gentlemen, as soon as we cross the causeway, we are at war and behind enemy lines. One wrong move can get yourself or the man next to you killed so forgive me if you find I've lost my sense of humour."

Jimbo clasped Goose's hand in a high five, biker handshake gesture, letting him know that as combat veterans, they understood each other.

The bikes kicked up a miniature sandstorm as they headed out of the desert, towards civilisation.

It took nearly five hours on the small capacity bikes to cover the distance from Almuzayri to Dammam. They took a necessary detour into Riyadh so that Mr Bennett could pick up his passport and leave a note for Mrs Bennett, telling her to stay put and wait for further instructions. Brodie's Ural was the slowest of the fleet with the sidecar filled as it was with bags of Goose's 'necessary hardware'. Despite its pedestrian pace, the outfit had been painstakingly prepared and was a bastion of reliability, an honour not normally bestowed upon this marque.

The Muslim bikers took a prayer break three times on route and by the time they reached Tubli it was well into the afternoon. They met up with the Arabs in the village square.

"Aarif, we aren't going to get much done now. The cab driver told us there's a comfortable hotel down by the sea: City Resort. I suggest we get ourselves booked in, grab forty winks, then have a little recce under cover of darkness; suss the place out," Goose suggested.

"You Westerners go book into the hotel. How do you think it would look: a bunch of dirty desert wogs booking into a posh resort hotel," Aarif replied. "Me and my men will check out the local mosque, find ourselves some humble, 'appropriate' dwellings, we can meet back here after evening prayer, say, at eight thirty this evening?"

"OK Aarif, I bow to your local knowledge, customs, culture and all that bollocks. See you back here at eight thirty."

That evening, the group experienced their first official call to prayer from the local mosque. In the desert, prayer had always been a close intimate ceremony. Jimbo, Jack and Goose had experienced the Muslim ceremony before and were accustomed to the devotion shown by the faithful. To Brodie, it was an amusing and enlightening experience.

"How come you haven't seen Aarif do his 'mumbo jumbo' before then Brodie? I thought you two were tight," Goose inquired.

"We were at uni together. Young guns drinking and screwing around. I don't think Aarif was practising back then. After that came the bikes and the club thing. Religion was the club; the 'cut' was our prophet. I guess all this came after he got back home," Brodie answered.

At around the agreed time, the men started to re-group in the town square. Goose beckoned for Aarif and his men to 'take a knee'.

"First off, we need to find the palace. Once we've swung that, what I'd like you to do, Aarif, is find a room or maybe a flat near to it; something private where we can watch the entrance see who comes and goes. Can you swing that?"

"I don't know Goose, this is a pretty upmarket town. Most of the houses here are probably owned by wealthy people. We may need to go a bit further afield," Aarif answered.

“As long as we can find somewhere with a clear line of sight we can use a telescope, otherwise, we are going to have to mount cameras with short wave transmitters,” Goose said matter of factly.

“You have all that shizzle with you?” Jimbo asked.

“Yes, why do you think I have no clothes?”

“I didn’t give it any thought, you’re a dedicated little fella ain't you?” Jimbo commented, genuinely impressed.

“Well, there you go. I can buy clothes anywhere, my hardware is unique, I need it with me,” Goose confirmed.

“How the hell did you smuggle that little lot through customs without anyone noticing?” Jimbo asked incredulously.

“Customs didn’t ask any questions, and you wouldn’t notice what I had with me unless you could eat it or take the piss out of it,” Goose replied.

“Touché, smelly,” Jimbo said with a grin.

“It’s getting pretty dark,” Goose cautioned, “I suggest we take a quick walk around the town, find the palace, then we can ask the locals a few questions about the occupants.”

“If we seem not to know who lives there, we will attract less suspicion than if we ask for Isa Al-Kooheji by name. We’ll make out we’re looking for some casual work, I’m sure they’re used to that.” Aarif suggested.

"Good plan Aarif. The four of us will take the beach side of town, moving towards the north. Aarif, you and your guys take the western sector and the south. There is an area called Isa Town that has to be an omen. I wonder if the fucking egomaniac has a town named after him," Goose said.

"Stalin had a city named after him," Jimbo added.

"Stalin named a city after himself," Aarif corrected.

"OK, let's shake a leg," Goose suggested. "It's getting really dark now and there ain't an abundance of street lights around here so I'm guessing we are running out of time."

"We will just need to stop by our lodgings; drop off our bedrolls and prayer mats, Goose," Aarif said.

"Are you very far away Aarif?" Goose asked.

"Not at all, just over there next to that..."

"Uh Goose," Jimbo interrupted, "look over there."

Goose followed the direction of Jimbo's gesturing finger towards an enormous walled sandstone compound lit up like a football stadium. "I'm guessing that's where Mr Aykay lives then."

After less than a two minute walk, they were stood across the square from the Al-Kooheji residence.

"So where's your digs from here then Aarif?" Goose enquired.

Aarif pointed at the tall sandstone building beside which they were standing.

“You are having a giraffe,” Goose exclaimed. “Don’t go telling me those windows up there are your windows?”

Aarif nodded enthusiastically.

“Allah be bloody praised,” Goose laughed. “I need to start going to this mosque malarkey if all yer prayers get answered that promptly!”

The unexpected supernova of illumination created by the opulence and paranoia of the palace's occupant proved a blessing for the motley group. Within the next two hours they were able to walk the entire perimeter. With fortuitous luck the windows of the sitting room of Aarif’s apartment offered a reasonably clear view of the main, and it would seem only entrance, which confirmed the intelligence which Natasha had previously provided.

CHAPTER THIRTY-THREE

Frequent visitor

The following morning Goose and Aarif were taking first watch of the Al-Kooheji mansion. Goose was busying himself with the setting up of equipment; Aarif was stood at the window aiming the 35mm single lens reflex camera in the direction of the entrance. The camera was kitted out with a formidable zoom lens allowing Aarif a very detailed view of potential comings and goings.

A man arrived at the door wearing a smart business suit, he was obviously an Arab but wore his facial hair very tidily trimmed in a western style.

"Goose, I think this could be your lawyer man: the 'fixer'." Aarif said.

"Let's have a look-see," Goose answered, taking the camera from Aarif. "Any ideas how we can positively identify him?"

"I can follow him, find out which mosque he prays in, then I can ask someone who he is," Aarif replied.

Goose was messing with the zoom lens. "Or I could just read it off his briefcase. Arrogant bastard has his name in gold letters across the front. YAZZAN RAHIMI, what a toss pot! Where does he think he is, primary school?"

A servant opened the door and the man was shown into the hallway.

"He likes to show that he is a successful man. Do you not ever show off a little Goose?" Aarif asked with a sarcastic laugh.

“Well, I did have a personalised plate on the Harley once, it read GEOF 1,” Goose confessed.

Just then, a bleary eyed Jimbo walked into the room to a fanfare of farting and butt scratching. “Act-churly, it read GEO 71E, so even if you were myopic enough to think it read GEOF, it undeniably read GEOF 1E or Geofie which made you look an even bigger knob than you actually are, which is saying something.”

Goose stared back at the mammoth for a while saying nothing before turning to Aarif and saying, “Anyway, we can pretty much say we have a positive ID on our ‘fixer’ man, so if we catch him when he leaves, could you possible follow him Aarif, find out where he lives, works or both?”

“Of course,” Aarif answered. “I’ll go and sit across the square facing you, signal me when he leaves and I will discreetly follow him.”

CHAPTER THIRTY-FOUR

Charmless man

"Aye aye," Goose exclaimed under his breath.

The group had divided into a 'home' team with eyes on the Al-Kooheji estate and a small team keeping eyes on the Rahimi residence.

Fortunately, not unlike the home of his boss, the 'fixer's' upmarket home opened out onto a bustling square, giving the 'away' team of Goose and Aarif the opportunity to linger without attracting too much attention. There was plenty of local colour and architecture for the pale skinned Goose to point his extensive array of camera equipment at without looking out of place.

Most of the day had been spent observing the gregarious, albeit wholly unsuspicious folk going about their daily lives. The last few moments more than made up for the tedium of wasted hours. He had just observed a scruffy individual dragging a young beggar urchin by the arm, shoving him roughly on to the elaborate marble steps of the Rahimi residence. The young boy was clearly reluctant to be there and was fighting, pleading with the man, it would seem, to be set free. Yazan Rahimi opened the door, conversed briefly with the man. An exchange was made, the man observed momentarily a sum of money in his hand before tucking it into his waistband and walking away, leaving the young urchin in the grasp of Rahimi. The boy was dragged protesting through the door and the door slammed shut.

"Bingo! Our man's a fucking paedophile," Goose whispered into his hand-held radio. He photographed the delivery man and spoke again on the two way. "Aarif, can you follow that guy, see where he hangs out? We need him."

Aarif, who had been crouched beside his little motorbike in the street, was glad to have something to do, there were only so many times you could take off and replace the side panels before it gets tedious and a little suspicious. "I'm on it boss," Aarif answered. He fired up the little bike and putted up the road, following the hurrying man from a subtle distance.

Back at the rented room opposite the Al-Kooheji residence, the bikers held an impromptu intelligence briefing chaired by Goose.

"We've got a credible lead. Home team have had no sign of Aykay hereabouts, but we've had a positive result at the home of his 'fixer' Mr Rahimi. Turns out our errand boy is a turd burglar with a penchant for little boys." He paused for a moment to let the information sink in before continuing. "We observed a pimp rock up at his gaff and drop off a little kid screaming and kicking."

"Did you drop the bastard Goose?" Jimbo asked. "I hope you did."

Goose sighed, "I wish I could have Jimbo, but we're not here to save one little kid and jeopardize the whole mission. I'm sure this wasn't a one off though; it's the flaw we've been looking for, somewhere we can jam a knife in and prise the top off the whole can of worms."

“I’m sorry Goose but you should have dropped the cunt, damn the mission. You shouldn’t have let that happen, we could’ve found another way in,” Jimbo exclaimed, angrily.

“Jimbo,” Aarif interrupted, “this is not your country, not your people. This is survival to these street kids. In my country, parents cut off the limbs of children, or blind them with hot spoons so they can make more money begging. This boy, he will have received a hot meal, a warm bed for the night and if he was good, he may be invited back making money for himself and his master. Don’t judge us Jimbo, this is not England.” He turned to Goose. “Do not chastise yourself, you did the right thing. You are not here to right all the wrongs of an alien culture. You have a just cause, to save your friend's life. Killing this man would have been akin to passing a death sentence on her. Perhaps by holding back we may find a way to exact a painful revenge on behalf of all the people these men have hurt.”

Jimbo looked a little embarrassed at the rebuke. “I’m sorry Aarif, I just can’t stand anyone hurting or taking advantage of kids, it makes me so angry.”

“You can’t change things in an instant my friend. If Goose had steamed in guns blazing and saved the boy, he would have returned penniless to his master and probably been flogged or killed for his failure,” Aarif added.

“Yeah, I understand. Sorry Goose. Heart rules me head sometimes,” Jimbo offered. The man mountain looked upset, almost tearful.

“Come 'ere you big lummox,” Goose said, pulling his friend into a clumsy embrace. Friendship restored.

“It makes my blood boil, people hurting kids. I just don’t think sometimes,” Jimbo said.

“Remember mate,” Goose said. “Up here’s for thinking,” he tapped Jimbo on the head, “down there’s for dancing,” he said, standing on Jimbo’s toe, “and here’s for everything else,” he said, punching his friend in the stomach.

“Oh you bastard,” Jimbo exclaimed between retching and holding his injured foot.

“I owed you that from yesterday,” Goose reminded him.

CHAPTER THIRTY-FIVE

Red herring

"What the fuck is going on Adiel? How is it that they know our next move before even we do?" Neil asked, exasperated.

"I don't know, Neil. It can't be coincidence, somehow we seem to be compromised at every turn. We cannot win against these odds; it is only a matter of time before our luck runs out," Adiel observed.

"We must have some sort of bug on us; it's the only sane explanation, they cannot possibly have known we would be in Italy, or even France," Neil concluded.

"You are right Neil, we must dump everything we have with us and start fresh, it's the only sensible thing to do."

"Wait a minute, do we have anything with us which we didn't buy ourselves?" Neil directed the question to the three of them.

"What do you mean Neil?" Natasha asked.

"Anything unsolicited? Anything you didn't specifically buy or bring along yourself, I don't know, just anything out of place, something which rings alarm bells?"

"I see where you're going Neil. I can't think of anything in my possession which doesn't belong," Adiel added.

"I can," Natasha confessed, searching in the depths of her rucksack. "Here, this lipstick, this was sent to me because I filled out a survey, I don't remember filling out a survey!"

"Shit," Neil exclaimed. "Why the hell did you bring it?"

"It's a lippy Neil, a harmless lippy. I never go anywhere without my lipstick," she said in her defence.

"Can I see it?" Adiel asked.

Natasha handed Adiel the innocuous cosmetic. He examined it in detail.

"Isn't it a gorgeous colour?" she said.

There was a faint crack as Adiel twisted the base, the two halves separated. He meticulously scrutinised the hollow base. "This innocent item is the bane of our lives!"

"Oh God no!" Natasha exclaimed in a resigned whisper.

"What do you reckon it is Adiel?" Neil asked.

"I would say that it is a simple tracking beacon, very short range, perhaps only a few miles, very limited. You would need to stay very close to this device for it to be effective."

"So our adversaries are very close, and have been from the outset. So what do we read from this?" Neil asked.

"Look, this is pure supposition, but I think we *were* being followed closely. I think that the attack back at the border was a bit of a 'red herring', possibly to kidnap Natasha, or maybe just to convince us not to trust the authorities, not to go to them for help. Since the attack on Alessandra, I think the need to track us has expired."

"That makes no sense. What about the bomb? Why would they try to kill her back in England, and then only track her here?" Neil asked, exasperated.

"Perhaps that bomb was meant for you Neil. Brodie said that the attack on you was not the IRA. Maybe you were the target?" Adiel questioned.

"That can't be. We know that the IRA were contracted to kill Natasha, not me, that's what Doherty told Brodie. They were supposed to kill her, even if the others were meaning to kill me."

"I don't know Neil. I'm not party to their course of thought. Perhaps after Anna contacted Natasha, they knew that information had been shared, perhaps they decided to see where it would lead. Either way, I think that we escaped a death squad back at the hotel. When we took off down the beach I think we got clear of the range of this little gadget, otherwise we wouldn't be breathing anymore."

"Give me that thing," Neil snapped. Snatching the bug from Adiel, he walked around the back of a German plated semi- truck parked on the café's forecourt and discretely poked the small device through a tiny tear in the trailer's curtained side.

"There, let the fuckers follow us now," he said as he returned to the phone booth. "I suggest we press on for a bit, put a few miles between ourselves and that fucking thing, then find ourselves digs for the night so we can go through the rest of our stuff; make sure that was the only little spy we had on us."

“I agree Neil,” Adiel answered. “We should stop and plan our next move; what to do with the ammunition we’ve found. I think we should stop as soon as it’s safe to do so.”

It was quite dark by the time they found a quiet motel in a place called Gemona del Friuli. The place hadn’t had much love invested in it since a terrible earthquake had demolished the majority of the buildings in the ancient town, most had been rebuilt and stood now proud and handsome, but this poor relic had escaped the battering and had been rewarded for its stoic resilience with neglect. The manager was pleased to have any paying visitors at all, and furnished them with the establishment’s most prominent rooms. To top that off, he allowed them to stow the bikes in a ground floor apartment which was no longer fit for human habitation. It was the perfect hideout to hammer out a game plan.

Neil and Natasha’s en-suite had a rusty enamel bathtub and a gas water heater.

“I’m going to have a nice long soak Neil. I’ve been feeling bloody lousy the last week or so, all the stress, eating on the hoof and that. I need to unwind and feel a bit girly again. You don’t mind do you? It’ll give you boys a chance to plan without me butting in.”

“You go ahead Natasha, have a little pampering session. Me and Adiel can look after the fort.”

This was the closest Natasha had come to heaven in a long while. The door was soon locked and a deep tub of steaming hot water drawn.

"I think we should cross over into Austria, then over the Alps via the Wurzen pass into Yugoslavia. What'd you reckon to motoring all the way down to Saudi, Adiel?" Neil suggested.

"To start off with I'm not all that keen to cross into an active war zone, Neil." Adiel answered.

"That's the beauty of it you see: we can slip over the Alps and into Slovenia, over into Croatia, then pretty much all the way down to Montenegro without going anywhere near the fighting, we then slide across to Albania and into Greece. Our enemies aren't going to expect us to do that are they?"

"And from Greece?" Adiel asked.

"Well I was thinking Turkey then on into the Middle East."

"We'd have to cross Syria or Iraq before we got to Saudi Neil. That would require travel warrants. Besides, you're talking some really huge miles we'd have to ride across quite barren desert; it would take us many weeks, even if we were up to the challenge."

"I didn't really think of that. Outside of Europe, I'm getting a bit out of my depth. Well, what about down through what used to be Yugoslavia, down through Greece, then a boat across to Egypt, or wherever, I don't know."

Adiel scratched his head and paced around the room. "You know Neil, I was thinking of a polite way of telling you that you're a meshugener, a madman, but you've got me thinking. If we could get over to Crete, or better still, Cyprus, I could get a boat to pick us up and take us home, that is, to my home,

Israel. From there we could cross into Saudi in secret without difficulty."

"So, what do you think, is it worth a shot?"

"Why don't we cross at Trieste? It's only an Alpine crossing away and we'd be straight into Croatia," Adiel questioned.

"Well I thought of that," Neil replied. "But I figured that the Mafia might, probably would, have some activity on the Pula peninsula. If we travel through Austria first we put a vigilant border between us and the Italian mob. The Austrians are virtually incorruptible, besides, the Wurzen pass is just one almighty great climb up over the Alps, probably take us no longer than all the twists and turns of the Trieste route. I know the Wurzen pass route well, the border is a pathetic affair more geared towards recovering all the stranded vehicles on the pass than a border control, at least, that's how it used to be. I know a further remote route up over the mountains from Slovenia to Croatia: part dirt track, part road with a huge polished stone across a ravine as a bridge. It's a perfect way to keep off the radar."

"Too slow Neil, we're not on holiday. We need to get there as soon as possible, not eventually. We have an expeditionary force already vulnerable; in the war zone do you not think it prudent for us to *mach shnell* and get ourselves into the battle?"

"I'm trying to keep us alive here. We're convinced now that these bastards know what we have and they mean to pry it from our cold hands. I think caution is going to bring us through this, not gung-ho haste."

"I'm sorry Neil. I think we must get to Bahrain as swiftly as possible. We have an ace to play, but we must work out how and when to play it before our opponents find a way to quash it. I think we should stop this cat and mouse game and just board a plane and fly to Saudi Arabia."

"We show up on the radar in Saudi, and we can kiss any chance of getting into Bahrain alive goodbye," Neil pointed out gravely.

Adiel sat silently, deep in thought before making a measured reply. "You are right Neil, perhaps we should take our time, keep our assailants guessing. That way, if we pop up on the radar, they will not be able to second guess our final destination. Also, it will keep our expeditionary spearhead a secret."

"We need to get a message across to Goose, let the boys know what we have and what we're doing. If they show their hand too soon, our tardiness could put them in jeopardy."

"Reaching out to Goose is a massive risk; if our communiqué was intercepted, it would compromise their security as well as ours. At present, I hope, their presence in Saudi, Bahrain, or wherever they are has not attracted the scrutiny of hostile forces, a mistake by us could change that, put them in grave danger and compromise any gains they have made."

"If we send a message to Mr Bennett, care of the Holiday Inn, I can't see the risk to us or them. We have to touch base at some point Adiel, we can't keep them in the dark."

"OK Neil, let's get to Austria, find somewhere comfortable and secluded to hole up for a few days, leave a message for Goose with our telephone number, then we can wait for him to make contact. That way, both our phones should be random and secure. You're right: it's time we let them know what we have and find out what progress they've had, perhaps filling the blanks in for each other will inspire us on a plan for the end game."

"Agreed, because frankly Adiel, I have absolutely no idea what we are going to do with the information we have."

"Neil, Al-Kooheji is so desperate to hide that information. We need to find out who he is so keen to keep from finding out about his dirty little secrets. If we can figure that out, we should know who our allies are and who can help us expose him."

A rush of steam filled the room as Natasha, bath robe wrapped around her body and her hair piled, turban style, in a hand towel, butted in, "We confront Isa with what we have, offer to give up everything in exchange for calling off the hit squads."

Neil and Adiel exchanged glances. Neil was the first to reply. "It wouldn't be a guarantee, that lousy bastard would promise anything to get his hands on that evidence. He would still have you killed."

"I know." Natasha sat down on the tired leather chair. Despite her best intentions, she sunk into the worn upholstery, exposing far more flesh to the men than she intended. Irritated, she immediately sat forward and said, "We offer him a deal: the evidence for the means to call off the hits. If he agrees, we draw him out. He will be expecting to draw us in and kill me; we have to make sure that we're a step ahead. That's the message we need to get to Goose, he can set up the trap, and I will be the bait."

"I don't like the sound of that," Neil confessed.

"I don't care. I want to face that bastard down, look him straight in the eyes when I kill him."

Natasha held Neil's gaze for a second, and in that instant he saw the hatred, all the hurt that his wife had tried hard to suppress conveyed in a fleeting moment, an expression of pure malevolence. He knew beyond a shadow of a doubt that Natasha intended to make good her threat.

"Look guys," she continued, "I was going to keep this a secret, but as it might compromise your safety too, I think I'd better come clean." She reached into the bottom of her bag and pulled out a muddy handgun.

"Jesus H Christ," Neil exclaimed. "Where the hell did that come from?"

"Natasha, you'd better give that to me," Adiel advised.

"Don't panic Adiel, the safety is on and I'm not planning on shooting anyone in the close vicinity. I took this off that bastard back in the woods, the one that Moss's man killed."

"Do you even have a clue how to shoot that thing, let alone make it safe?" Neil exclaimed, alarmed.

"This is a Glock 26 semi-automatic pistol Neil, a 'baby' Glock. I'm not that familiar with it because it has only just been released for issue, but I am very familiar with the Glock 22 which I've fired a lot. It has a full magazine and one in the chamber: 'one in the pipe' in gun speak, 11 rounds, and yes, I *can* fire it, and I'm also a bloody good shot."

"I am gobsmacked, I share a bed with a total stranger. When the hell did you become a gunsmith?"

"I joined a gun club after I moved to Saudi Arabia. I'm also trained in martial arts, although, after the ordeal I went through my confidence was shot through, but that was then, and this is now, my time, and I can tell you Neil, I want this, I want to hurt that bastard for what he put me through."

"Well then, I say we get across to Saudi as quickly as possible, get the ball rolling," Neil said.

"Agreed," Adiel concurred. "Austria, Vienna, then straight to Tel Aviv, from there we can acquire false passports for both of you then we smuggle you across into Saudi Arabia."

"But we will show up on the radar either leaving Vienna or entering Tel Aviv, we'll still be putting our forward party at risk," Neil warned.

"I've got that covered Neil. My organisation can arrange for two people matching your descriptions to fly out on your genuine passports, destination Austin, Texas. It will be plausible, and will draw the heat away from us."

"That will put Warren in danger won't it?" Natasha asked.

"I don't think so. Warren is obviously under observation. It's you they're after; it's just going to intensify their vigilance. I can't see that would be justification for hurting him," Neil answered.

"Well, I think that might buy us enough time to plan something with Goose and the boys," Natasha said. "So I'm game if you are."

"OK, agreed. So tomorrow, we motor across to Austria and catch a flight to Tel Aviv. We should have had you in on the planning sooner Natasha, you've a head for it," Adiel added.

"Yes well," she said, "I'm getting a little sick and tired of being a passenger in my own life. No offence to anything you guys are doing for me but it's time I took a little responsibility on my own shoulders."

"You will need to lose the Glock though hon', we can't expect to pass through departures with that little tool in our luggage," Neil commented.

"Well I can carry it through customs for you, let you have it back when we get to Tel Aviv. I am Mossad, I have, how do you put it? A licence to kill," he said, "like your 'James Bond'. I won't risk phoning ahead, so it will take a few days to put things together in Israel."

"Your people will be cool with this?" Neil asked, opening the mini bar and examining the miniature liquor bottles.

"No. They do not want the Americans to suspect our involvement at all. It would prove very damaging to our relationship with them were they to discover our intent. However, my team are very loyal to me and we are fairly autonomous, so we will get the job done before anyone loses his nerve and pulls the plug. The result will be worth the pain. Besides, the Americans will not admit to any part of their master plan once it blows back in their faces, so a successful outcome will be a happy one."

"Adiel, you must know the best way for a girl to conceal such a little gun?" Natasha said. "I feel a lot safer when I know this little toy is close to me."

"I don't know how difficult it will be to take a gun across to Bahrain; we will see what Brodie's Saudi friends have to say about that when we get to the Holiday Inn in Riyadh. I can show you how female agents conceal weapons to pass all but the most thorough searches though if you wish."

"I'd appreciate that Adiel. I want it close to me, at least while we're on that bastard's home turf," she answered.

"Please excuse me Neil," Adiel said, rising to his feet. "I'm afraid I have to take certain liberties with your wife."

Neil nodded his somewhat confused approval.

"Natasha, please stand up and open the top of your robe. Show me your breasts."

With a look of puzzlement, but without hesitation, Natasha opened the robe exposing her breasts to Adiel's scrutiny.

"You have a generous sized natural bosom Natasha, just as I thought," Adiel confessed. "That is ideal." Taking the 'Baby' Glock between the index finger and thumb of his right hand, he turned the pistol over so it hung upside down from the trigger guard. Adiel lifted Natasha's breasts with his left

CHAPTER THIRTY-SIX

Observe

In the small apartment overlooking the home of Isa Al-Kooheji, Goose was holding one of his frequent mission briefings. "Guys, I need some eyes inside the fixer's home. I want to record everything that goes on in there so that when the others get here, we have an idea how to maybe take our man down." He thought over his next sentence then added, "We need to get inside his home, undisturbed, for about an hour so that I can plant a few short-wave cameras about the place."

"The old cleaning woman who comes and goes every day. She has a key. Why don't we steal her key and let ourselves in?" Aarif asked.

"Well you see now Aarif," Goose explained, with just a hint of sarcasm, "I haven't a clue how to go about dipping someone; I'm a surveillance expert, I'm afraid I was absent on the day we did 'picking pockets 101'."

"Ah yes my friend, *you* may have been absent on that day, but we thieving '*camel jockeys*' were not." To prove his point, Aarif produced a Bic lighter, which up until a few seconds ago had resided in Goose's top pocket.

"Impressive Aarif," Goose commented with a smile. "Remind me not to keep any nude pictures of me girlfriend up there."

Jimbo suddenly jumped up. Patting his top pocket and searching frantically he said, "Shit, where's me nudey pictures of Goose's mum gone?"

"Ooh, you are a bad man Jimbo," Goose cursed. "I'm going to tell Mum you said that."

Jimbo laughed and replied, "She knows about them mate, she was there!"

Goose was winding up for some serious retaliation when Jack butted in with, "C'mon you two, we need to get our heads together and decide on a plan of action. No horseplay in a war zone, remember?"

"That's right," Goose agreed. "OK, Aarif, if you can organise dipping the old trout, get us the key. In the meantime, I'll sort out the hardware."

The plan worked like clockwork; Aarif and one of his henchmen carried out a textbook perfect distract and dip manoeuvre. Goose was able to use the stolen key to enter the house.

The Rahimi home was a lavish affair arranged in a Western style with bedrooms on the upper floor and a sumptuous living area below. Goose had only a limited number of the short-wave cameras, so chose the two main bedrooms upstairs and the comfortable sitting room downstairs to place them.

Working quickly, Goose had little time for subtlety. As luck would have it, the house had an air conditioning system which circulated throughout the rooms via ducting in the walls. This pipework, with slated grills of 6 inch by 12 inch square, entered the rooms about a foot from the ceiling, offering the small cameras an ideal vantage point, and more importantly, somewhere to conceal the 12v motorcycle batteries which Goose had procured to provide motive power to them for as long as was likely to be required.

With his objective achieved, Goose left the house, locking the door as he left. He casually dropped the key onto the step in the hope that the cleaner would find it upon her return and the whole incident would not be reported to Mr Rahimi.

Luck was on the side of the righteous on that day as the old woman did indeed turn up, exhausted from running the distance from her house to her employer's, and was ecstatic to find her keys lying on the step outside. The exaltation she showed on finding the keys safe and sound illustrated to those observing her that Mr Rahimi would probably not have been best pleased with her had she reported the loss to him, and it was unlikely that he would indeed be informed of her indiscretion.

CHAPTER THIRTY-SEVEN

Unexpected visitor

With the cameras up and running, Goose was having some trivial issues with the range of the cameras which was easily solved by placing a small signal booster into the crumbling brickwork of a building midway between the fixer's house and the small apartment they were using as a base. Within a few hours, the glitches were ironed out and the first images were gathered and recorded onto VCR. Taking first watch, their plan was to record constantly, but observe everything in two man watches so they could re-load used tapes to stretch their finite resources. Jack and Goose had the first watch, with Goose watching from the window and Jack watching the camera action on a split screen monitor.

"What do you make of this Jack?" Goose questioned as a well-heeled white man in his sixties approached the door.

Jack left his vigil in front of the monitors and approached the window. Goose had already moved quickly to catch the man's image on 35mm film.

"Jesus Goose, that's Dan Ruthers, he's a goddamn high ranking CIA agent, what the hell is he doing here in a hot zone, alone, no security detail?"

"I don't know Jack, but I'm damn sure we're going to find out," Goose answered.

"Can we get sound with your cameras Goose?" Jack questioned.

"We can, but it'll mean shutting down all but one camera as the sound is on one frequency. It'll take me a while to bring them back online afterwards as I'll have to scan for the signal from the booster. My kit's a bit limited I'm afraid, I didn't have a great deal of space, and the kit Aarif's got me's all a bit ad-hoc."

"Then we should wait until we get Dan Ruthers and Rahimi together, listen in to what they say."

The two men greeted each other warmly on the steps, and then moved inside. Goose waited until they were settled into the sitting room area before taking the bedroom cams offline to allow the microphone frequency to be monitored. After some minor adjustment, the sound frequency came through quite clearly.

"Yazan, we are getting a little impatient to move our little mission along. Your man seems somewhat preoccupied with his house cleaning and not putting enough energy into the program," the CIA man said.

"Despite my employer's best efforts, and of course with your very generous help, the prey still seems able to outwit and out-manoeuvre us at every turn. I fear our adversaries are somewhat more cunning than we at first believed," Rahimi replied.

"Where is our man now?" Ruthers enquired.

"He is in the field, doing as you wish, moving the mission along."

"So who is overseeing the clean-up effort then?"

“That task is being overseen by Mr Al-Kooheji’s own head of security, Mohamed Zakrem. Mr Ruthers, I engaged the services of the Irish contingent as requested, but it seems that despite there being numerous and diverse teams in the field, all are still missing the target. As I said, they seem to have the ability to acquire allies at will, quite formidable allies too it would seem.”

“Look, I can’t take this task on,” Dan Ruthers continued. “It must look like a criminal operation connected with...” At this point, the sound died. Goose frantically adjusted the frequency of the sound channel in an attempt to re-instate it.

“Goddamn it, another 5 seconds, we would have had enough to fry the bastard. Get it back Goose for mercy’s sake!” Jack shouted.

“Shit, I’ll have to scan for the sound. Something’s upset the booster frequency; it’s going to have to re-set,” Goose exclaimed, frustrated.

After a tense five minutes, the sound once again came through clearly.

“Right, let’s just hope it holds this time; bloody ‘made in Hong Kong’ crap,” Goose complained, fixing his gaze back onto the screen.

Rahimi and Dan Ruthers were still seated in the living room. The dialogue had moved on but was obviously concluding the same item of business. “I’ll see to it that all flights, trains, borders and buses are screened. If they show up, you will hear about it immediately.”

“That will be most useful Mr Ruthers, the last message I received was that Mr Zakrem lost track of them in Italy and has not been able to pick them up since."

"Do they still have the evidence in their possession?"

"It would appear so. It was certainly delivered to them from a member of the Italian authorities. That was our opportunity to 'kill two birds with one stone' but I'm afraid that our mercenaries fell short of the task."

"So where are they now?"

"I believe that they are heading back into France. Probably not sure how to use what they have found. My instinct tells me that they will attempt to make familiar ground, either England or America, somewhere they feel safe. After that, I think they will most likely approach the authorities with the evidence."

"Let's hope that's what they do. I could arrange for them to be detained at immigration, either in the UK or the US, makes no odds, then we'll have to play it by ear," Ruthers said.

"If you do that, you will be exposed; there will be many witnesses, many listeners for them to tell their story to."

Well, if this goes sour, we're all for the guillotine anyway. Just you try to bring things to a close the way we planned, that way I won't have to create a plan B. Who has the kill switch on all this if things go south and we need to abort? You?"

"With our Irish friends, yes, but not, I'm afraid, over Mohamed Zakrem, he answers only to Mr Al-

Kooheji. I can offer him advice when he calls in his bulletins, but I cannot give him instruction. That is the way Mr Al-Kooheji works; he is a most distrustful man."

"What about the Irish then, when are they going to give their money's worth?"

"The Dutch woman has been taken care of; a random act of violence, as prescribed."

"Good. Let's hope they are successful with the Curland woman then we can all move on. On a lighter note Yazan, any entertainment planned for this evening?"

"Will you be staying the night Dan, as usual?" Rahimi enquired.

"Yeah Yazan, I could sure do with the unwind. Can you indulge me at such short notice?"

"Of course Dan, such things are never far from my thoughts and here in Bahrain, never far from my grasp."

"Good man. Sound man. Usual room? D'you mind if I go get some shut eye while you get things organised? I'm feeling a tad jet-lagged. Don't want my performance to suffer y'know!" Ruthers laughed.

Yazan smiled. "Your room is ready Dan, just make yourself at home. I will organise everything. We will have a delightful time my friend."

Ruthers smiled at the Arab's quaint turn of phrase as he climbed the familiar stairs to his room.

The Arab must have made a phone call because within half an hour, a nervous looking man stood at the door. Rahimi spoke a few words to the man and handed him a sum of money. The man, hat in hand, nodded profusely, almost bowing before taking off down the road towards the seedier part of town.

Goose constantly monitored the cameras, glancing periodically at the small timer set up to give him an idea of the remaining battery life. So far, all were still healthily within the green.

Dan Ruthers was sleeping in the smaller of the two bedrooms and was being constantly monitored by one of the cameras. Rahimi was active in the downstairs and would appear periodically in view of the sitting room camera before moving off again.

Goose was taking the window shift when a man appeared at the door to Rahimi's house.

"This is getting interesting Jack," Goose said. "Remember the Charlie from before, the old beggar bloke who brought over the little street urchin? Well he's back, this time alone."

Jack picked up the 35mm and snapped off a few shots.

Rahimi once again appeared at the door. Once again there was a short exchange and the old man disappeared off to do his master's bidding.

"I wonder what he's gone to get," Goose whispered, the question rhetorical. "No wonder Ruthers is in mufti."

CHAPTER THIRTY-EIGHT

Vengeance

The beggar man returned some time later, this time with a young boy and urchin girl; the girl must have been no more than eight or nine years old.

Goose, staring at the screens, looked over at Jack who had just put down the 35mm and turned his attention to the action on the split screen monitor. The young girl could be seen fleetingly, dragged by her armpits, passing by the open door of the sitting room, only to appear again a minute later in the bedroom occupied by Dan Ruthers.

"I'm not sure I can do this again Jack. To do nothing is to be a party to it. I don't know what to do."

"I don't know Goose, maybe we have enough already. I think we should stop this!"

The young boy it would seem was putting up something of a fight and Rahimi had obviously enlisted the help of the beggar man to drag him kicking and screaming up the stairs as the boy was manhandled into view of the second upstairs camera by the two Arabs.

Rahimi made some exchange with the beggar man which was not relayed to the observation post as all three cameras were running. Rahimi then shut the door from inside, leaving the beggar to let himself out of the house.

"What do we do Jack, what do we do?" Goose questioned nervously.

On the screen, Rahimi dealt the boy a savage blow, rendering him impotent with the force.

"That's it Jack, I've seen enough. Time to do what's right." Goose grabbed his backpack and fetched out a black pistol.

Jack was still hypnotised by the action on the screens as suddenly another figure appeared in the view from the guest bedroom. "Jesus Goose, what the hell's going on?"

Goose spun around. It took him a second to focus in on the small divided screen. "Holy cow, who's this?"

The figure on the screen hesitated for a second as if struggling to comprehend the nature of the situation: the slender, naked body of the frightened young girl, the sweaty overweight man on his knees, his obscene wrinkled digits encircling the fresh innocent flesh of his captive, the fingers touching, probing. In a moment, the man had seen enough and lunged at Dan Ruthers. The blade flashed a number of times and the CIA agent fell forward onto his face.

"Holy shit almighty," Jack said. "He's run the bastard through."

"Christ on a bike, what do we do now Jack?"

"Keep the cameras running and get ready to move. We can't let those kids get hurt no matter what," Jack answered.

Rahimi, obviously hearing the commotion, was hurriedly dressing. For a while he was in a part of the room which was out of range of the camera. When he returned into view he was carrying a pistol.

The man in the guest bedroom grabbed the young girl and her discarded rags into his arms and fled the room, quickly alighting the house and running up the road at pace. By the time Rahimi entered the guest bedroom, he and the girl were gone.

“That must have been her dad,” Goose suggested.

“I reckon you’re right. Hell, that sure was divine intervention,” Jack replied.

“What about the boy?” Goose asked.

“We’d better just keep watching. The boy hasn’t seen anything, with any luck Rahimi will just let him go.” Jack watched the screen for a few seconds longer before deciding what to do. “Quickly Goose, fit me up with an earpiece. Just keep an eye on the screens. If I need to drop him, you’d better tell me when. Don’t let him hurt that kid.”

“Wait up Jack, we’ve got enough on this bastard.” Goose reached into the duffel bag on the floor and pulled out another handgun. “It’s fucking showtime!”

CHAPTER THIRTY-NINE

Protocol

The front door was still open from the fleeing father and daughter. Goose and Jack ran up the stairs three at a time, bursting into the guest bedroom behind Rahimi.

"Drop the gun you bastard, drop it!" Goose screamed.

Rahimi twisted round, bringing the gun up to bear when he saw Goose and Jack stood behind him, pistols raised.

"Drop the goddamn gun, *NOW,"* Jack reiterated.

Hearing the American accent, Rahimi wrongly concluded that the cavalry had arrived and did as he was commanded and dropped the gun.

"It was not I who stabbed him, it was a beggar man, a thief. He ran from the house moments before you arrived," Rahimi protested.

"We know. We saw him," Goose agreed.

"Thank goodness. How is he, is he still with us?"

Jack was examining Ruthers, feeling for signs of life. "Barely. He won't be for much longer though, without hospital treatment. He has a punctured lung."

"Yazan, we need you to go next door and send the beggar boy home. Get some money from your safe, pay him what you normally would plus a nice tip, then get him out of the house. While you're in the safe, get us the protocol that takes off the IRA hit. We need to close down that operation until we can extract Mr Ruthers; he's not supposed to be here. Do you understand?" Goose said, pressing home the advantage.

"Yes, yes," Rahimi stammered and hurried from the room.

"This could fucking work," Goose whispered to Jack.

A few minutes later, a breathless Yazan Rahimi rushed back into the room carrying a dossier. Goose scanned it quickly, identified it as the document they required before tucking it into his waistband.

"And the other team, Yazan, how do we shut down Mr Kooheji's back up unit?" Jack said.

"Mohamed Zakrem answers only to Mr Al-Kooheji. He will not, cannot be stopped unless ordered to stand down by Isa Al-Kooheji himself."

"And just where is Mohamed Zakrem now, Yazan?" Jack questioned.

"I do not know. His last update was from Italy after he had lost contact with the fugitives," Rahimi answered truthfully.

"Where do you *think* he is?" Jack persisted.

"Wherever the fugitives are," Rahimi delivered matter of factly, before looking Goose square in the eyes and saying, "We should be getting help for Mr Ruthers."

"Where's his gun Yazan?" Goose asked.

The Arab was slow to reply.

"His gun, Yazan," Goose repeated. "We can't cart him off to hospital with his gun in his pocket; he's not supposed to be here. Help me find his gun."

Yazan Rahimi dropped to the side of the bed and lifted the edge of the mattress as Goose looked under the pillow.

"A good CIA agent would not leave his gun far from his hand," Jack commented.

"Here, I have it," Rahimi said, and handed the pistol to Goose.

"See if you can pull the knife out of his chest man, quickly, we haven't got all day, he needs to get to hospital," Goose said, putting the man under considerable pressure after he was already way out of his comfort zone.

Rahimi was slow on the uptake. The events of the last half an hour had overtaken his mental agility and he was doing as he was told like an automaton. Without question his hand went to the knife, ensuring his fingerprints were stained into the bloody handle.

"Cheers mate. Now this is for all the little kiddies you've abused, some Dutch woman you never met and for my mate Jimbo."

Rahimi was slowly beginning to comprehend the situation: sitting beside the bed where a top ranking CIA agent was dying with knife wounds to the chest, and him, with the murder weapon in his hand. Yazan was about two seconds away from his adrenal gland receiving an order from his brain to flood his heart with adrenalin, heralding the fight or flight instinct, and readying his body for the battle to come. Milliseconds before that process began a hot metal projectile pierced the front of his face and by very effectively severing the link between gland and brain, ensured that the order wouldn't be received. Seconds later, devoid of any electrical activity, his heart stopped beating.

"Damn Goose, we could have gotten more intel out of him," Jack protested.

"He was starting to wise up Jack. We wouldn't have got anything more out of him. Anyway, job jobbed!" Goose said, matter of factly, wiping his prints off the gun. "Talk about lucky breaks. Let's take on matey's gun; he don't need a gun at a knife fight. Wrap old pervy Dan's fingers around his gun, I'll go and whip all my cameras out then we can be off. Leave this for the local plod to discover. Should raise a few eyebrows."

"What about Ruthers?"

"He ain't got long to go. We'll just leave him to bleed out. Good riddance."

"You're a cold son of a bitch Goose," Jack observed.

"I do have me moments," Goose replied. "Let's get the fuck out of here!"

CHAPTER FORTY

Cut and run

Back at the observation point, Goose briefed the forward party on the outcome of the Rahimi mission. After the obligatory back slapping and congratulations, Goose was breaking down the bullet points from a list he had hastily created.

"Brodie, can you deliver this protocol to the Irish ASAP? Might be an idea to give your mate in Dublin a ring too, let him know about developments," Goose said.

"Consider it done man. I'll get on back to the hotel, make some calls."

"Go for it," Goose added. "We need to call off the Irish wolves as soon as we can; God knows how close they are to our Italian team. Haste could make the difference between life and death."

Brodie took the dossier and left the OP.

"Jimbo," Goose said, writing a number on a piece of foolscap. "Can you nip out and find a pay phone, ring the Holiday Inn back in Riyadh, leave a message for Mrs Bennett. Give them our phone number back at the hotel; let them know that we need them to call urgently. We'd better keep a vigil on the phone back at the hotel in case they try ringing."

"I'll take the first shift then," Jimbo replied. I could do with a night back at the hotel."

"What's up mate, you feeling a bit crook?" Goose asked.

"Not feeling too special mate, my arse has been eating grass for days. I need to shit for England, and when I do, it ain't gonna be pretty. Pebble dashing, or a light bulb with the consistency of wet cement, I'm not sure," Jimbo explained. "Either or, the smell is going to strip paint. Best I do it back at the hotel on my own!"

"Oi, too much fucking information bud!" Goose exclaimed.

"Well, you fucking asked," Jimbo grumbled, snatching up the telephone number and storming out of the apartment.

"We'd better get back to the hotel too Goose," Jack said.

"When the local militia find our VIP casualties, this place is gonna go into lockdown. We'd better go back to looking like tourists for a few days."

"Good point Jack," Aarif interrupted. "I think I'd better send some of my guys home. We'd better try not to look or act suspiciously. What about all your surveillance gear Goose? That's going to look bad if the law go house to house."

"You're right Aarif; we'd better all clear off back to your gaff for a while. Jack, can you go and tell Jimbo not to send the message. Better tell him to stow his big shit; we're on the move again," Goose said impatiently. "If you could stay on, Aarif, try to keep tabs on developments here. If Aykay shows his face you can call the Holiday Inn, I'll park myself there for a few days. We need to be back in communication with each other. This was a stupid idea; should have brought cell phones."

"Cell phones have little coverage here. Leave me the phone number for the Holiday Inn; I will phone in every day with a bulletin," Aarif said.

"I just hope we can make contact with Neil and Natasha. We desperately need to touch base," Goose commented gravely.

CHAPTER FORTY-ONE

First contact

The group checked out of the hotel and called a taxi to take them back across the causeway to where they had previously stowed the bikes. Aarif's men were already waiting to escort them back to Almuzayri.

They travelled through the night, stopping only for the ritual of morning prayer. By sun up, they had reached the safety of the compound on Saudi soil.

"I'm going to press straight on back into Riyadh, sit by the phone in the hotel. I'll let you guys know as soon as I hear anything," Goose said.

"I'll come with you mate," Jimbo said.

"No, best you, Brodie and Jack stay here at the compound with Aarif's guys. I'll go back with my 'Mr Bennett' passport, that way I won't cause any curtains to twitch. I need to extend my stay anyway; pay up for a few more weeks. We don't want to lose the room."

"OK, but you just take care of yourself mate," Jimbo said.

"I'll let you know as soon as I hear something."

"Goose," Jack called over. "Best you take yourself into Riyadh and buy yourself some decent threads before you go back to the Holiday Inn. You look like a saddle tramp."

"Right," Goose acknowledged. "See, I don't think of these things. I'll get myself some jeans and a shirt, that'll do."

"And some shoes," Jimbo added.

Goose shot Jimbo a filthy look.

A grubby but well-dressed Goose presented himself at the reception desk at the Holiday Inn hotel in Riyadh to collect his room key. While he was there, he booked and paid for the room for a further three weeks.

"Has Mrs Bennett checked in yet?" he enquired, casually. The receptionist scanned the arrivals book and answered, "Mrs Bennett has not booked in or indeed requested the key as yet Sir."

"Has she picked up the message I left, or left one for me?"

The man shuffled across to the pigeon holes and returned with a note, it was the note Goose had left for Natasha and a piece of foolscap with a note and a telephone number written on it.

Goose quickly read the note, it said, 'Ring urgently, will be here for two nights only'.

"Do you have an international phone book?" Goose enquired.

The clerk took a book from under the desk and handed it to him.

"When did you receive this message?" Goose asked.

The clerk quickly looked through his log before replying, "About a week ago Sir."

"How do I get an outside line from the room?" Goose asked.

"Just press nine Sir," the clerk replied.

He hurried up to the room and rang the number using the code for Austria. As he dialled, there was a knock on the door. He grabbed his pistol from his duffel bag and stood with his back up against the wall on the handle side of the door.

"Let us in Goose," the voice from the other side called.

Goose recognised Neil's voice immediately and opened the door.

It was a tearful reunion for the four of them. Goose had no idea if Neil and Natasha had been successful, had no idea what challenges or danger they had faced. He was naturally overjoyed to see them, and they him.

Goose went first and briefed the trio on all the events which had taken place in Bahrain, taking particular pleasure in informing Natasha that the IRA hit at least had been called off.

Neil gave Goose a potted history of what had happened to them since they had parted, then showed him the photos from Warren.

"Bloody hell!" Goose exclaimed.

"Yeah, it's pretty shocking isn't it?" Neil said.

"No, it's not that. This guy Warren mentions, Ruthers, Dan Ruthers, the crooked CIA boss,"

Goose explained. "He's busy lying on a slab in a Bahraini morgue."

"Did you kill him?" Adiel asked.

"I was thinking about it, and then the dad of the little girl he was raping did it for me."

"Raping? Where was he?" Neil asked.

"At the fixer's house. The bastards were having an 'all you can eat' paedo party at Rahimi's house," Goose explained.

"Did Rahimi call off the IRA hit?" Neil questioned.

"Not exactly," Goose said. "Brodie made the call; Rahimi couldn't get his thoughts together."

"I'm not with you," Neil said.

"Neither's Rahimi," Goose concluded.

Neil smiled and touched the side of his nose with his index finger.

"Where are the others?" Adiel asked.

"They're all at a safe house, out in the desert. We should get out there," Goose said.

"Give us an hour to get cleaned up," Natasha said. "We've been travelling across the desert all night, I for one need a shower."

"Good idea, I'll join you. The safe house is a bit crude when it comes to sanitation," Goose said.

Natasha raised an eyebrow, "I said Mr Bennett sleeps in the bathtub, I didn't mean with me!"

Goose blushed profusely and grinned at Neil. "Sorry guys, I didn't mean at the same time."

The trip back across the desert to the safety of Almuzayri passed without incident. As they entered the gates, Goose observed that the compound had retired for the night with only the Arab guards burning the midnight oil.

"I'll show you guy's where you can bunk down. Should I wake the boy's, they'll be well pleased to see you two," Goose said.

Neil looked at a dozing Natasha and said, "If you don't mind mate, we really need some shut eye. Can we leave the reunion till sun up?"

"Sure thing Neil. Everyone's going to be so made up to see you two," he replied. "You can bunk down in my cot; I'll take a turn on the floor. I'm sure we can find you somewhere in the morning."

CHAPTER FORTY-TWO

Treachery

Brodie awoke suddenly, sitting bolt upright. Something wasn't right; the compound was devoid of its night sounds. The ever present howling of the guard dogs and the perpetual whinnying of the horses was absent. He reached for his prosthetic leg. Suddenly, a knee to the chest pushed him back onto the bed, the cold steel of a knife pressed against his throat.

"Aarif, what the fuck…?" he protested.

"Silence Brodie. Do not make a sound or I will cut your throat and pull your tongue out through the slit," the Arab threatened in a hoarse whisper.

"OK man. Just tell me what you want," Brodie said.

"Your people arrived with someone in Riyadh, who was it?" Aarif asked.

"Aarif man, I wanted to trust you with this, I was outvoted see."

"Who was it Brodie? Do not lie to me," Aarif warned, menacingly.

"Alright, it's a Jewish guy OK, a member of the Israeli secret services," Brodie confided.

"Why have you lied to me Brodie, tricked me into helping a Jew?"

"Look Aarif, I haven't tricked you into helping a Jew. Everything we've told you is the truth; the only bit I've kept from you is that the Israelis are helping us too."

"I cannot trust a Jew Brodie; if you are working with the Jews then you are my enemy."

"For fuck's sake Aarif, take the blade off my goddamn throat and I'll explain. Better still, I'll take you to meet the guy and you can hear what he has to say, judge him for yourself."

Aarif relaxed his hold on the knife then lifted his knee from Brodie's chest, allowing the big man to regain his composure.

"Thank you." Brodie sat up on the cot. "I'm not going to try to explain to you the bigger picture Aarif, tell truth, I'm not really sure about it all myself. What it boils down to is that everything I told you is true. The Israeli dude has uncovered some sort of big power play going on with this Al-Kooheji guy and the US: my lot. Seems the CIA are grooming him as some sort of Arab King-cum-Chief of all the terrorist factions. The CIA think it will create some sort of United States of Arabia. The Israelis think it will blow back on them when it all goes tits up."

"And it will all go tits up," Aarif agreed.

"Exactly. The Jewish guy just wants things to stay as they are, he's afraid of a power vacuum swallowing up the whole region and us Americans running away. Thing is Aarif, we just want to stop this asshole from killing my friend's wife. Taking him down is what the Israeli wants too, so we're in bed together, there ain't nothin' sinister going on."

"Why couldn't you have come to me with this in the first place Brodie? Do you not trust in me as a friend?" Aarif asked.

"Yeah, I do, but it wasn't my call. The Israeli said that you would never trust a Jew."

"So what do we do now my friend?"

"We go and speak with the guy, let him put his case to you. It makes no difference to me; we have to take down Al Kooheji to save Natasha's life with or without the Kike's input."

"OK Brodie, take me to meet this Mr Zeev, we'll see what he has to say."

"How the hell did you know his name?"

"I know much about Mr Zeev, Brodie, I just wanted to see if you would tell me the truth."

"And if I hadn't?"

"Then you would be wearing your tongue as a necktie."

"Not with that dull blade, I could ride all the way to Big Spring on it and never split a hair," Brodie answered, confidence returning his sass.

"I'm glad I didn't have to kill you Brodie. Come out and speak to your friends, reassure them. We will talk in the morning."

CHAPTER FORTY-THREE

Strange bedfellows

Aarif left him to dress and walked out into the compound, barking orders to his men in Arabic.

By the time Brodie followed him out, a bonfire was raging in the centre focal point of the compound. In the light from the dancing flame Brodie could see his friends and companions in various states of undress grouped around the fire. He walked across to Neil and grabbing his hand in welcome, said, "Jesus Neil, good to see you buddy, I'm guessing you got the knife to throat wakeup call too then?"

"Yep. It was looking pretty grim too until their leader came out and shouted something at them in rag-head, then they just let us go and went back inside," Neil said. "I don't know what you said to the boss man but it seems to have worked."

"Aarif, that's Aarif. He's an old, dear friend of mine. I told him about Adiel," Brodie said.

"Was that wise?" Neil questioned.

"We're still breathing aren't we?"

"So, now what?" Neil asked.

"Aarif wants to meet with Adiel, hear what he has to say."

"We can't take him to Adiel. What if he just wants to kill him?"

"He won't do that."

"What makes you so sure?" Neil pressured.

"Because he won't. It would be discourteous. Despite what you may think of him, Aarif will do no harm to Adiel while he is under our protection. If they met in different circumstances things might be different. My friends are not snakes in the grass you know."

"They felt pretty low sneaking in and putting a knife to my throat. Pretty bloody snake like too."

"Welcome to Saudi Neil. Where's Natasha?" Jack asked, nodding to Neil before glancing around the fire.

"They didn't disturb her, left her sleeping like a baby. I guess they didn't think this concerned her," Neil replied.

"You see what I'm saying: well mannered," Brodie said.

"Oh God yes! Very considerate. Take her husband and his friends outside and slit their throats, very couth indeed," Neil hissed, "He's fucking lucky she didn't wake up, he'd likely be picking 9mm slugs out of his arse."

"Stop whining buddy, you're still alive aren't you?" Brodie berated.

"Yes, but I wish it was down to the calibre of the man rather than just because you got a multiple choice question right."

"Look, Aarif was pissed because we lied to him OK?" Brodie explained. "Now I can sympathise with him there; I wanted to tell him about Adiel from the outset. All we have to do is take Aarif to meet with Adiel so that he can be sure that helping us isn't going against the interests of his own people, then everything will be fine and nobody's blood gets spilled."

"Just Aarif?" Neil asked.

"I guess so. Most of the others don't speak English, so I'm guessing Aarif will come alone," Brodie said.

"We'll have to insist on it Brodie, we can't turn up at the hotel with a lynch mob."

"OK Neil, I'll speak to Aarif in the morning, make sure he's OK with that," Brodie concluded. "Let's get everyone back inside, we aren't going anywhere until morning.

Brodie didn't feel much like sleeping and sat by the fire until dawn brought the Arabs and their prayer mats outside once again. Once the morning ritual was finished, Aarif walked over.

"I take it you did not return to your bed last night then Brodie?" he asked.

"Well call me old fashioned Aarif, but I find it hard to settle when there's a noose hanging from every tree."

"I am truly sorry Brodie but I had to be sure that you could be trusted, besides, it's not like we aren't both outlaws. Didn't we both choose this life knowing that it could end quickly and violently?"

"Yeah, but hopefully not at the hands of an old and very dear friend," Brodie reasoned, his voice etched with sincerity.

"I must reserve judgement at this time my friend, but if this man is indeed on the side of right, then I will apologise unreservedly for my mistrust."

"Well," Brodie said, "we've got the green light to go speak to Adiel, but it will have to be just you on your own. Are you cool with that?"

"Why wouldn't I be Brodie? I'm sure your Jew poses me no threat," Aarif answered.

"Look man, we're in your debt for all you've done so far. I'm really sorry for keeping you out of the loop. Hear the man out, if you don't like what he has to say, then me and the others will clear out and leave you in peace," Brodie said.

"And will you undo the things we have already done, stop things we have put in motion?"

"Hell man, we've done nothin' that didn't need doing, you know that."

"Come then Brodie let's you and I go alone, hear what this Jew has to say."

Brodie and Aarif drove to the hotel at Riyadh. Brodie made the introductions, then at the request of both of the men, left them to talk and thrash out their differences.

Centuries of mistrust needed to be cast aside for Aarif to even consider what Adiel had to say. A lesser man would not have been up to the task.

Adiel spoke to Aarif in fluent Arabic. "We are cultural enemies you and I, but in this instant we are working for a common goal, against a common foe.

The Americans feel that they have achieved something working with the Mujahidin against the Russians. They feel that they now have allies in the Middle East. They are wrong, you and I know this. Once again, the Americans see themselves as 'Kingmakers'. They will put all their considerable resources at the disposal of Al-Kooheji; they will do all that is necessary to exalt him to the highest position. Al-Kooheji is a power hungry megalomaniac, he will do as they bid. Our countries will suffer the consequences as heads of state fall and a power vacuum is left." Adiel let his speech sink in a little with Aarif before adding, "The Americans would not get their 'United States of Arabia'. I think what we would have would be more akin to a Sunni Caliphate. You as a Shia Muslim would not benefit from that."

"How would you, a Jew, know what sect I belong to?"

"If I was in your company for half an hour, I would know. As it happens, I asked Brodie, he was fascinated by your prayer rituals, he was able to describe in detail how you and your men pray. You are all Shia not Sunni. Under a Sunni Caliphate, you would be put to death as apostates."

"I am ashamed to say that you are right," Aarif concurred. "The removal of borders and heads of states by a militia of Sunni, Wahhabi and Salafi would lead to the reprisal of old hatreds. Wholesale defeat and slaughter of Shia Muslims would undoubtedly follow."

“So you see, for once Jew and Arab are not mortal enemies. It is in our mutual interest to see that this plan does not grow legs,” Adiel concluded.

“Agreed. You can accompany us to the compound in Almuzayri. Until our business is concluded you will be under my protection and will not be harmed. We can call Brodie back in.”

Brodie was waiting in the hallway, ear practically against the door, hoping that neither man would need rescuing.

“Brodie, we can return to the compound. Mr Zeev will be accompanying us.”

“Well that’s mighty fine news. The others will sure be glad to see us. I’m supposin’ they’ll be getting a might anxious by now,” Brodie said, lapsing into broad Texan.

Aarif laughed. “What is it you say Brodie? You can take the man out of Texas, but you can’t take Texas out of the man!”

CHAPTER FORTY-FOUR

Reveal

"I don't know how you pulled that off Brodie, but well done," Neil said as Brodie, Adiel and Aarif dropped from the cab of the Hilux.

Jack and Jimbo greeted Adiel cordially, clearly pleased to see him safe and sound.

Brodie made a bee line for Natasha and embraced her in a sincere 'bear hug'.

After the introductions and reunifications were complete, Neil beckoned for all the English speakers to sit down around the dust bowl. "Right, I think it's time we all sat down and talked about what we have," Neil said. "Because right now I have no idea what to do with or about any of it, so I'm going to say my bit, then throw the floor open to suggestions. We have a sample of DNA, which if analysed should show that Aykay fathered a son to his own Mommy. We have Italian and Bahraini statements to the effect that this sample belonged to Mahmoud Al-Kooheji. We have a dossier by a senior FBI agent, outlining a CIA plot to create an 'Arab King'. We have explicit phoney photographs of a very dear friend performing lewd acts with a now deceased minor. We have a dead paedophile 'Mr fix-it' hot shot lawyer and all round git, and we have a dead paedo senior CIA officer who is probably responsible for the death of aforementioned minor, and a good few besides, and to top that off, we have Rahimi and Ruthers on tape discussing the hit on Natasha.

"Question to the floor is: what do we do with all this great information to bring Aykay and his associates down?"

Aarif was the first to offer an answer. "The countries with the most to lose from the American plan would be Iran and Iraq. As the most dominant Shia territories, I would assume that they would be very interested in the information we hold."

"Granted Aarif," Neil answered. "But *if* we were able to get the information to the authorities in either of those countries, what guarantees would we have that the information would be used the way we want: to bring Aykay down and exonerate Warren?"

"There is one individual who may be able to help us," Aarif said. "Hamad bin Isa Al Khalifa: the Crown Prince of Bahrain. The American plot will depose him, prevent him from becoming Emir. The Prince is promising reforms when he becomes head of state, promising the Shia majority better representation in the political arena. But making contact with the Crown Prince would be impossible."

"We could call him and arrange a meeting," Natasha offered.

"I beg your pardon Natasha," Aarif answered with incredulity, "one does not simply call the future king of Bahrain."

"One can if one is friends with him," Natasha answered.

Neil looked on with his mouth agape.

"I know the Prince, I've been for lunch at the palace. I'm sure if I call him he will return my call,"

Natasha said, playing down the magnitude of what she was saying.

"I'm not sure I want to know how you know the Crown Prince of Bahrain," Neil said, quietly.

"He plays golf Neil, he was a regular customer. He's a very good friend of Warren's."

With this, Neil relaxed slightly. "Oh right."

"For heaven's sake Neil he's nearly old enough to be my father," Natasha chastised. "Besides, he already has four wives, I'm sure he's not looking for a fifth."

"So where do we start? I'm sure you don't have the Crown Prince's phone number conveniently in your little black book, and we are unlikely to get the number from directory enquiries," Neil commented, with an air of sarcasm.

"Warren would have his number, but I don't suppose calling him is an option?" Natasha questioned.

"Not safe. Any contact with Warren at this stage could potentially compromise everything," Neil confirmed.

"In that case, I suggest we take a trip to the golf club in Dhahran. They will have the Prince's secretary's number. It might take a while but I'm sure we will be able to touch base. Worst case scenario I will get a message to Sheia, his second wife. She and I were roughly the same age. We became quite friendly when the Prince visited the course. Her little one, Khalid, was the same age as

David. It was at her invitation that I visited the palace."

CHAPTER FORTY-FIVE

Rekindle

In an effort to keep the visit casual, Neil borrowed the pick- up from Aarif, and he and Natasha made the trip to Dhahran alone. As they entered the pro shop, the manager instantly became stressed and hustled them into the back office. Once out of sight, Natasha introduced Neil to her former boss.

"Mr Curland I am so pleased to meet you but I fear that your wife may be in grave danger," he said, grasping both Neil's hands with surprising familiarity. Neil was finding customs somewhat strange, despite Natasha's attempts to acclimatise him to the ways of the Muslim world.

"You may speak directly to my wife sir, please do not stand on ceremony," Neil said.

The manager continued to hold onto Neil's hands as he said, "Mrs Curland, I am so pleased to see you well. I fear there are people who seek you. These are not good people my friend, I fear they will do you harm."

Natasha rightly interpreted that her former manager felt awkward speaking directly to a woman while her husband was present and so suggested that he conduct the conversation with her husband and that she would just listen in.

"Men have visited on several occasions sir, wanting to know who your wife befriended during her tenure here with us."

"What kind of men?" Neil asked.

"Not the secret police sir, but men every bit as dangerous."

"You mean like private security?" Neil suggested.

"I would say more like private militia sir. Men who made me feel very vulnerable despite my own considerable security staff."

"What did they want?"

"Information sir. Names, addresses, anything to do with your wife: her friends, who she befriended during her employment with us."

"What did you tell them?"

"I told them the truth sir, that you wife was friends with everyone from our VIP guests to the lady that cleans out the bathrooms. With all due respect sir, your wife is well revered by all who come into contact with her. She was a great asset to the club."

"Did they seem interested in anyone in particular?" Neil asked.

Alarmed, Natasha interjected, "Sheila. Oh please God no."

"Yes, our former cleaner. They demanded I furnish them with a last known address for our cleaner, your wife's business partner, Miss Sheila. They were most persuasive I'm afraid," the manager confirmed.

"Did you give them Sheila's address?" Natasha asked.

"I gave them the address we had when Miss Sheila worked here. I did not give them her current address," the manager answered.

"This next matter is of grave importance," Neil stressed. "We must make contact with one of your VIP clients. I cannot overstate the importance of this request," Neil added.

"Sir, if it is in my power to comply with your wishes, I will," the manager confirmed.

"We have critical information which we can only share with the Crown Prince of Bahrain. I implore you sir to help us, help my wife to make contact with the Prince."

The manager looked thoughtful for a while. "Your wife was on intimate terms with the second wife of the Prince I believe?"

"That's correct," Neil confirmed.

"I cannot request that the Prince speak to Mrs Curland directly, but it would be permissible for me to contact the Prince's personal secretary, ask him to request the Prince permit his *wife* to contact Mrs Curland."

"If you would be comfortable doing this, I would be in your debt," Neil added, quickly learning how things are conducted in the Muslim world. "I'll leave a number on which we can be contacted. I must add that this is a matter of life and death for those involved. A swift result would be most appreciated." Neil was learning that to hurry or hustle a Muslim was an act of great insult. Encouraging expeditiousness had to be approached with great subtlety.

"We must find Sheila," Natasha said. "She's in great danger."

CHAPTER FORTY-SIX

Mortal danger

"Where is she living these days?" Neil asked.

"Here in Dhahran, my apartment. Give me the keys," she said, snatching the keys to the pick-up from Neil's grasp. "It'll be quicker if I drive."

"*Your* apartment?" Neil asked.

"Yes Neil, Sheila lives in *my* apartment in Al-Khobar."

Natasha gunned the old Nissan along the familiar route from the club in Rolling Hills to her old apartment in the upmarket suburb. Not a word was spoken between them during the ten minute drive. Natasha screeched the truck to a halt in a palm tree lined avenue before opulent crescent shaped apartments, each facing a private beach and the sea.

"This is where you lived?" Neil asked. "You never brought me here."

"David was here. I didn't want you to meet until I was ready."

"Have you got the Glock with you still?" Neil questioned.

"Yes."

"Do you want to let me have it, just in case?"

Natasha looked at Neil, he could see the strength and determination in her eyes. "Look I'm not dissing you in any way Natasha, but I'm the ex-serviceman,

I think we have better odds if I'm the one with the gun."

Seeing the common sense in his argument, she reached under her top and pulled the little pistol free of its Velcro strap, handed it to Neil, then turned and ran towards one of the beach front condos with him in hot pursuit.

Natasha ran straight up the familiar marble staircase and through the maze of corridors to the front door like a woman on a mission. Neil, a visitor for the first time, was lagging behind slightly. Seeing the door slightly ajar, she charged straight on into the apartment. Neil heard her scream as he crested the last few steps, and burst through the door just in time to see a surprised and bewildered Arab levelling an automatic weapon towards his wife.

Neil fired once. The round took the man centre chest and the weapon dropped before it could finish its upward arc. A burst of automatic fire ricocheted off the marble floor as the forearm muscles of the dying man tensed the tendons in his finger one final time in spasm.

Outside the apartment, they heard the tortured squeal of tyre rubber as a vehicle was hurriedly driven away.

"Bollocks," Neil cursed. "Now we're compromised."

Natasha quickly looked around the condo. All around there were scenes of a struggle. Sheila was gone and so was her daughter.

"They've taken her. They've taken her, Neil. We've got to get her back. We've got to save them!" Natasha was distraught, but surprisingly coherent.

"We should get back to the golf club," Neil said, "bring the manager up to speed. He needs to get us an audience with the Prince sooner rather than later. If our enemies put two and two together, then he's not safe either."

"I don't get it Neil. Isa knew I owned this flat. Why did he send his guys to the golf club?"

"I guess he didn't know you still owned it, or at least he didn't know Sheila lived here. Anyway, he knows now." Neil looked at Natasha. "Are you good? Are you OK to drive back to the club or do you want to direct me?"

"I'll drive," she said, quickly retracing her steps to the truck.

Recognising that his own life may be on the line, the manager was quickly convinced to expedite their request, and by convincing the Prince's personal secretary that the kingdom was in grave danger, a meeting between Neil, Goose, the Crown Prince and his security advisers was arranged for the following day.

As they drove back towards the compound in Almuzayri, Neil broke the silence by saying, "We get all the evidence we have into the hands of the Crown Prince, that should reverberate through your Mr Al-Kooheji's world and send him on the run, or at least smoke him out. That's the best thing we can do for Sheila. Other than that, we're after a needle in a haystack."

"He's not *my* Al-Kooheji, Neil. He's a sadistic, murdering bastard, and I intend to kill him!"

"Sorry, I didn't mean it like that."

"Let's just press on Neil; I'm not much in the mood for small talk."

"We've a four hour trip ahead of us; it will pass a lot slower in silence."

"Well let's just get a move on can we?"

"The trick is to develop a callous on the outside, stay soft on the inside. If you let it, this stuff will dry you up and turn you to stone."

"Sorry Neil, but I didn't join the forces like you did, I don't want to develop a callous on the inside or the outside, I just want to be me; I want to stop causing my friends suffering."

"You're not the cause of this Natasha; you just got drawn into some other bastard's fucked up world. I'm just as much to blame for that as you are."

"Please Neil, I just want to zone out for a bit, I'm bloody emotionally exhausted."

Neil stared at the road ahead and gave Natasha her space.

After half an hour of complete silence, she turned to him and said, "Thanks for back there. You saved my life."

Neil answered with sincerity. “I’d give my own life for yours, you know that.”

“I’m sorry for being such a bitch.” Within a few minutes, she was fast asleep.

CHAPTER FORTY-SEVEN

Preparation

Natasha was still not feeling in the mood for discussion and decided to leave Neil to brief the others on the recent developments while she drove back to the Holiday Inn for a shower and to check for messages.

"Take the Toyota," Aarif said. "It's faster than the Nissan and it has a cell phone and shortband radio, just in case."

"You get reception out here?" Neil asked.

"Closer you get to Riyadh, the better the reception. By the time the cell loses reception, you're usually close enough for the shortwave. It works OK for us. Channel five: we monitor it 24/7. "

Jimbo and Brodie volunteered to act as her escort. The three of them jumped up into the Land Cruiser, with Natasha in the driving seat. Aarif took a few minutes to orientate Natasha with the new vehicle.

"Are you familiar with the transfer gears, and that Natasha," Aarif asked, "in case you need to use four wheel drive?"

"I think so Aarif. Do I need to lock the front hubs?" she asked.

"Not from outside, just push this yellow button on the dash," he said pointing to a prominent knob on the dash. "I've fitted electric locking hubs. You don't want to be jumping out of the cab in the middle of the desert."

They said their goodbyes and Natasha drove out of the compound, back towards Riyadh.

"Take a knee guys," Neil said. "I've got quite a bit to tell you. We've had a bit of an eventful trip."

Neil brought the group up to speed on the forthcoming audience with the Prince, the development in Al-Khobar and the apparent kidnapping or abduction of Natasha's friend Sheila.

"Jesus Neil," Goose exclaimed, "do we have any clues at all as to where the lunatic may have taken her?"

"Not a one Goose. I am hoping that the audience with the Prince will smoke him out." Neil directed his attention towards Jack. "What do you think Jack? Will the Prince have the necessary clout to shut the American scheme down or will they be able to tough it out?"

"Well, I'm no expert in the relationship between the Prince and his US allies, but I would say that the US needs to sustain the rosy relationship they have with the Bahraini regime. This is going to blow back heavily in their faces. I can't see them being able to placate the Prince without him seeing a lot of sacrificial heads roll. This is not a plan hatched by the present administration, Neil. It's likely that this is a CIA or internal security agency operation, possibly backed by the previous regime, certainly behind the back of the current President. At the end of the day, the Prince was one of the heads of state who would have been deposed by an American backed coup. I can't see this turning against us."

“I think that you should be with us tomorrow Jack; your former position will add credibility to our argument,” Neil added.

“The Crown Prince is an educated man Neil,” Aarif interjected, “a Western educated man. I read somewhere that during his spell at university he studied with fascination the rise and fall of empires; Roman, Ottoman, Austro Hungarian through to the British Empire and its ultimate disintegration. He will probably not be too surprised by the American scheme.”

“Hey steady on Aarif, the British Empire is still alive and well mate,” Goose corrected. “The Falklands, Bermuda, Christmas Island, Gibraltar, and we’re renting some council flats in Hong Kong still. Oh and don’t forget, the Isle of Wight.”

Aarif laughed, “OK Goose, I stand corrected; the British Empire has not yet taken its last gasp.”

“Glad you agree Aarif, otherwise I would have had to list all our other ‘dependencies’ like the Isle of Man, Guernsey, and Jersey. Need I go on? There’s the Scottish islands and Highlands too, and Northern Ireland.”

“OK Goose, the British Empire is still alive and well. Now can we please continue?” Aarif conceded. “The point I wished to make is that the Crown Prince will see the logic in the scheme. I believe he will threaten to expose the plan. The Americans will sacrifice Al-Kooheji for the better good. I would put money on it, and I am not a betting man.”

The sun had not long come up. Morning prayer was about to commence. The Toyota was observed speeding towards the compound, its tyres kicking up a sandstorm in the arid desert heat. Behind the Toyota, and slightly obscured by the cloaking sand, sped a veritable cavalcade of cars, the incandescent flashes of small arms fire clearly visible despite the backdrop of sand and shimmering sunlight.

The radio crackled a sombre message: "Get the welcome wagon ready guys, we're coming home and we're coming in hot!"

CHAPTER FORTY-EIGHT

Clash of clans

On route to the hotel, Natasha told Brodie and Jimbo about the day's events, about how it appeared that Isa, or his cronies, had kidnapped her friend Sheila.

At the Holiday Inn, she called at the reception desk and collected the key.

Distracted by the delicious aromas drifting across from the restaurant, the normally diligent and observant men were discussing the merits of a Western diet, and failed to notice the man behind the desk pick up the phone as they left.

"I'm going to take a shower guys," Natasha said, as they entered the room. "Why don't you call room service and get yourselves something decent to eat?"

"I could really use a change from goat," Jimbo said.

"Ditto," Brodie agreed, "I'll see what's on offer." With that, he rummaged through the numerous leaflets and tourist shizzle lying on the bureaux, until he came across the restaurant menu. "Hey Natasha," he called out, "did you want anything?"

"No ta Brodie," she answered, "I'm still feeling a bit off colour."

Brodie did the honours and by the time Natasha came out of the bathroom, the two men had devoured a number of courses of food. "Feel better?" he asked, seeing that the colour had returned to Natasha's cheeks.

"Yes thanks Brodie. How about you two?"

Jimbo belched out a short reply.

"Fed and satisfied thanks girl," Brodie replied politely. "Should we be getting on back to the compound now?"

"Do you mind if we stay here, just a few hours? I am so exhausted; I really need a few hours in a comfy bed," Natasha asked.

"Hell, why not?" Brodie said. "It's not as though me and Jimbo have anywhere to be in the morning. You go through to the bedroom and catch some z's, me and Jim can stretch out on the couches here in the day room, watch ourselves some TV. We'll wake you up bright and early so we can get back to the compound in time for tomorrow's business."

"Thanks guys. I really do need to sleep," Natasha said, and then retired to the bedroom leaving the door slightly ajar.

After a short while, Brodie and Jimbo overheard her softly sobbing into her pillow.

"What should we do?" Jimbo whispered to Brodie.

"Nothing man," Brodie replied, in equally hushed tones. "She needs it I should say. Some kind of release after the shit she's been through; poor mare."

"She's a brave soldier right enough," Jimbo commented.

"She'd charge hell with a bucket of ice water," Brodie concurred in his uniquely Texan style.

It was about an hour before sunrise when Brodie decided to wake Natasha. He knew from living with Tarina that women took a while to get ready in the morning. He knew also that women such as Tarina and Natasha didn't take kindly to being rushed, so an early start was a wise call.

She looked so peaceful lying there, her eyes all puffy from crying herself to sleep. He recalled the first time he'd seen her in a hospital bed in Austin. He feared the same haunted look would be in her eyes again when she opened them.

"Hey Natasha," he called softly. "Hey girl, time to wake up. I know I'm about as welcome as a wet shoe, but it's time to put the chairs in the wagon, and get down the road a piece."

Natasha mumbled and started to rouse. Brodie preserved her dignity by making his way back into the day room, and closing the door behind him.

Jimbo was staring intently out of the window. "Brodie, I've got a bad feeling," he said.

"Rich food," Brodie laughed. "Today's goat will see you right."

"I'm serious mate," Jimbo reiterated. "See these guys down there on the street? Well I've been watching them. There are around four white sedans parked around the back of the hotel, plus the Hilux you see out front. They're together. I saw one guy get out of that pick-up and walk away. I nipped round and watched him out of the bathroom window. He went round the back, to each of the other cars in turn. They're watching for us, I'm telling you."

Brodie looked at the truck out front, then from the bathroom window at the cars at the rear. "Well supposing you're right, we gotta get Natasha out of here safely."

"Agreed, but how?" Jimbo asked.

"OK, here's the idea. We go downstairs, get the valet to bring the Toyota to the front of the hotel. When he gets to the door, we barrel out, tackle him into the passenger seat and motor off. Hopefully, our tail will think that all three of us are in the Jeep and will be on our tail," Brodie answered, thinking on his feet.

"What about Natasha?" Jimbo asked, alarmed.

"Well if the bad guys are after us, she can catch a Johnny cab to the compound later," Brodie answered.

"What do we do if we get them to chase us then?" Jimbo enquired.

"Lead 'em back to Almuzayri," Brodie replied.

"That'll please Aarif I'm sure," Jimbo cautioned, sarcastically.

"I'll call my man on route, let him know company's coming and to add a cup of water to the soup."

They explained the plan to Natasha.

"I'm coming with you guys in the Jeep," she said.

"It'd be safer for you if you follow on later," Brodie advised.

"I'm coming with you; no discussion. Your plan is rubbish. I'm sorry Brodie, but with your leg you aren't about to go leaping into the truck 'Starsky and Hutch' style, they'll see what's going down, and I'll be a sitting duck on my own. I'll take my chances with you guys. They're obviously going to wait until we're out on the highway to pounce, so I suggest we lock the front hubs, shove the crate into four wheel drive high range then take to the desert. That'll give us an advantage over all but the pick-up."

"Hell girl," Brodie said. "When did you get so much snap in your garters?"

"I told you Brodie, I'm not a passenger in my own life anymore. I'm doing the driving. We'll see how well these bastards keep up."

At the front of the Holiday Inn was a separate covered lane for dropping and picking up as you would find at airports. The valet brought the Toyota up to the main doors, under the bright glare of security lights and cameras. The inconspicuous sedans remained inert in the long term car park. Clearly their occupants weren't brave enough to mount such an audacious attack.

As they pulled out onto the highway Jimbo exclaimed, "They're coming!"

"Let 'em come," Natasha growled, gunning the 4.5L six cylinder petrol engine.

"Holy shit, this thing's quick," Brodie remarked, oblivious to the fact that his Arab friend and fellow engineer had fitted a turbocharger from the 3L turbo diesel.

They were pulling away from the pursuing cars at a respectable rate. Brodie grabbed the cell phone and dialled the land line back at Almuzayri. The call cut off as the cell lost signal. "Shit, shit. We'll have to put our faith in the two way," he said, picking up the hand-held radio. "It won't give them much of a heads up but hopefully it'll be enough."

"We're losing them," Jimbo said, staring out into the night through the rear window."

"Decision time guys, either we lead these creeps into an ambush or we power on and lose them in the desert," Brodie reasoned. Natasha's foot gently let the pressure off the gas pedal.

"Unanimous Jimbo?" Brodie asked.

"I'm with you," the voice from the rear seats confirmed, as Jimbo busily checked the magazine on his handgun.

Once off the highway, the pursuit was in full swing. The assailants had no doubt that their cover was blown and that further subterfuge was pointless.

"Let's have a little fun with these fuckers," Natasha said, turning off Highway Forty towards virgin desert.

"Keep focused Natasha," Brodie advised. "These bastards mean business."

"So do I," she growled in reply. "Trust me; I know what I'm doing." Natasha hit the yellow button on the dash and snicked the transfer box into high range four wheel drive.

The Toyota dropped into a wadi which was almost a mile wide. The sedans bravely kept pace, probably hoping Natasha would make a mistake, making their job easy.

Natasha aimed the car towards the face of the wadi and gave it full beans, putting several hundred yards between her and the lead pursuit car. The Toyota powered up the steep slope at speed. The slope was far rougher up close than it appeared from a distance; nevertheless, she kept the engine screaming.

"You know what's on the other side of this Natasha, right?" Brodie questioned with a note of caution.

"Yes I do," she answered. "Trust me."

Just as they reached the top of the slope, she ran the Toyota right out of steam so it crested at little more than walking pace before hitting the lee side with little more than a wobble before powering down the slip face at a ferocious pace.

The lead pursuit car had to carry considerably more momentum to reach the summit without the benefit of four wheel drive. As they popped over the top of the ridge, for a few moments the car continued on up without any solid ground beneath it before the inevitable free-fall as the heavy car pitched nose first into the lee slope. It flew end over end all the way down the vicious slope spraying its occupants through the windows and into the air, or pulverising them in a cauldron of hot twisted metal and glass.

The other sedans held back, leaving only the Hilux to follow on over the ridge.

“Well, that’s one down!” Natasha exclaimed. “Bastards must have two way radios. I was hoping that would catch them all out.”

“I thought we were leading them into a trap?” Brodie questioned.

“I don’t care how they die,” Natasha said.

“Jesus girl, you’re as cold as a cast-iron commode,” Brodie remarked.

“It’s kill or be killed Brodie. They knew the score,” she answered.

“I suggest we try to keep some of them alive, it’s just possible we might interrogate them, find out where they’re keeping your friend,” Brodie cautioned.

“You’re right Brodie, I wasn’t thinking straight,” she concurred. “OK, let’s take it back onto the track; give these clowns a fighting chance.

“Is the pick-up still on our tail?” Natasha asked Jimbo.

“Yep, about a hundred yards back,” he answered. “They have a body in a parka stood up in the flat bed, looks like he’s trying to get a bead on us with a rifle.”

As they headed towards a second wadi, Natasha had an idea. "Strap in boys, were coming to a bumpy bit."

She had spotted a dried up river bed running across the route they were taking. In a stroke of luck, it was between them and the route back to the beaten track. Aiming the Toyota into the bed she took the ascent at an angle, pitching onto three wheels in the bowl before powering up and over the bank, and down the other side. As the Toyota once again reached the flat, Natasha leapt out of the truck with the little Glock in her hand. She gestured for Jimbo and Brodie to follow. Exactly as she anticipated, the Hilux crested the bank and beached itself, throwing the occupants into the windscreen and catapulting the man on the flat bed over the cab, down the bank, head first into the back door of the Land Cruiser.

"Take care of him!" she screamed to Jimbo, gesturing for him to neutralise any threat posed by the jettisoned man. Natasha pressed her body in firmly against the bank so that the wheels of the pick-up spun dangerously above her head. Without hesitating, she pointed the Glock towards the thin steel floor pans of the cab and fired twice, once into each side. The screaming engine dropped revs abruptly as the driver's door swung open and a whimpering Arab staggered from the vehicle clutching at his bloodied genitalia. Jimbo saw him first and dropped him with a head shot.

Natasha hurried back to the truck and, pointing at the guy from the flat bed, said to Jimbo, "Get him into the back, Jimbo. We'll interrogate him when we get back to the compound."

"Holy fucking shit!" Jimbo exclaimed. "Would you look at this?"

Jimbo pulled the Arab's jacket up: he was wearing a bomb vest. "What the fuck were these fucking sand monkeys planning?"

Jimbo patted around the man's torso looking for the detonator. "You bastards! Packed with steel balls for max carnage."

"Jesus Jim," Brodie hissed, "should you be bumping that shit around, don't you know that stuff goes bang?"

"Don't panic Brodie, this is C4 not TAPT, these muppets have money to spend, we aren't dealing with street terrorists. Soon as I get the detonator out it'll be as safe as a house brick."

"I've seen what a house brick can do in the wrong hands," Brodie mused.

Jimbo pulled a short device out of the vest. "Here we go, electrical discharge detonator, remote controlled. No delay, no fuss." In a pocket in the man's parka was the remote trigger. Jimbo carefully removed the 9v batteries from the assemblies and shut the lot away in the glove compartment of the truck. "No wonder he was wearing a parka. I thought he might just have poor circulation."

"Chuck that shit away Jim. Why the hell do we want to babysit that?" Brodie protested.

"This *shit* is better in our hands than theirs. Jack will know what to do with this. It could prove useful," Jimbo decided.

"Gents," Natasha butted in agitated, "could we please get a move on before our pursuers catch up?"

With the unconscious Arab pressed into the rear foot-well, she gunned the Toyota back towards the road. As they did so, the motorcade of sedans came into view some distance behind.

"Sorry I wasn't much help back there," Brodie confessed. "My goddamn leg came off, left me as much use as a one legged man in an ass kicking contest."

"That's what I meant back at the hotel Brodie," she said, "we've got to play to our strengths; recognise our weaknesses."

"How the hell did you know their truck would get stuck?" Brodie questioned.

"This is a short wheelbase," she answered, "the Hilux is a long wheelbase. It was a sure thing."

"Jesus Natasha," Jimbo said. "I always thought you were a smoking hot model, no offense, but when did you become a bloody terminator?"

"Life hasn't always dealt me the long straw Jim, you know that. I've had to learn, to adapt. Luckily being wealthy and single in Saudi Arabia gave me lots of opportunities to learn life skills; one of those was off-roading."

"Thank fuck for that!" he concluded.

CHAPTER FORTY-NINE

Fourth of July

It was fortuitous that Aarif, as the best English speaking of the Arab clan, was within earshot of the two way radio when the frantic warning came in from Brodie, announcing that they were approaching at speed and with hostile company.

Instantly, orders were barked in Arabic and English; a call to arms which saw the walls of the fortified compound bristling with armaments within seconds.

Two of Aarif's men positioned themselves at the steel gates and opened them, allowing the Toyota passage to the sanctuary within.

The truck barely slowed as it cleared the threshold. Natasha again proved her skill and confidence, deftly slewing the beast sideways slowing it rapidly in the soft sand, and narrowly avoiding a collision with the cliff wall behind.

The first pursuit car was carrying too much speed to abort. Aarif screamed an order to the gate keepers and they resisted the temptation to close the gates, instead allowing the sedan to power on through the gates with full momentum.

The sedan driver had neither the skill nor the equipment to emulate Natasha's manoeuvre. With nowhere to go, and no time to stop, he crashed spectacularly into the unyielding cliff face. Aarif again barked orders and a number of his soldiers, armed to the teeth, left the barricades and ran to check on the occupants.

With the gates firmly sealed, the remaining sedans skidded to a halt. The lead car, precariously close to the gates, was already taking small arms fire from the camp battlements. The occupants quickly de-camped and from the comparative safety of behind the vehicle, began to return fire. Aarif shouted once more, and the encampment was suddenly filled by a deafening staccato thunder from an unknown source. The lead sedan was lifted from the sand and thrown around before settling back to earth in several pieces; its former occupants gone, erased.

Jimbo, an ex-tankie, was the first of the Westerners to comprehend what had just occurred. "Holy shit, you've got a Dushka!"

The occupants of the remaining sedan, seeing what had happened to their comrades, were attempting a reverse gear escape from the mighty anti-aircraft gun's range. Two wheel drive on soft sand, versus a .50 calibre heavy machine gun, the outcome was inevitable. The deep rasp of the Russian made 1940s DShK anti-aircraft gun barked one more 3 second burst and the sedan erupted into flames.

"Where in hell did you find a Dushka, Aarif?" Jimbo asked, in awe.

"Ah, that would be telling my friend," Aarif answered, and then asked, "I am something of a 'Del Boy' no?"

"No," Jimbo corrected. "If you were, that thing wouldn't have worked."

Neil ran from his place at the battlements and embraced Natasha. “Are you OK darling? Jesus, what happened?”

“I’m OK Neil, we’re OK, just another fucking day at the office.” Despite her blasé reply, Natasha hugged Neil with more conviction than she had in quite some time.

“Your bird’s a fucking cast-iron superhero Terminator Neil,” Jimbo said, flinging a gigantic arm around Natasha’s shoulder. “I think you’d better invest in some man sized pinnies when you get home bud; she ain’t going back to doing the dishes!”

CHAPTER FIFTY

Regal

Security was tight around the Crown Prince, only Natasha was spared the embarrassment of a full body search, though on this rare occasion she was not carrying the little Glock pistol.

The Prince's security detail were sceptical at the rushed and somewhat unorthodox approach; they were leaving nothing to chance.

After passing security scrutiny, their files and the all-important safe box containing the physical evidence and all the surveillance video and photographs was returned to them, and they were ushered into a large, low ceilinged room in the basement of the palace.

Once they were all seated, the Prince stood up and gestured for the others to remain seated. At the table were military heads of staff, civilian security chiefs and numerous generic 'suits'; most probably representing the 'secret' wing of the Bahraini security services. After the necessary introductions, the Prince was the first to speak. "Greetings gentlemen." Uncharacteristically he turned his attention to Natasha. "How are you my dear, and how is my good friend Warren? He has not blessed us with his company for the last couple of years. I miss the opportunity to play against an opponent who is truly as bad at the game as I." The Prince made a swing with an imaginary golf club, illustrating to what he was referring. "Most of my people let me win when we play, whereas Warren I could beat with only my superior skill." The Prince laughed, finding his own anecdote amusing.

Natasha made to rise, but the Prince gestured for her to remain seated. "I fear that Warren is not in the best of places," she began, "I'm afraid that he finds himself on the wrong side of this heinous plot, just as we do your Highness. Warren's honour, and perhaps even his life, hangs on how we proceed with the problem facing us."

The Prince raised a hand to stop Natasha from speaking further. "In that case, let us make haste and discuss this matter that we may quickly recognise the threat we face and decide what to do about it."

Each member of the party in turn took the opportunity to brief the Prince on what they knew. The dossier was passed around the table, each relevant department head taking the opportunity to flick through the evidence.

When the last of the party had delivered what they had to say, the Prince pondered for a while before saying, "How far along do you believe this plot is? Just how many organisations has this Al-Kooheji recruited?"

Jack picked up the baton. "Your Highness, in my experience, I would say that Mr Al-Kooheji was on the 'putting his own house in order' phase of the plan. I would say that he has the sympathy of a good number of terrorist factions, but he needs the religious and moral high ground and the blessing of the Imams before he can become the 'man of the oppressed' which the plan requires. My own government will be hanging back at this stage, waiting for him to have all the pieces in place before they show their hand. It's my belief that if you act now and detain Al-Kooheji, break up his organisation, the Americans will walk away, leaving him to his fate."

"I must say, this all comes as a bitter pill to swallow. My country has recently fought conflict in Kuwait as allies of the United States. We have encouraged the US to establish its bases on our soil. We consider them an important friend in the region," the Prince declared.

"Trust me your Highness," Jack reassured, "this is not the present administration, the armed forces, or the American people's will at work. This whole plot centres around a tight little group of Capitalists, Oligarchs, greedy, power hungry CIA agents, and unscrupulous, ambitious 'two bit' politicians."

"Will exposure take away their power?" the Prince asked.

"I would say that's very unlikely your Highness. They are pretty well entrenched. Heads will roll, but I suspect the band will play on. You will have to keep vigilant," Jack said.

"Well we should concentrate on the task at hand. Mr Al-Kooheji is an influential man in Bahraini society, without the added danger of his terrorist and US allies; we will have to be very sure before we detain him," the Prince stressed. "Please give me some time to absorb this information. I must speak with my security advisors; the King must also be consulted, informed at the very least."

"Your Highness," Natasha interjected. "Please forgive the interruption. We have very good reason to believe that Al-Kooheji has kidnapped my ex-business partner and her child. I fear if we dally, we may seal her fate."

"I'm sorry Natasha, I will do what I can, but matters of State take precedent over individual lives. We must deliberate on what is to be done." He added, "Take a tour of the palace and grounds, my guards will see to your needs. I will consult my advisors and we will summon you when we have made a decision." He beckoned them away with a wave which left no doubt that he was not to be argued with.

After an age, they were called back to the conference room.

The Prince addressed the seated assembly once again. "We are agreed that this predicament presents a clear and present danger to our kingdom. We have agreed to isolate and confine Mr Al-Kooheji. We have also despatched a delegation to our esteemed neighbours in Saudi Arabia. We have a close working relationship with the Saudi establishment. King Fahd is a personal friend. It will be beneficial for them to be party to our planning, especially as much has already played out on their soil. Hopefully the Americans will leave this as an internal issue and will choose to abandon Mr Al-Kooheji to his fate; either way that is our problem." The Prince rose, walking towards the door. He beckoned to Natasha to join him. "Come Natasha, walk with me; we can let our respective experts iron out the creases." He waived his personal security detail away and they climbed the short flight of stairs which led to the gardens. "You have blossomed into a strong young woman Natasha; a fine role model. Sabika campaigns for the rights of women in Bahrain. In many ways, you remind me of my wife."

"Which one?" Natasha blurted out, engaging mouth before brain. "Please accept my apologies your Highness. This has been an exhausting episode in my life, I'm afraid that my manners have become somewhat diluted."

The Prince opened the bullet proof glass doors and led Natasha out into the breathtakingly beautiful gardens of the palace. "Please Natasha, I am not offended. I realise our culture is somewhat alien to you. I cherish my wives. I know polygamy is not the way of the western world, but you must remember that I too had limited choice; my marriages were arranged through promises and obligations not of my own making."

"Forgive me your Highness, but you have children with all of your wives; as a woman, that would make me feel somewhat worthless."

"Ah Natasha, as I said, my marriages were arranged along lines which I was not old enough to be party to. Families expected to be gifted with children within the royal lineage. What sort of a man would I be to deny my wives this fulfilment? My love is to my future queen, my first wife Sabika. We were both born into this culture; she bears no resentment.

"You and your friends are welcome to stay here at the palace until Mr Al-Kooheji is apprehended, Natasha. I feel it will be safer for you that way."

"If you don't mind, your Highness, we have pressing business back in Saudi Arabia; my friend is still missing. I must do all I can to help to find her."

"My lawyers will have to take signed depositions from each of you before you leave. We will need to know everything which has happened to you since this whole affair began. From what you have said, there is a body count stretching half way across the world which will need to be explained."

"Of course, you are right. Half the police forces in the Middle East and Europe must be looking for us and our friends by now, your intervention on our behalf would certainly take the heat off, allow a lot of innocent victims to go back to their normal lives." Natasha was thinking of Moss and his men who would more than likely be in hiding, avoiding arrest by now.

"That will be taken care of my dear, have no fear. I hope that despite all your suffering this should at least bring a happy ending and convince the American authorities to indulge in a little 'house cleaning'. They are not bad people, they just have little or no understanding of our ways. How different things would be were it not we who were blessed to sit on the world's oil reserves."

"I don't know much about the politics your Highness, I just know that a lot of innocent people have died as a result of me, as a result of things I've done, set in motion. So many innocent lives."

"We are all but threads in life's rich tapestry, Natasha. We cannot know how one move, one decision, can influence the future. You never set out to hurt anyone, you are too positive a force for good to knowingly do others harm. Now come, I will take you to see Sheia; she is excited that you are here."

After signing off their sworn affidavits, the party spent a comfortable night in the opulence of the Prince's palace. In the morning, they were summoned once again to the conference room.

They were addressed by the man who'd been introduced the day before as the head of state security. "The Prince sends his apologies, he is busy with affairs of state and is unable to brief you today so I have agreed to deputise." He sat down and gestured for the others to follow suit. "Dawn raids were carried out on all Al-Kooheji's properties in both the kingdom and in Saudi Arabia." The man used a projector and microfiche maps to illustrate the areas they had raided. "We encountered considerable resistance at a number of properties, however, Mr Al-Kooheji was not present at any of these locations."

"No sign of Sheila Carter or her daughter?" Neil asked.

"I'm afraid not Mr Curland. We have confiscated a vast quantity of papers from the Al-Kooheji residence which may yield clues. I'm sorry to say that the local authorities have been bought off by the Americans. The residence of your Mr Rahimi had been stripped bare; there is no sign of Mr Ruthers's body, only the body of Mr Rahimi. Your beggars and their charges also seem to have disappeared."

"Damn it!" Goose exclaimed. "If the Americans covered up what really went down, Al-Kooheji must have thought that one was down to us."

"That is possible. So we can assume that Al-Kooheji is already on the run. We are tracking down all his employees and known associates. I'm afraid that with all his alleged terrorist connections, he could be anywhere in the Middle East. He will be impossible to track down."

"Surely you have the influence to track down a man as high profile as him?" Goose interjected.

"My friend, if I were Mr Al-Kooheji, I would be hiding out in the desert now; in Afghanistan or Iraq perhaps. He knows that we have no meaningful dialogue with these somewhat lawless countries. Only the Americans *might* have the sophisticated hardware to track him down, but they are unlikely to offer to help us," the man answered.

"We're on our own again then," Jack exclaimed.

"Not entirely. All Mr Al-Kooheji's considerable assets, both here and in Saudi Arabia, have been frozen. I assume that the Americans will also have cut off any accounts which connect them to him, so I think we can assume that he is now running around with no more than pocket change. He has not the means to buy freedom so he will be at the indulgence of friends, and brothers-in-arms. My guess is that he will have sought refuge in Afghanistan, where he has friends in the Mujahidin."

"That's a bloody big country!" Neil said

"Yes it is Mr Curland. Even if we had the cooperation of the Afghan authorities, which we do not, you would be looking for the proverbial pin in a haystack, a turbulent and hostile haystack."

"Needle," Goose chimed in, his impulsive obsessive behaviour overruling good manners.

"Indeed," the man agreed, missing the impertinence.

"Well, if it's OK with the Prince, I'd like for us to get on back to the compound; brief the others on what's up," Neil said.

"Of course, your party are free to leave. Give me a moment and I will arrange a security detail to escort you back to your compound." With that he pressed the intercom and a number of plain dressed Arab secret service men filled in to ensure them safe passage back to Almuzayri.

CHAPTER FIFTY-ONE

Persuasion

Back at the compound the royal party briefed the others on how they had fared in the meeting with the Prince.

"Did we get any useful intel from our prisoners?" Neil asked.

"Only one survived from the sedan: the passenger. Of course we have the one from the pick-up truck too," Aarif answered.

"Have you interrogated them?" Neil asked.

"Not yet, we waited for you. Brodie tells me that Jack has a foolproof technique to extract information, one that does not result in death or blood. If you all agree, I think we should let him try."

"Waterboarding?" Neil said. "Hasn't that been around since the sixteenth century? Chinese water torture, Spanish Inquisition and all that?"

"Well Neil," Jack answered. "Water's certainly been used as a method of torture for some time, waterboarding's more a sort of 'forced dry drowning', it's closer to stuffing rags down a man's throat than conventional 'water torture'.

"Is it safe?" Neil asked.

Jack raised an eyebrow. "You going soft on me Neil?"

"I can't kill a man in cold blood Jack," Neil replied. "It's not in my nature, I'm a soldier."

“Safe is too unequivocal a word Neil. Carried out carefully, it shouldn’t prove fatal. It depends on the man’s resistance. It can kill through neurogenic pulmonary oedema, just depends on the way the subject’s wired up. If his brain is convinced that it’s drowning, it might drown.”

“Just try not to kill him then,” Neil said.

Jack placed his hand on Neil’s shoulder. “Trust me Neil, I don’t give a damn if this guy lives or dies, and neither should you.”

“I’m not sure I would trust the word of a man who cries before he bleeds,” Aarif said.

“That’s just the macho man in you talking Aarif. Men will break quickly; you just have to find their weakness,” Jack said.

Aarif led them into the cave where the bikes were kept. The man from the pick-up was there, hands and feet secured with zip ties.

“Where’s the other one?” Jack asked.

“We kept them separated. The other one is in the food cooler,” Aarif replied.

“Get him in here,” Jack said.

Aarif barked a few words in Arabic and his man scuttled off, returning with a battered and bloody passenger from the crashed sedan.

“I thought you said you waited for us?” Jack questioned.

“That is all from the impact with the cliff face. We have not laid a hand on him,” Aarif protested.

"OK Aarif, ask him which of them is higher in the pecking order, him or the guy from the pick-up."

Aarif spoke a few sentences in Arabic; both the men simply shook their heads. "They refuse to cooperate."

"Okey dokey," Jack said. He pulled the Beretta M9 from his belt and fired twice directly into the face of the guy from the flat bed.

"Jesus Christ Jack!" Neil shouted.

"Get out Neil!" Jack spat, gesturing with the business end of the recently fired gun.

Neil held Jack's gaze for a few seconds, then after a long look at the corpse on the floor, turned and walked out of the cave.

The sedan passenger suddenly became very communicative and fired a stream of Arabic towards Aarif.

"He says he will tell you everything he knows. He asks what you want to know," Aarif translated.

"Ask him where Al-Kooheji is," Jack said. "Ask him where his yellow-bellied boss has run off too, leaving them to fend for themselves."

Aarif rattled off another few sentences in Arabic. The man answered, all the time making praying gestures to his interrogator.

"He says Mr Al-Kooheji has not communicated with him since before he took off."

Jack put the barrel of the pistol into the Arab's mouth and said, "Then how come he knows that his boss has taken off?"

Again, Aarif translated Jack's words to the terrified man.

"He repeats that he knows nothing," Aarif confirmed.

"OK, let's test the theory then," Jack said. "Aarif, can you get me a hose pipe, or at least a few buckets of water, and a thick towel or blanket, preferably something you can't see through."

Aarif passed on Jack's requirements to one of his men who hurried out to fetch the required equipment.

Under Jack's instruction, Aarif's men strapped the prisoner to a plank of wood, his feet bound with gaffer tape and taped to the board, his arms pulled under the board and zip-tied securely. The board was then laid with one end propped on a chair so that the prisoner's head was lower than the rest of his body. They then wrapped the towel around the man's face, binding it tightly with gaffer tape so that he could not move his head at all.

"Ready?" Jack said, and began pouring water from the bucket onto the towel. Within seconds of the water flowing over his nose and mouth, the prisoner began to gag and retch. Despite the water not being sufficient to kill him, the automatic gag reflex was preventing him from drawing life-giving breath. He was drowning.

"I'm not good with this Jack," Aarif said. "Do you mind if Adiel deputises for me? He speaks Arabic like a native."

"OK Aarif, send him on in." Jack resumed the torture, this time pouring an entire bucket slowly over the towel. When he paused, his coughing, vomiting victim was wailing for his God to intervene.

Aarif passed Neil as he left the cave. Sensing the questioning in Neil's eyes, he paused. "This does not sit well with me either Neil. I think we are warriors you and I. This is work best left to spies."

Adiel entered the cave just in time, knelt down next to the suffering man and whispered something in his ear. He immediately started screaming and crying out.

"Give it to him again Jack, this time two buckets, no break."

Jack slowly poured the contents of the first bucket over the towel. Adiel waited with the second bucket so there was no let up between them. When the session eventually came to the end, the prisoner was barely breathing. This time he was singing like a canary.

"OK Jack," Adiel said, "I think he's cleansed his soul now. Anymore and he'll be telling us who he bullied at school and which girls he pushed over in the playground."

"So what did he say?"

"He believes that Al-Kooheji will be hiding out in Pakistan. He has a secure compound in the village of his mother's birth. A place called Allai."

"Where the hell is that Adiel?"

"Northern Pakistan. On the border with Kashmir. It's bloody bandit country. Not a good place to be a stranger, or for that matter, a Jew," Adiel answered.

"What did you whisper to him that broke him?" Jack questioned.

"I just told him that I am a Jew and that I would kill him and see to it that he is buried in the ground in the belly of a pig, to a prayer from the Tanakh."

"Oh that old nugget," Jack grinned.

"Yes, but coming from a Jew I think he believed it. He's given me some pretty good intelligence on the fortress too Jack: the security, some useful stuff about the security cameras."

"Jeez Adiel," Jack replied, "the whole nine yards. That's information which our man Goose can use."

Brodie and Goose walked into the cave. "Aarif and his men ain't too happy about what you're doing to this guy Jack. Thought I'd better come talk to you, see if it's really necessary, what with us being the good guys and all."

"He's good Brodie." Jack ripped the tape from the captive's arms and legs and allowed him to regain some composure. "See, this one we water-boarded, he'll live to stab us in the back another day. That one there," he pointed to the man with no face, "he got the same fate he was offering to you."

"OK man, but we need to respect our host's feelings. The Arabs feel that this is torture without honour; these guys are pretty big on that. I don't need to remind you that without Aarif's hospitality we'll be out where the buses don't run," Brodie said.

"Well done for getting the whereabouts of Al-Kooheji out of him in good time and without killing him Jack," Jack chided sarcastically.

“Sorry man, I just ain’t too big on torture. Been through it myself, and it ain’t a fun place to be,” Brodie confessed.

“Right well, let’s get this new information to the table, and see what we do next,” Jack concluded.

“Do we know who he is?” Goose asked.

“Who?” said Jack.

“Old ‘Achmed’ the terrorist. Do we know who he is?” Goose repeated.

“Zakrem, he said his name was Mohamed Zakrem.”

The name sounded familiar to Goose, so he made his excuses and took off by himself to interrogate his surveillance tapes.

CHAPTER FIFTY-TWO

Excursion

"OK, Neil's spoken to the Prince's people. They can help us with an excursion into Pakistan. They'll help us with supplies, weapons, and they'll give us safe passage to Karachi, from there on, it's our mission," Jack said.

"Why don't we dock at Gujarat and make our way up through India and Kashmir?" Goose asked. "I'm thinking that we catch a train from the south coast all the way up north. Travelling the length of Pakistan will take forever and will be bloody dangerous," he said. "We can cross the border from Kashmir or India, whichever's the more straightforward."

A voice piped up from the rear of the group, "Why don't we just charter a plane to take us from here to Islamabad?" Natasha had been pretty quiet since returning from the palace, that was about to change.

"Sorry Natasha, I forgot that you know your way around here," Jack confessed. "What were you thinking?"

"Well I figure that Isa's whole operation has been closed down right?" She paused to let her words sink in. "So why are we still creeping around as if 'Big Brother' were watching us?"

"Crikey, she's right you know," Neil said. "What about weapons and stuff? We won't be able to take any hardware on a plane trip to Pakistan."

"Don't worry about that Neil, in Pakistan you can buy Kalashnikovs and ammunition at any street market," Natasha reassured.

"I can confirm that Neil," Aarif said. "The streets of Pakistan are awash with Russian small arms."

"Actually Neil," Natasha interjected, I suggest you call Warren, find out if the skies have cleared for him."

Jack's face lit up, "That's a damn fine idea Natasha, that will give us a clear indication of where my people are in terms of strategic withdrawal from this debacle. With the CIA stood down, we should be clear to go where we please with whatever we please."

"Will the info have filtered down so quickly though mate?" Goose questioned. "Last thing we want is to be captured in the middle of bandit country by some trigger happy 'Z list' agent whose carrier pigeon hasn't arrived back at the coop yet."

"We'll just have to take that chance Goose," Natasha said. "My friend's life and the life of her child are in serious danger. I've been the recipient of all your thoughts and prayers long enough. It's time for me to start thinking of others."

CHAPTER FIFTY-THREE

Clear skies

Neil, Goose, and Natasha took the Toyota and drove back in the direction of Riyadh. Upon spotting a payphone, Neil pulled up and used the public phone to call Warren while Goose kept watch.

"Warren, it's Neil."

"Hell Neil, let's shoot out the lights and party. How's our girl, is she OK?"

"She's fine Warren, she's right here with me."

"Neil, if I felt any better, I'd think it was a setup."

"How are things your end Warren? How are things, have the storm clouds passed?"

"Well that's the damndest thing Neil, I've had me an iron curtain of suits around me for the longest time, then this morning, 'poof' all gone, the phone doesn't even click when I pick it up, and you know what, this morning I get a call from Tom Berrington who has just slipped his feet under the desk as the new chief of the CIA. Guess what, he tells me that I am completely cleared of any wrong doing, he has curtailed all surveillance operations directed toward me, and he would like to speak to me soonest on a matter of national security. I don't know what you did Neil, but it did the job with bells on."

"Well, probably still best we don't say too much over the phone right now," Neil cautioned. "We can communicate through our friends, that worked a treat and the dossier you sent was a game changer.

Got a lot to tell you Warren, but for now just know we're all OK, but the struggle's not over yet."

"Can I do anything to help Neil? I feel like I'm burning daylight when I should be helping."

"You've helped already Warren. Just you talking to me confirms that the race is nearly won."

"I'll keep this appointment with our chief of spies Neil, then I'll touch base with our friends; get a direct line to you and we'll swap stories."

"OK Warren, I look forward to it."

"Hey Neil, you need anything, money, planes, hardware, boots on the ground, you just name it. The bank of Warren just re-opened for business."

"That's very reassuring Warren. I think we're through the worst, but I'll let you know if we need anything."

"Let me speak to Natasha, Neil, I haven't stopped thinking about her."

"Hi Warren," she said, "I'm so sorry I've dragged you into my mess again."

"Are you OK? That's all that matters to me right now," Warren said.

"I'm fine Warren. I love you. Give my love to Nell too."

"I love you too little lady. You just look after yourself and come and see us soon as you can. We got so much catching up to do."

"You bet Warren. See you soon." Relieved, Natasha put down the receiver

The next call Neil placed was to the offices of ‘Fizzy Door Productions’ in Beverly Hills.

CHAPTER FIFTY-FOUR

Computer age

"Karl, it's Neil Curland. Did you mean what you said when you offered to help us?"

"Hey, for sure Neil. We owe our success to you and Warren Bateson, now if you're in trouble we're at your service," Karl answered.

"You guys would have made it without us. We just helped with the logistics," Neil assured him.

"Whatever Neil. Your money and Warren's exposure opened doors though, I can tell you. Now what can we do?"

"Look, I've no idea if any of this is feasible, but what we're thinking we need is some bogus camera footage; something we can feed into some bad guy's surveillance system. We need to create a spectacle outside a fortress; something which will have the guards running around like headless chickens. We need a big, spectacular diversion."

"Can you get me photos or better still video of exactly what the camera sees?" Karl asked.

"Hold on, I'll pass you over to my technical man, he's better equipped to explain what we need." Neil passed the receiver to Goose.

Goose smiled. His analytic mind coupled with his OCD meant that he would remember everything that was needed and some besides.

"Hi Karl, my name's Goose, I'm the guy that's a bit handy with surveillance. What do you need to know?"

“Hi Goose. You will need to find out if their cameras are digital or analogue. Find out if the signal is encrypted. Have you got the equipment to patch into them at all?” Karl asked.

“My equipment is simple and crude. If they’re using wireless analogue units it will be a breeze, digital could be tricky, but still possible as long as any encryption is simple. I’ve got some portable hacking software but it would take time. These guys think they’re the only clever bastards on the block, so as long as the cameras aren’t hard wired I’d say we have a fair chance.”

“Right,” Karl replied. “Do you have access to email?”

“I should think I’ll be able to access a modem back at the Bahraini Embassy,” Goose answered.

“We have internet access at the glove factory in Mansehra, Goose. We can use the facilities there,” Natasha interjected.

“OK Karl, it seems that we *do* have access to email,” Goose corrected. “Exactly what do you need?”

“OK Goose, what we need is a few seconds of good quality footage of what the CCTV camera sees, we can use that to create your diversion. It won’t be our best work, but at VGA quality, it should fool the uninitiated,” Karl replied.

“It’s going to be a bloody dangerous assignment though, because if it’s exposed, with no cover, I’m not sure how I’m going to go about it.” Goose mused.

“Well dude, it’s a slow process producing CGI, the sooner we can get started the better. Make and model of their equipment and the equipment you’ll be using would be handy too if you can get it. Better to iron out any problems here rather than over there,” Karl said.

CHAPTER FIFTY-FIVE

Flight of fancy

Thanks to the warm relationship Bahrain and Pakistan enjoyed, it was no problem for the Crown Prince's staff to provide the entire expeditionary party with diplomatic status to fly directly from Muharraq to Islamabad without the worry of customs scrutiny. Natasha could even carry her trusted Glock openly with her.

A short walk across the tarmac at Muharraq airport saw the party boarding a twin turbo prop Fokker 50 charter plane which they would have to themselves.

Neil sidled up behind Natasha as they waited on the windy tarmac to load their baggage into the hold.

"Just like travelling on a coach isn't it," he said, wrapping his arms around Natasha's waist and slipping his hands into her flimsy jacket pockets. "Good grief!" Neil exclaimed as his fingers made contact with the butt of the little Glock. "You're inseparable from this little designer pistola aren't you?"

"I can't wait to be rid of it Neil," she said, "but until all this is over, the gun stays close."

"I used to find lippy and tissues in your pockets," Neil remarked.

"It's just having a short break from its usual uncomfortable living quarters, then it's back into the bra holster.

"Do you think we can ever go back to the way we were?" he asked.

"There's no going back Neil," she said. "We can never get back the innocence we once had. We can only hope that we find something in our future as good as what we've had to leave behind."

"That seems so fucking sad," Neil said.

"Well it's up to the both of us to make sure it's not all we're about. We've the help of two gorgeous children, fantastic, loyal friends, and hopefully a long life ahead of us to put all of this behind. We've all been in this together, and together we'll work it out."

Baggage stowed, they climbed the short steps up to the passenger cabin and waited for the others to board.

Down on the tarmac porters were loading what looked suspiciously like a coffin into the cargo hold. "Jesus Jack!" Brodie exclaimed, watching the loading of the unscheduled freight. "Tell me that ain't who I'm thinking it is?"

"Well my Texan friend, just who are you thinking it is?" Jack asked his fellow countryman.

"I don't know Jack," Brodie answered, shaking his head, "and I don't think I want to know."

"I can live with that big man," Jack said grinning.

As they took their seats in the cabin, Brodie sat down in the aisle seat opposite Jimbo and Goose. Leaning across the aisle he gestured to Jimbo who leant towards him to hear what he had to say. "He ain't wearing his buddy's parka is he Jim?"

"Come again?" Jimbo said, clearly puzzled.

"The man in the coffin, is he wearing a vest?"

Jimbo coloured up immediately, embarrassed. "Uh, he might be mate, possibly."

"On a damn plane," Brodie exclaimed, "and me shit scared of flying. I'm telling you Jim, you guys are all missing a few buttons off your shirts. That thing goes up in this little plane, and God's gonna make us as welcome as a porcupine at a nudist colony."

"Don't sweat it Brodie," Jimbo said. "I'm telling you, that stuff's benign with the detonator removed."

"Calm down Brodie," Jack said as he shuffled between them on his way to his seat, "or do we have to medicate you same as old Achmed back in cargo?"

The 5 hour flight was largely undramatic. Shortly after they touched down at Islamabad, they were met by a delegation from the Bahraini embassy, charged with seeing them, their luggage, 'dead' body, and equipment safely to the Embassy grounds from where they could plan their next move.

"Look at this place, surrounded by squalor, in a country where most of its citizens don't have access to a toilet or running water. They certainly know how to spoil themselves these diplomats don't they?" Neil remarked to Natasha as they were shown their way through the ornate white marble arches into the cool opulence of the inner Embassy.

"It is beautiful isn't it?" Natasha agreed rhetorically.

"So where is he then?" Brodie asked Jack.

"Who?" Jack replied, innocently.

"Your man, Achmed. Did he survive the flight in the hold or is he opening himself up a worm farm?"

"He survived. We've got him a snug little room down in the basement: no windows and just one metal door with strong locks. He'll be safe until we decide what to do with him."

"The Embassy staff good with all this man?" Brodie questioned.

"Hey Brodie," Jack replied. "We got the Prince's blessing. We can do no wrong my man."

"I'm going to ring Daggy at the glove factory," Natasha said. "He's practically a local; he can be our guide while we're here."

"Can he be trusted Natasha?" Neil cautioned. "You said yourself that Pakistan is pretty lawless."

"Daggy loves Sheila," she replied, "he owes everything to us. He's going to be in a hell of a state over her kidnapping. I guarantee that he will want to help and he's 100% trustworthy."

Daggy it seemed had received a heads up from the manager of the golf club back in Saudi Arabia. When Natasha called him, he was already fuelled and packed for the drive over to them. The distance from Mansehra to Islamabad was a little over 100 kilometres, nevertheless, the poor condition and congestion on the roads made the journey take the biggest part of 3 hours.

The group had established a command centre in a little used back office in the Embassy.

Introductions made, the group sat down to discuss impending action.

“We’ve spoken to some computer boffin friends back in the States. If we can get them some good footage of Al-Kooheji’s stronghold, they reckon they will be able to create us a little cinematic diversion to get us inside with a minimum of death and destruction,” Neil said.

“I don’t follow, Neil,” Jimbo commented. “We’re going to invite ourselves round to watch a video? Shall I get some beers and a curry?”

“These boys are into ‘Computer Generated Graphics’, they reckon that with a bit of footage of the place and its surroundings, they should be able to create us some sort of diversion to plug into their security cameras.”

“Right,” Jimbo said. “So one of us is going to walk up to the mad-man’s hideout, and ask him to pose for some snap-shots?”

“Not one of us,” Goose confirmed, “me.”

“Are you up for this Goose?” Neil asked. “You’re going to be out there with nothing but your dick for protection.”

“Piff and tish,” Jimbo chimed in. “I’ll be going with the little bugger to make sure he comes to no harm.”

"How do you think you're going to pull that off then Jimbo?" Neil questioned. "If there's no cover out there, it's going to be bad enough trying to secretly get Goose and all his kit and caboodle within range of the place, let alone with a great big white bugger like you in tow."

"Well see now," Jimbo deliberated. "I've had one of my 'once in a lifetime' good ideas, and I must say I reckon it's gotta be cleverer than a canny squirrel who's just swapped the theory of relativity for a big bag of nuts."

"That's making my head hurt. Explain Jimbo, please," Goose pressured, shaking his head.

"Camels!" Jimbo exclaimed, a big smug smile across his face.

"Camels?" Goose questioned. "Not squirrels then?"

"The squirrel was merely an irrelevant metaphor my dear Watson," Jimbo said in his best 'Old Etonian'. "What I propose is that we get Aarif and his boys to score us a camel train, some goats and shit, and then we rock up outside the bunker and set up camp for the night, just a bunch of wandering Bedouin tribesmen. Hell, we could go right up and bang on the door, offer to trade some goat's cheese or blankets for water, tobacco or something. By the time they get us moved on, Goose should have had enough time to get what he needs."

Goose stared at Jimbo for a moment before saying, "Hell Jimbo, are you sure you were a tankie, that plan is worthy of a Jedi."

Brodie, who had been listening in silence said, "I'll run it past Aarif, you'll have to bung him some 'splash cash' though Neil if he is to run up goats and camels in a hurry."

"The Embassy staff have good knowledge of the area. They've briefed us of a couple of possible fortified bases in the area of Allai," Jack said. "Our prisoner Achmed has indicated that the Al-Kooheji stronghold is in the Himalayan Mountains close to Allai. I'm inclined to believe him; the jig is up for him, he has nothing to gain by lying. Allai is in the fucking mountains not remotely desert. We can scrub Jimbo's camel train idea, it just don't cut the mustard. Maybe some goats, but we ain't gonna justify a platoon of men to drive a couple of mangy goats. Besides, the Bedouin are from Syria."

"So what's our 'Plan B' then Jack?" Neil asked.

"We're gonna have to get 'Navy Seal' bud; cover of darkness, the whole nine yards. Think you boys are up to it?" Jack replied.

"Well," Neil said, "we seem to have done OK so far. I reckon we'll give it our best shot."

"We are going to need to acquire some gear," Goose said. "We're going to need Ninja suits, night vision goggles, weapons, binoculars..."

Daggy butted in, cutting Goose off mid-sentence. "I think I can help you." Now he had the attention of the room. "I have a cousin of my sister-in-law who has a gift for getting things people need; he is a useful man, but I'm afraid not an honest one. This cousin, he supplies military equipment to anyone with the money to pay."

“What kind of military hardware are we talking about?” Jack asked.

“Whatever the Pakistani military has, this cousin has,” Daggy answered.

“Before anyone gets too carried away,” Goose cautioned, “we aren’t here to start a war. It’s important we get in and out without causing an international situation. We need to use the big brain we keep in our heads, not the little one we keep in our trousers.”

“That goes without saying mate,” Jimbo commented. “I’m not suggesting that your flea infested Cumberland sausage wouldn’t effectively infest the whole stronghold with incurable venereal disease, but it’s a time issue, we just don’t have the time to hypnotise the enemy into being willing to have sex with you.”

Natasha, Daggy, and a few of the Arabs, who were either too polite or simply didn’t understand Jimbo’s scathing wit, smiled politely or bit their tongues. The rest just erupted into uncontrolled laughter.

“You’ve got to make me look a cunt haven’t you Jimbo?”

“You do that yourself mate, I’m just your commentator,” the big man said, holding himself in a stoic expression of seriousness.

“It’s the way he tells 'em!” Neil said.

“It’s water off a duck's back Neil,” Jimbo said. “That’s why we call him ‘Goose’.”

"You finished?" Goose asked, too exasperated to retaliate.

"Guys," Neil said, "can we have everyone with an opinion sit down and write a list of our procurement needs for Daggy?"

"Come again?" Jimbo asked.

"Our QM stores order mate," Neil said, "What are we going to need?"

"Gotcha boss," Jimbo replied. "Remember, we don't all speak Shakespeare.

The group sat down to debate what equipment they would be likely to need.

"Put down some nine mill Parabellums for my Glock would you?" Natasha added. "Oh and can you get a couple of black burqas for me Daggy. I don't want to chance being recognised."

By the early evening, Daggy was ready to take the order to his sister-in-law's cousin.

CHAPTER FIFTY-SIX

Covert action

Daggy's contact came through in spades. Much of the equipment was pretty much state of the art American hardware which had been supplied to their then prominent regional ally prior to the fall of the Soviet Union, after which the 'friendship' had cooled somewhat. For the group's needs the equipment was better than expected.

A reconnaissance party consisting of Neil, Jimbo, Aarif, Adiel, Jack, Goose and a number of Aarif's men were dispatched to find lodgings in Thakot, a tribal town some 15 clicks west of Allai, in order to mount an excursion to assess the hideout and its fortifications. Daggy, as the sole non-combatant, was taken along for his local knowledge as a spotter but would be left a safe distance from the objective. Despite her protestations, Natasha was persuaded to remain behind at the embassy with Brodie and the rest of Aarif's men. Although she had proven her worth on numerous occasions, she was the one member of the party who could be recognised by numerous members of Al-Kooheji's 'inner circle', potentially compromising the mission.

Thakot proved to be a good choice to set up a forward base. A sapphire sifting operation along the Indus River basin provided dilapidated mobile homes to house the scores of migrant miners flocking to the area during the dry season. A modest sum of Pakistani Rupees secured the party a double caravan for the duration of their stay, no questions asked.

Isa had chosen the location for his fortress bunker well. The village was nothing more than a collection of huts clustered on the side of a rugged hilly landscape set against a background of mountainous terrain. Even under the cover of darkness, covert approach would be impossible.

“This is a non-starter Jack!” Neil exclaimed. “Under cover of darkness and carrying equipment, we have no way of negotiating 15 clicks of rough mountain terrain on foot. In vehicles, we will have no element of surprise and we’ll be sitting ducks. We’re bikers for fucks sake, not Navy Seals.”

“I’d like to run this past Daggy as he’s a local,” Goose said, turning his attention to the Pakistani. “What do you reckon to getting a few horses for us, then me, you, Aarif and some of his guys take a ride up there and check it out, see how well defended the place looks?”

“I cannot ride a horse my friend,” Daggy interrupted, putting the dampers on Goose’s preliminary plan, “but I think I may have an idea.”

“Right now I’ll take suggestions from all comers buddy,” Jack replied.

“There are preliminary talks between Khyber Pakhtunkhwa Provincial authority and various outside interests to dam the Indus River and create a power station. It is my knowledge that an Austrian company is in talks with the authority as we speak.”

“Go on,” Neil urged, intrigued.

“Most locals in Allai will not speak a foreign language and could easily be fooled by an Arab interpreter. You could be a joint delegation from

Austria and the authority discussing the impact of the project."

"That's genius Daggy," Neil concluded, excited. "Me and Adiel speak German, Aarif and you speak Arabic, we fit the bill like a hand in a glove. As long as it covers us snooping around the mountains, and prevents the villagers from raising the alarm, we should be good to go."

"I have some garment label samples and a small sewing kit in my truck, if we could find some coveralls and I can mock up corporate uniforms," Daggy said.

"That's awesome Daggy," Jack praised. "I saw a mine back a ways, we could backtrack there, probably pick up coveralls, hard hats and some safety boots to complete the picture."

The mining company were only too happy to comply with Daggy's request; 15,000 of Neil's Pakistani Rupees saw a stack of overalls and hard hats sitting in the back of the truck. Within an hour, Daggy had deftly sewn little-known golfing brand badges to a number of the coveralls, giving them a distinct corporate identity. Unless the terrorists happened to be keen golfers, the subterfuge should work.

It took a further hour to retrace their steps and continue on into the mountains towards Allai.

A group of heavily armed villagers were blocking the mountain road, preventing the strangers' entrance.

"Looks like someone knows we're in town," Neil said to Adiel, who was sitting in the back of the first truck next to him.

Aarif, driving the truck, said, "It's the village elders coming out to greet us and ask our business. Relax, it's normal practice in tribal regions."

Aarif pulled up to the party and spoke quickly and quietly to the head man. One of the men handed his AK47 to his colleagues and squeezed himself into the back of the truck beside Neil and Adiel.

"What's all this then Aarif?" Neil asked.

"It appears that we have hired a guide, Neil," Aarif replied. "It is of no consequence, he will help us to blend in."

"Can we still go where we want to?" Neil questioned.

"I think so Neil. I have told him who we are and where we want to go. He should be a bonus."

For the first couple of hours they skirted around, picking up and bagging rock samples in the convenient apparel bags Daggy had provided. As they climbed up out of the village, towards the mountains, the whereabouts of the terrorist stronghold became apparent. The area was vast. The group were able to get a pretty good idea of the layout whilst remaining a safe distance from it.

Fortuitously, a tributary of the Allai Khwar River fell in a spectacular waterfall just above the fortified gate of the Al-Kooheji hideout. The falls appeared to fuel a plunge pool somewhere within the stronghold, providing the inhabitants with their supply of fresh mountain water.

"Aarif, can you tell him that we need to examine the flow rate of the falls? Ask him if we can get access to that compound," Goose said.

Without warning, they were surrounded by well-trained militia men armed with an array of modern Soviet weapons. Aarif and their local guide rattled off a quick string of Arabic and local dialect, explaining the agreed cover story. One of the soldiers turned to Neil and spoke in near fluent German.

"Was machst du hier?" the soldier questioned Neil, asking what they wanted here.

"Grüße dich meine Herren. Untersuchen wir die Geologie des Bereichs. Hydroelektrizität Ingenieure sind wir." Neil answered, confirming that they were hydro-electricity engineers conducting a survey.

"Wir möchten den Wasserfall untersuchen. Ist das eine Möglichkeit?" Adiel asked, getting straight to the point and asking if they could go in to examine the waterfall.

The soldier laughed and rattled of a sharp sentence to Aarif, once again speaking in his native Arabic.

"What did he say?" Neil asked Aarif in English but with a mock German accent.

"He says no!" Aarif answered. "He says for us to leave here quickly."

"Let's agree and move further into the mountains. I need some photos of that compound," Goose whispered to Neil.

"Please apologise for our intrusion," Neil said. "Tell them that we will examine the falls further up and obtain the information we require."

Aarif passed the information to the militia men. They laughed and made gestures with their weapons for the group to move on before melting back into the rugged landscape.

"That was fucking scary!" Neil said. "I felt like Richard bloody Burton in 'Where Eagles Dare'. Thank God he questioned me!"

"It was a close thing," Jack agreed. "They'd have seen straight through my 'Clint Eastwood' that's for sure."

"They're running their own Ninja patrols. That's a worry," Goose said.

Well above the terrorist sanctuary, Goose broke out the telephoto lenses for his high power digital surveillance camera.

"Bingo guys. This is pay dirt," he said. "I can practically see the rivets on the back of the gate. We've got some serious security cameras on duty here. It's a wireless system so we're in with a chance."

"You got what you need Goose?" Jack asked. "I'm worried that patrol could be keeping an eye on us."

"Just need to scan for a radio frequency, see if I can patch into their security cameras." Goose set his equipment up on a flat rock above the waterfall. Donning a discrete pair of earphones, he began twisting the dials and knobs on his wireless scanner. "Damn, we're still such a distance away; I really need to be much closer," he complained.

"Well we ain't getting any closer, not on this recce." Jack said. "Do what you can Goose." Jack addressed the whole group, "Listen up everyone: concentrate. Pace out the path back, remember any obstacles, anything that we can get behind or need to climb over. We may need to come back under cover of darkness. Goose, get as many shots of the area and the terrain as you can. The more familiar we are with this place, the better."

"You reckon we'd be up to a night mission now Jack?" Neil asked.

"Looks like we might have to Neil," he said, "At least we know where the place is at now. It's the Ninja patrols that have me spooked.

"Let's get our asses back to Thakot," Goose said. "I need to transfer these images onto my laptop and see what we can email across to the boys in Beverly Hills, get them started."

"You really are a 'gadget man' Goose," Neil said. "Where would we be without you?"

"In my business Neil, it pays to stay one step ahead of the competition," Goose said.

CHAPTER FIFTY-SEVEN

Trojan horse

Back at their digs, Goose had successfully loaded the images from the camera to the laptop and had saved anything useful to a series of diskettes for transfer to Daggy's computer at the glove factory.

"Eureka!" Goose exclaimed. "I've got it. I know exactly what spectacle we need to get the main gate open."

"We're all ears mate," Neil replied.

Goose drew Neil's attention to a still photo of the security gate. "See the manufacturer's plate on the rear of the gate Neil?" he asked, the question rhetorical. "That's a well-known German make; I reckon that it operates on a single button system: one press for open, one for close."

"How does that provide a 'eureka' moment then?" Neil asked.

"If I'm right then the gate has to open completely before it can close."

"That's how mine works, that's pretty normal for electric gates isn't it?" Neil questioned.

"Let's hope that's how they work," Goose said with breathless excitement. "We can use the stills I got with the telephoto for the guys to work their magic, and then Jimbo's goat herding ploy to get us close to the fortress. At the precise moment we get the raiding party in close enough to the main gate, we fire up the CGI footage and get them to open up."

"I still don't see the bunny jumping out of the hat. What are you going to feed them to get them to open the gate?" Neil asked with a raised eyebrow.

"Simple bloody genius Neil," Goose said, "us lot, approaching."

"And they are going to open up to let us in?" Neil asked, his tone more than a touch sceptical.

"Ah, no Neil, they're going to close it you see, because they're going to think it's already open," Goose concluded with a smug smile.

"You're right, that is bloody genius; a Trojan horse for the 1990s, nice one!" Neil said. "The factory in Mansehra is much closer to here than the Embassy. Soon as you've got what you need, me, you and Daggy fire off to the glove factory and get it sent off to the boys in Beverly Hills OK?"

"Roger that Neil. I can make some calls regarding the gate from Daggy's factory. If I'm right, the sooner we can get Karl and his boffins started on my plan, the sooner we can bring down the city of Troy."

The trip to Mansehra passed off without a hitch. The stills were successfully dispatched to Beverly Hills via the glove factory internet connection. A call to the manufacturer in Germany confirmed that the gate was indeed a single open single close design as Goose had suspected.

The cherry on the cake came from Karl who recognised the brand of security camera used within the compound, and could predict with confidence what frequency range they would be operating on. This information would mean that a night sortie wasn't necessary.

Upon their return to their lodgings in Thakot, Jack called a meeting to order to discuss a timetable for action, and to formulate a plan.

"Right guys," Jack said. "We've got mountain terrain, roving Ninja patrols, possible civilian interference, and of course, a kidnapped non-combatant mum and daughter, possibly hostages. What else do we know?"

Goose brought the others up to speed on his ambitious 'Trojan Horse' plan, and filled them in with further updates from their trip to Mansehra.

"Clever plan Gee," Jack said. "Might just work."

"It's going to be impossible to gain entrance to that place without a fire-fight Jack," Neil said, "and we've got the Ninjas to worry about."

"It's time to break out our secret weapon," Adiel chimed in.

"We have a secret weapon?" Neil questioned.

"I'm with you Adiel," Jimbo exclaimed. "You mean old Achmed and his body warmer."

"That is precisely what I mean Jim," Adiel concurred. "I propose we dress him up with some chain and padlocks, and then send him through the gate with a two way radio tucked into his parka."

"I'd be all up for shunting old Achmed through the doors dressed in his best vest and parka, then blowing them all to hell. Only fly in the ointment is the hostages. We can't detonate the vest with them in there, and if we go through the front door we can kiss them goodbye. Worse still, they get cut down by friendly fire."

"What say we post a sniper up above the stronghold," Goose suggested, "a safe distance off then give the terrorists an ultimatum to release the hostages or we detonate him."

"We will need to take the Ninjas down first," Neil said. "This plan is sketchy at best but relies heavily on us having the run of the outside, and a monopoly on the high ground. Can't chance having them take our sniper out; he'll be our only eyes on the compound."

"I can put a wireless camera on Achmed," Goose said, "it'll only give us about 20 minutes of surveillance, but at least we'll be able to see inside in real time."

"I don't know guys," Jack cautioned, "what's to stop them just shutting the inside door and letting old Achmed detonate harmlessly out in the yard? How do we know Al-Kooheji's going to give a monkey's what happens to Achmed?"

"Our Achmed is really Mohamed Zakrem: Aykay's chief of security and unofficially, his second in command. He could prove to be an important puzzle piece," Goose said.

"How come you didn't share that Gee?" Jack asked. "I thought Zakrem was just a grunt, one of

Aykay's soldiers. This information could be a game changer."

"Sorry Jack, I thought I'd best keep that under me hat until we got here. We've let a lot of strangers into our confidence on route, just thought I'd keep that one to myself for a bit."

"Whatever Boss, I'll stand by your call on that. Let's get a hold of Brodie, get him to bring Achmed and the bomb vest on over," Goose said. "Maybe he will have something on Al-Kooheji we can use."

"You'll be lucky," Jimbo said. "Brodie hasn't the stomach to play with C4"

"Give him a call," Jack said, "tell him to get Achmed and the vest ready for the off at a moment's notice. While we wait for your boffins to come good, I suggest we see what we can learn about the security patrols. I think the power company should do another daylight recce, see if we can get any intel from our local guide."

CHAPTER FIFTY-EIGHT

Observation

Over the next few days the group carried out a number of daylight patrols disguised as power company engineers with their local guide in tow.

Fortunately, the terrorist roving patrols were not experienced 'special ops'; their patrols followed the same daily routine. This was confirmed by the local guide who advised them on where to be to avoid further confrontation with the guerrillas.

Goose decided it was important to have eyes on the stronghold 24/7 in the run up to the offensive, in an attempt to adapt to any unforeseen developments.

"Aarif, would a couple of your guys be up to lookout duties in the village?" Goose asked. "Keep eyes on the coming and goings for us? It'll be easier for them to talk their way around than us pushing our luck as visiting engineers. That excuse is wearing a bit thin."

"They will do as I bid them Goose," Aarif replied.

"Great. Just get them to watch the approach to the hideout. They can't get in too close, but they can report on who's travelling the road. Sort them out with one of the Paki army 2 ways. Tell them to keep it switched on all the time in case we need to contact them. Best give 'em a stack of 9 volts too."

On the fifth day of waiting, an urgent Fed-Ex parcel arrived at the mining site in Thakot for the attention of Geoff Duckworth: 'Goose' to his friends. Inside the package were a number of digital video diskettes and some highly technical and expensive electronic gadgets designed to hack into security equipment and broadcast video footage over surveillance camera frequencies.

"I need a day to familiarise myself with this new equipment, Jack," Goose said. "After that, soon as you're ready, we can make our move."

"Right," Jack said. "Let's get Achmed over here so we can have another pop at him; see if he has anything which might be of value to Aykay. I think that we're all agreed that our first priority is to get the hostages released. If we can terminate Aykay in the process, then that's a bonus. Primary objective: release the hostages."

"I agree Jack," Neil said. "Aykay's threat has been neutralised now. His death is the desired outcome but not a necessity. I'll make the call to Brodie. He's a brave guy, I'm sure I can talk him out of his fear of explosives. Brodie and a couple of Aarif's boys can escort Achmed here."

Back at the Embassy, Natasha took Neil's call and agreed to relay his instructions to Brodie.

"What are they up to?" Brodie asked, eager for an update.

"They want us to take the terrorist across to them," she lied, "complete with the bomb vest and detonator."

"OK," Brodie said. "I'll tell you what we'll do. To be on the safe side, you take Achmed, the vest, and two of Aarif's guys in the lead truck. Me and the last guy can follow behind with the detonator and remote trigger. That should make things safe."

"Whatever Brodie," she replied. "I don't mind nurse-maiding him. Jimbo says that stuff is safe, that's good enough for me."

"Sorry Natasha but that stuff just freaks me out. You sure you're good to carry it?"

"Sure I'm sure Brodie. C'mon, let's get the job done."

The remaining trucks, acquired in a rush by Daggy, were manual shift. Brodie couldn't drive a stick shift with his prosthetic leg so jumped into the passenger seat with the detonator, remote trigger and batteries, leaving Natasha, dressed from head to foot in the anonymous ambiguity of the black Burqa to drive the lead vehicle with her VIP passenger, the bomb vest, and the remaining two of Aarif's men.

They set off on the N75 national route before cutting across the mountains on the arduous Ayubia National Park road which although slow and torturous, was a quieter and more direct route to the N35 which would take them to Thakot. The trip would take them the biggest part of a day due to the poor state of the road climbing and traversing the steep escarpment of the breathtakingly beautiful Himalayan foothills. The route was chosen as the safest option considering the value and vulnerability of the convoy.

Coping up a steep gradient through the sparse pine forests of Changla Gali, Brodie momentarily caught a glimpse of a large lorry as it crashed through the saplings of the forest to their right, on a collision course with his truck. Before he could begin to shout a warning to the driver, the lorry struck, crushing the driver instantly and sending the Jeep careering down a 20ft slope before coming to a rest on its side in a shallow stream.

Brodie remained unconscious for an indeterminate time. When he came to, it took him a further few minutes to orientate to his unfamiliar surroundings. The driver of the Jeep, one of Aarif's men, hung limply from the steering wheel, impaled by the lorry and crushed beyond recognition; the man was dead. Brodie had been forcibly removed from the vehicle whilst still unconscious, his jacket had been torn from his back. The detonator, remote trigger and batteries were gone.

Still dazed and shaken, it took him a few more minutes to successfully struggle to his feet. His prosthetic leg was damaged; it would make the climb back up to the road even more challenging.

"Oh Jesus! Natasha!" he shouted, remembering the mission he'd been on.

Scrambling up the embankment, he saw the other Jeep, the engine still running, sitting on the side of the road some 100 feet up the road.

Half running, half shuffling, Brodie moved as quickly as his damaged right leg would allow. Aarif's men lay splayed out on the shingle, both shot in the head. Natasha and Mohamed Zakrem were gone.

He jumped into the idling Jeep. Forcing his damaged leg onto the gas pedal, he jammed the truck into gear and roared away. Gear changes were achieved at full throttle; he hadn't the time for mechanical empathy. Ten minutes further along the road he came upon a newly opened hotel, built to accommodate the increasing tourist trade to the higher altitude ski resorts of the national park.

Brodie drove into the car park on full throttle, skidding to a messy halt as he rammed his left foot on the brake pedal at the same time as killing the Jeep's engine.

The hotel receptionist rattled at him in Urdu.

"American, English, English, phone, phone!" Brodie screamed tossing a handful of notes onto the desk.

"Here, Sir. Here," the receptionist said, guiding him to a phone behind the desk.

"Neil, it's Brodie. He's taken her, Neil. He's taken Natasha!"

CHAPTER FIFTY-NINE

Desperation

"Oh Jesus Christ!" Neil screamed into the handset. "How?"

"They ambushed us," Brodie confessed. "They took Natasha, Neil, they took Achmed too."

"Oh my Christ." Neil turned to Goose and the others. "It's Brodie; they have taken Natasha, captured her, and they've got Mohamed Zakrem back."

"Have they got the vest and detonator? Have they got the remote and everything Neil?" Jack questioned.

"Do they have the vest and everything Brodie?" Neil asked.

There was a pause before Brodie answered, "They've taken everything Neil." Another pause. "Aarif's men are all dead."

Jack took control of the situation, snatching the phone from Neil. "Brodie, when did the ambush go down?"

"What?" Brodie answered, confused.

"How long ago man? How long ago were you ambushed?"

"Oh Jesus, I don't know, a couple of hours ago at least. I was knocked unconscious."

"Are you mobile?"

"Yeah, I've got one of the Jeeps."

"Can you get to our OP Brodie?"

"Negative, I can make it to the intersection with the N35. I can't duel the suicidal rag-heads on the busy highway with my leg."

"I'll send some guys out to bring you in, where are you?"

"I'm at a hotel. Hang on." Brodie gesticulated towards the receptionist to come over. "What's the name of this place? What's the address of this hotel?"

The receptionist handed Brodie a card.

"OK Jack, you ready? It's the Naseem Hotel & Restaurant Nathia Gali-Abbottabad Rd, Tauheedabad, Nathia Gali, Khyber Pakhtoonkhwa. You got that?"

"Got it. Just sit tight Brodie, we'll come to you. The roads through the mountains are hairier than hell; we don't need any more fuck ups."

"I'll press on towards the N35 Jack. Aarif's men are spread out all over the road back aways. If I hang around here, it's gonna get hotter than Hades; there'll be questions to answer, and I don't fancy sitting by myself in a Pakistani jail."

"Fair enough Brodie. Take it easy, I'll get them to meet you at the intersection."

Breathless, Aarif came running into the caravan office. "My man has just called in. A car has just passed him on the track leading to Al-Kooheji's fortress. He says that they had a woman dressed in a Burqa in the back, and that they were holding a gun to her head."

"That's it then," Neil said. "We raid now, and we raid hard."

"I agree," Goose said. "No sense in waiting now; we've lost the element of surprise. They have Natasha and Achmed, it's only a matter of time before they break her, and then they have the Trojan horse too. We make our move now!"

"What have we got in the arsenal that makes a big bang?" Jack asked.

"We've some claymores," Jimbo answered, "some grenades, smokers, flashbangs and some mortars. We weren't planning on full on bunker busting. We're heavy on sniping and Ninja gear and a little light on frontal offensive stuff."

Neil handed a wedge of cash to Daggy, "Can you motor back to the mine and score us as much dynamite as you can carry Daggy? We are going to need to get from the compound into the bunker within a heartbeat otherwise this rescue mission becomes a clean-up op."

"Forget that Daggy, you go and fetch Brodie," Jimbo said. "There isn't time to fuck around waiting for dynamite. Anyway I have a better idea."

"You OK bud?" Goose asked Neil.

"No Goose, I'm fucking angry! Now let's get this done."

"OK," Jimbo said. "Guys, grab all the claymores, a couple of mortars and the propane bottles off the caravans, stick them all in the back of the Jeep. Everyone grab all the firepower you can carry: grenades, smoke grenades flashbangs, rifles and handguns, and then follow me up to the fortress."

"OK Jimbo, what's your plan?" Goose asked.

"Get me into the compound mate, just get me into the compound and then cover me when I make me move."

Aarif radioed ahead to his lookouts to take up positions in the mountains behind the hideout to act as snipers and to protect the offensive from the roving patrol.

CHAPTER SIXTY

Armageddon

Thankfully, due to the increased frequency of their visits, the village neglected to dispatch the usual welcome party to intercept them.

Jimbo's heart was thumping fit to burst. He had to bite down hard to stop his teeth from chattering.

Sitting up the dirt track leading to the hideout, he had gaffer taped the claymores and mortars to the outside of the propane bottles. The propane bottles were then ratchet strapped tightly together with the claymores and mortar bombs squeezed between them, high up towards the valves. The whole shooting match was laid out with the valves pointing towards the rear of the Jeep.

In his clammy hand, Jimbo held his crude timer, a single thermite grenade with a five second delay pin and lever fuse.

He was wearing a flak vest, although it wouldn't offer much protection if the plan went south.

The two-way radio sat on the passenger seat beside him, waiting to crackle out the signal from Goose, the signal which would tell him that the gate was open and he had the green light to go.

Goose was parked just behind him in a Jeep with Aarif at the wheel, and Neil and Jack in the rear. Adiel and the rest of Aarif's men were parked up just behind them. All were armed to the teeth.

Goose was frantically scrolling a wheel and pressing buttons on what looked like a sophisticated

'Ham Radio' set. A series of tiny neons lit up one at a time on the radio set. When the last light lit up, Goose keyed the mike on the 2-way and whispered, "Amber." Goose flicked out a forward gesture with his hand, and Aarif dropped the clutch spinning the wheels as the Jeep shot forward towards the gate, with Adiel and the others close behind.

A few yards short of the entrance, Goose pressed the play button on the video camera and the two vehicles skidded to a halt just past the gate with all the combatants disembarking weapons at the ready, waiting for Goose's signal.

Inside the bunker an exhausted guard, waiting eagerly for his shift to end and for his relief to arrive, was shocked to see the security gate open. In the ensuing panic, he didn't notice the flashing light normally indicating an open door, which was conspicuously dark. Just as the attackers had hoped, he instinctively hit the button to close the gate. The gate began to slowly open.

"Green light Jimbo, green light!" Goose screamed into the radio, then grabbing his M16 rifle he leapt from the Jeep and joined the assault party.

The engine of Jimbo's Jeep was screaming in low gear as his powered through the partially open gate to the sporadic staccato sound of small arms fire. Seconds later the compound echoed to an enormous explosion.

Jimbo's plan had far surpassed his expectations. The thermite grenade detonated just as his body hit the ground, pitching and rolling clumsily away from the speeding bomb. A fraction of a second later, the claymores erupted, sending balls of white hot steel through the propane bottles. As the jeep struck the inner wall of the stronghold, the mortar rounds and propane erupted into a cataclysmic pyrotechnic crescendo.

Only Jack, with his Navy Seal experience, was able to function clearly immediately after the blast. "Go, go, go. C'mon, let's go, nuts to butts!" he shouted, galvanising his warriors to action.

The inner sanctum was of reinforced concrete construction, set back into and below a natural outcrop of mountain. The entire entrance was obliterated; a massive smoking hole exposed two levels of the hideout blowing the entire side out of a stairwell connecting the ground and upper floors. The blast had taken out a huge swathe of electrical wiring, plunging the entire artificially lit complex into pitch darkness.

Jack was the first through the hole, wearing night vision goggles followed closely by Neil, Adiel and Aarif, all wearing head torches: for the time being, turned off. Goose hesitated for a second, instincts telling him to check on Jimbo. Remembering the gravity of the situation, he flung a smoke bomb over to where his best friend lay and jumped through the gaping hole with the others.

"Jesus fucking Christ," Jack exclaimed as his goggles picked out what at first appeared to be a terrorist clutching a glowing shell. "Ignore him," he shouted back, "he's tango uniform. Keep nuts to butts boys, I'll lead you in, return fire after my lead."

The bottom half of a propane cylinder had struck the unfortunate Arab in the centre of his body before crashing through the rear stairwell wall, impaling him in a macabre standing position with his hands seemingly holding the object.

The first wave of the operation was proceeding successfully with the attackers moving swiftly, clearing the complex room by room as the defenders failed to rally after the confusion of the initial assault. With the advantage of Jack's night vision, they were sweeping upwards towards the rear and into the natural caverns, killing the terrorists or pushing them back deeper into the mountain. They were moving with considerable speed and confidence considering the unfamiliar maze-like layout of the complex.

Jack rounded a corner and immediately encountered bright light and a large open and occupied space. The solar panel on the goggles reacted before his eyes could and the goggles switched to clear. Snatching them from his head he dived back into the cover of the concrete wall. "We got live ones here," he hissed back to the others. "They've got the lights back up. Flashbangs, quick as you like," he said, gesturing for the others to hand over what they had.

The stronghold was surprisingly ill-equipped for defence, perhaps more intended as a hideout rather than a last line of defence. Just beyond the corridor where the attackers had come to rest was an open chasm which led into the open cave chamber wherein the terrorists had chosen to make a stand. Just beyond the chasm was a small tunnel separated from the main chamber by at least 3 feet of solid rock. The tunnel was of indeterminate depth, created naturally by the overflow from the waterfall's sump. The floor of the tunnel was covered by a few inches of fast flowing freezing water from melting snow from the high Himalayas.

Jack tossed a number of the flashbangs and a smoke grenade into the chamber. As the flashbangs exploded with devastating effect, he, Neil and Adiel crossed the open chasm and found sanctuary behind the thick wall of the tunnel.

After 20 seconds of concentrated M16 fire from the two strategic points, the cavern was silent, the defenders suppressed.

"Where to now Jack?" Neil asked.

"Shhh! What the hell's that?" Jack questioned.

A sound like a wounded animal howling could be heard from the tunnel.

"Probably just the wind," Adiel suggested.

"Bollocks the wind!" Neil said, rising from his crouch and running down the slippery stream bed of the tunnel towards the sound.

By the time Adiel and Jack caught up to him, Neil was half cursing, half crying, his muscles straining, trying to prise open the bars of what appeared to be a medieval prison cell hewn from the bedrock. Inside the cell, a naked woman lay chained, spread-eagled on a pile of empty ammo crates. Inert and unresponsive, her battered and bloodied body bore the evidence of sustained punishment. The cries came from a soaking wet child sitting against the wall in the corner of the cell. "It's Sheila; it's Sheila and her daughter. I think Sheila's gone."

Adiel pulled Neil to one side to let Jack get to the cell door.

"Listen honey," Jack said. "We're the good guys. We've come to save you. I want you to get down behind the boxes where mummy's lying, that's a good girl. Quickly now, we need to get you out."

The girl did as she was told. Jack pulled out his pistol and fired a round into the mortice lock. The lock parted with the second round.

CHAPTER SIXTY-ONE

Labyrinth

"Is she..." Neil asked, as Jack checked Sheila for signs of life.

"She's still with us but only barely. She's hypothermic. All this freezing spray makes it as cold as a fridge down here. This poor bitch has been left to freeze to death."

"C'mon Jack," Neil urged. "We have to find Natasha."

"Someone has to get these poor wretches to safety Neil, Sheila's a goner if we don't act fast."

By this time, Adiel, Aarif, Goose and a couple of Aarif's men had caught up.

"Send your guys back out with these two Aarif," Goose suggested. "They've more than done their share. Tell them to call Daggy on the two-way, get him and Brodie up here. They can take the two girls and Jimbo back to safety."

"How is Jim?" Neil asked.

"He was down," Goose said, "but moving. Couldn't see if he was hit, but I didn't see any ketchup so I'm hopeful. Reckon he was just stunned."

Aarif gave his two men their instructions and then started on releasing Sheila from the chains.

Recognising Neil, Sheila's daughter wrapped her arms around his leg. "Listen honey," Neil soothed, "these two men are goodies, I want you to trust them, they will take you and Mummy somewhere safe; somewhere they can get help to make Mummy better. Uncle Neil has to go and help Aunty Natasha now because the bad guys are hurting her. OK honey?" The little girl held out her hand and one of the Arabs took it and whisked her up into his arms. The other man carefully lifted Sheila onto his back in a fireman's lift.

"Tell them not to forget Jimbo," Goose said. "He's the fat useless fucker that got us in here."

Aarif relayed the reminder to his men.

"So where do we go?" Aarif asked, watching his men climb back up the tunnel towards the brightly lit cavern.

"I would say on downwards," Neil said. "Rats always have a bolt hole."

They followed the path of the water flow onwards down the steep decline for a few hundred feet.

"Turn your lights out," Neil said.

"What is it?" Jack asked.

"Look, there's natural light coming in," he answered.

Just above them was a fissure in the rock ceiling. On the cave wall you could see a series of well-worn hand and foot holds carved into the rock face, creating a well camouflaged stairway through the fissure.

Neil positioned his head lamp at an angle and started up through the hole. "Fuck! The clever bastards!" he exclaimed.

"What is it?" Jack shouted up through the fissure.

"They've got a fucking steel ladder up here," Neil said, "set into the wall, this is some sort of a shaft, and it goes all the way up to the outside. C'mon up, there's like a ledge just past the fissure. I'm going on up the ladder."

"That's where the Ninja patrols came from," Jack concluded.

"You can bet your ass that's how that sneaky bastard's got away, and with my fucking wife. We'd better get after him."

Neil, Jack and Goose ascended the ladder leaving Adiel and Aarif on the ledge just in case it was an ambush.

Jack tapped Neil on the ankle, and handed him the night vision headgear. "Here Neil, stick this up through the hole first, if they're waiting for us, at least you only lose a hand."

"Good thinking Jack," Neil said, hanging on to the rails with one hand to grab the goggles.

There was no reaction to the headgear's ascent so Neil quickly jumped up out of the hole and ran for the cover of a nearby rock. Quickly surveying the area, Neil called out to the others to join him. Aarif and Adiel began the ascent as Jack and Goose joined Neil behind the cover of the rock.

"Well. Where do you think he's taken her?" Jack asked.

"Not up for sure," Neil said. "Look at that fucking cliff face. Without ropes and shit, you'd have no chance of making that climb, especially with a pissed off Natasha in tow."

"He's run for the village then," Goose concluded.

"That's my hunch too Gee," Jack said. "He's not going to head back to the compound, it's a war zone and he doesn't know how many men we've got down there."

"Follow the path then," Neil said, and they set off on the steep descent down towards the village.

As they rounded the first corner in the track which zigzagged its way between huge rocky outcrops and sparse pine forest, Neil spotted the corpse lying on the rocks some 50 feet below their present position. Taking a set of field glasses from his tac-vest, his heart was racing as he focused in on the body.

"One of theirs?" Jack asked.

"No. I think it's Ahmed, one of Aarif's guys."

Aarif took the glasses from Neil and confirmed, "It is Ahmed. He was one of the two snipers I set to watch for patrols."

"They came this way then," Jack concluded.

The trail twisted around the back of a steep outcrop, then dropped abruptly 15 feet or so courtesy of some rough-hewn steps. As they dropped down the steps Goose noticed a splash of blood on the rocks behind them, followed by a steady spray of blood following the trail down. Something or somebody was bleeding heavily. "What is it?" Jack asked.

“Looks like movement among the boulders down there.” Goose pulled the field glasses from Jack's tac-vest and scoured the area. “Yep, there’s something moving behind the boulder down there.”

“I’ll go down,” Aarif said. “I am like a mountain goat. Climbing mountains is second nature.”

“And there was me thinking you were a ‘sand monkey’ Aarif,” Goose said.

“In me beats the heart of many animals, little duck,” Aarif replied. “I will descend to where the drop re-joins the path and meet you there.” He then stepped off the path and began the difficult descent down to where they’d spotted the movement.

It took them five minutes to zigzag down to where Aarif was breathlessly waiting.

“What was it Aarif?” Jack asked.

“It is Basr, the other sniper I sent into the mountains.”

“Is he dead?” Neil asked.

“No, he attempted to shoot Al-Kooheji as he was fleeing; unfortunately, they saw him and fired first. A round caught his gun and it exploded in his face.”

“I’m sorry Aarif, is he a goner?”

“No Neil, on the contrary, Basr will be OK. He broke his leg when he fell. They thought him dead and so went on their way. Basr was able to follow their progress from his position using the telescopic sight on his rifle.”

“You mean we know where they are?” Neil asked, excitedly.

"Indeed we do Neil. Basr was able to show me the house they fled to; where they are still."

"Is Natasha with them?" Neil asked impatiently.

"Who? How many?" Jack asked, interrupting Neil.

"Al-Kooheji, Mohamed Zakrem and Natasha," Aarif replied. "And there is more good news. Ahmed it seems managed to shoot Mohamed Zakrem in the groin, wounding him seriously."

"That is good news," Jack said. "Between dealing with a seriously unhappy Mrs Curland and a wounded comrade, Aykay's options are going to be limited."

"There is also some unnerving news," Aarif said. "Mohamed Zakrem: he has the bomb vest with him."

"Shit," Jack said. "Let's hope he's not planning to end on a high note."

Towards the bottom of the cliff, the track began to level out to a sparsely wooded plateau, beyond which the track was lost in a myriad of crossing animal trails. The red tile roofs of the village made the choice of path unequivocal.

Moving at a fast pace, Jack almost ran headlong into the prostrate figure of Mohamed Zakrem, abandoned and bleeding out in the dirt of the forest.

"One moment my friends," Aarif said, "I must quickly speak with this man before his life is over."

Aarif asked the man a number of questions.

"What's he saying Adiel?" Neil asked.

"He asks if a fatwa of death has been passed on Natasha," Adiel said, holding his hand up for Neil to let him listen further.

"The man says there is no fatwa. He also says that

Al-Kooheji will use the bomb vest if he is cornered," Adiel said.

"Can we trust what he says?" Goose asked.

"Aarif has made him an offer he cannot refuse," Adiel concluded. "I will let Aarif explain when we have time."

With Aarif still crouched over him Mohamed Zakrem expired.

"Come," Aarif said, "we must make haste."

The buildings were arranged in a simple terraced grid arrangement showing good prudence in the management of building materials, but leaving little cover for exposed invaders. The building where Al-Kooheji had taken refuge was somewhere in the middle, enveloped by other buildings.

As they started forward in a conventional tactical advance, they faced a wall of stern faced, armed villagers. Aarif shouldered his M16 and moved forward to address the group while Neil, Goose and Adiel, skirted around them and continued on towards the target by another route.

Soon, they were once again surrounded by angry armed villagers. It seemed that they had taken up positions around Al-Kooheji's hideout.

"This could get ugly," Jack said.

Aarif soon caught them up. He had their former guide in tow. The man addressed the village militia and their hostility promptly ceased.

"Again we have Allah on our side," Aarif declared. "The villagers are Shia, not Sunni, they will not intervene. They have no loyalty to the man they call the 'Bahraini Sheik'. He has taken this house by force and is holding a local family hostage. The villagers are on our side."

"So what's the plan then Jack?" Neil asked.

"I'm kinda out of ideas Neil. We can't blast our way in with flashbangs; Aykay's got the vest, which gives him all the cards. We're going to have to go in softly; see what he wants; stay fluid; react as the plot unfolds."

"Well he hasn't blown himself up yet," Neil concluded, "that must mean he wants to deal. Let's go and see what his demands are."

The house was one of a few two storey dwellings in the village. Neil and Goose stood with their backs to the sandstone wall adjacent to each of the two ground floor windows and waited for further instructions. Jack, Adiel and Aarif positioned themselves at the door. Jack gave a slow count of three fingers. On the count of three, Jack gently pushed the door open. Neil and Goose dropped to a crouch and swept their M16s from left to right across the ground floor of the open plan dwelling.

Inside the room Isa Al-Kooheji stood with his left arm locked around Natasha's neck. In his right hand, he held the trigger. His thumb hovered over the button. He screamed at them, "Get back. Get out, otherwise I will take all of you with me." He dragged Natasha kicking and screaming up the narrow stone staircase.

On the narrow landing, Natasha seized her opportunity and sank her teeth into Isa's arm. He released her momentarily but as she attempted to run towards the stairs, he lunged at her, sending her crashing against the wall, knocking her unconscious

Back on the ground floor, Aarif released the terrified family who had been tied up with their own clothing. They ran from the building to screams of relief from the concerned villagers.

CHAPTER SIXTY-TWO

Retribution

Isa dragged the prostrate Natasha through the door of a small room and threw her on the floor behind him.

As Neil and the others, hot on his heels, reached the corridor, Isa shouted to them, "Do not enter this room otherwise I will take all of you with me."

"It's all over Isa, we can talk about this. We just want Natasha back and safe. Put down the detonator," Neil implored.

"You, Son of Satan. It is thanks to you and your perverse sexual acts that have brought these woes down upon me. If the last breath I take on this earth serves to take out your worthless infidel lives, then my Jihad will have been just," Isa hissed.

"I'm not the one who got jiggy jiggy with my mum now am I you two faced bastard," Neil retorted.

"I loved Natasha. I would have made her my wife and given her the world if you hadn't planted your ungodly seed inside her belly." Isa's thumb was poised over the remote trigger button.

"Don't fucking push that button yet, you and me have unfinished business," Neil persuaded. "She was my bloody girlfriend, my fiancée. OK, I was a bit off the rails, but I didn't even know you existed. As far as I knew, my ungodly seed was the only seed that should have been there."

"You Kafir pimp, you infidel whoremaster. You were sending her out to sleep with other men to satisfy your own Satanic desires. You deserve a thousand deaths. I should take your head off with my bare hands."

"So take the bloody bomb vest off then and take your best shot. Fight me man to man."

"I loved Natasha. I wanted her with me, I wanted our son," Isa confessed.

"*My* son," Neil retorted. "Do you have any fucking idea what that psychotic bastard you set on her did to her? He had her gang raped around the clock, in every way imaginable. He beat an unborn child out of her, and then kept right on going till he'd beaten the womb out of her too. You ordered him to do that; paid him to do that, you, Mr motherfucking pure Allah worshipping Muslim. You fucked your mother, killed your own son; killed your whole damn family. Where do you think you're off to when you push that button, paradise, seventy odd virgins? I think not. When you leave this world it will be in a body bag filled with bits of Christians, atheists and a Jew. No promised land for you scumbag."

Isa's thumb hovered menacingly over the trigger button; Neil's attempts at diffusing the situation were failing dismally.

"You filthy infidel pimp, what do you know of the trials which I have faced, you dare to judge me? I didn't choose my situation, it chose me. You have followed the path of Satan not I," Isa cursed.

"OK, I admit I've brought all this down on you, on Natasha too. I know, maybe I don't deserve any better than this, but she does. Her only mistake was to fall in love with bad men. Let her go, take me with you instead."

Neil gestured for the others to leave the building before carefully edging inside the door and closing it behind him.

"You are a fool infidel, now you have sealed your own fate too."

"You push that button mate and you will be off before me. You won't get to see me suffer because you'll already be vapour. Who knows? Maybe I'll get lucky and survive. Stranger things have happened you know; vest bombs are mighty unpredictable. Tell you what though, you let me call my friends to get Natasha out of here and I'll give you my gun, you can take me out first; see me dead before you check out."

Natasha was stirring. Neil could see her movements in his peripheral vision. He had to concentrate hard to avoid focusing on her. He only hoped they hadn't discovered the little Glock pistol she carried around everywhere with her.

This offer made Isa hesitate, his brain picking through the possible scenarios which a loaded gun afforded him. He didn't really want martyrdom, the border with Afghanistan was close; he wanted escape. He had friends over the border, he could start over. The bomb vest only afforded escape of one kind; a loaded gun however presented an entirely different prospect.

Isa's mind was in turmoil, he stared intently into his opponent's eyes, reading for any sign of treachery. Too late he saw the focus shift, saw the momentary glimpse of Natasha leaping up from the floor reflected in the dark pools of Neil's eyes.

Neil was already moving, lunging towards the remote trigger as Natasha's baby Glock pumped six rounds in quick succession into the back of Isa Hashim Al-Kooheji's neck, instantly severing the brain's activity from the nervous system of the body. Neil wrestled the trigger from his grasp before his body hit the floor.

"Are you OK?" he asked a still groggy Natasha.

"Oh marvellous thanks. Are we done now? Is it finally over? Can we possibly go get our kids and go home?"

Their passage down the stairs was blocked by the overwhelming bulk of Jimbo, still wearing his flak jacket. "Oh don't tell me I've gone and missed the whole fucking show?"

"Jim," Neil shouted, "you *were* the fucking show mate. We thought you were a goner."

"Ah bollocks, I was just winded from jumping out of the car. Then numbnuts here," he had Goose in a headlock, "threw a bloody smoke bomb at me. I got fucking lost. Time I found me way in, everyone was gone."

CHAPTER SIXTY-THREE

Endure

It had been a slow month for Rocco Montisi. His duties had mainly involved dull enforcement work; teeth and toenails stuff. Rocco had followed the outcome of his last 'real' assignment with considerable interest. He'd never even heard of Dextrocardia let alone experienced it in one of his 'patients'.

He'd been thorough; he always was. This time was no exception. The girl had really put up a fight, he'd actually begun to root for her, but the outcome was inevitable.

The internal damage could not be reversed. The doctors had fought a valiant battle to keep her alive, but she was simply too gravely hurt; too weak for the extensive surgical procedures needed to give her a fighting chance.

She'd died hard; really hard. The Italian press, renowned for their celebration of the macabre, had reported how the machine breathing for her had emitted smoke from her seared lungs on the exhale stroke, and how the nurses treating her had vomited from the smell emanating from the putrefying tissue inside her body. She'd clung to life for over a week. Time enough for her to have made any number of statements to the police, but Rocco doubted that had been the case; she was probably unconscious or heavily sedated throughout the whole ordeal. Besides, months had passed; he'd have been arrested by now if they had anything on him.

Rocco smiled quietly as he let himself into the apartment. The scene had already been prepared; the victim was securely taped to a chair silently waiting in the kitchen. Rocco opened the cupboard drawers and searched for some interesting implements he could use to strike terror into the heart of his latest ‘patient’. His attention was caught by a small blending device used for dicing baby food. It looked powerful enough to do serious damage to vulnerable appendages. Break off the bottom guard and it would just about fit into an eye socket.

“Good evening my friend. My name is Mr Montisi; I will be your torturer tonight,” Rocco began, his usual ice cold patter designed to strike terror into the heart. This time the victim, a known Mafia ‘rat’, was someone who would know his captor well, by reputation if not in person.

Too late Rocco noticed the paper tape around his victim's wrists and ankles, heard the faint noise behind him and then felt the sharp scratch of the hypodermic as it was thrust into his neck.

Rocco was a clever soldier; he knew not to show all his cards at once, so as his consciousness returned, he first gathered information with his senses. He could smell heat, like the smell of a dry pan cooking on the hob. He was laid on his back on a bed, he was naked. He discretely applied pressure to his wrist and ankle bonds. They were fast, they wouldn’t give.

“Open your eyes dickhead,” the voice said. “You’re not fooling anybody.”

Rocco opened his eyes. He was spread-eagled. He didn't recognise Ludo or Adriano Armenti. Why would he? He glanced around the room, saw the curling tongs on the locker, the steam iron sat on the dresser, the bottle of cooking oil.

"You're going to die hard my friend," Ludo Vincelli said. "Before you die, I want to hear you pleading with the soul of Alessandra Armenti to forgive you in the next life."

Rocco soiled himself.

CHAPTER SIXTY-FOUR

God's Miracle

Sleeping in her own bed, in the company of her exhausted children and the man she loved unconditionally, the man she owed her life to, Natasha finally felt at peace. The news that Sheila was making a good recovery from her ordeal filled her with euphoria. The wind had changed; now anything was possible.

Natasha felt it. She knew, since the old passion had returned in the chateaux months ago. She felt that something in her body had changed. The mood swings, the temper, the fierce desire to protect what was hers. The queasiness she had felt, the sickness. Tingling in parts of her body which had lain dormant, dead, unresponsive since the fateful day Brian Dix had unleashed his barbaric cruelty upon her. She knew that the doctors would tell her it was stress, unfamiliar diet, the water, but Natasha just knew.

She made the trip to the chemist alone and in secret. She didn't want the doctors to know. They would be supportive, tell her it was impossible, and prescribe her counselling, anti-depressants. Alone in the bathroom, she held the strip in her trembling right hand and waited for it to repair her soul, to return her to a full woman or to dash her hopes, her dreams, and torment her with feelings, cruel memories like ghosts from a past life. The minutes passed interminably slowly, seeming like hours, days. The strip began to blur as Natasha's eyes filled with tears. She blinked them away, rubbing them with her free left hand. The strip came into clear focus. It had changed from pale to bright blue. She grabbed for the chart and held the printed card against the strip, scarcely believing her own vision, but there it was, screaming unequivocally: positive.

She was pregnant.

CHAPTER SIXTY-FIVE

Legacy

"That whole messy business with the girl has been erased Warren. I had no idea that was going down, I'm sorry. Dan Ruthers crossed the line."

"I'm sorry too Tom. What made that mad, bad son of a bitch frame me up like that? He could've had all the cooperation from the Curlands if he'd just asked; her husband's an ex-soldier, a patriot. They would have complied with any demands if he'd just asked. All they wanted was to be left in peace."

"Warren, I don't need to tell you what a bad man Ruthers was, a bad man who made a lot of bad calls, but I've had to step on a few backs to get where I am, and I'm damn sure you have too."

"That poor girl died needlessly and a good friend of mine, a father and an outstanding FBI agent, lost his life along with no doubt countless others."

"I know that Warren. To be fair, it seems that the decision to eliminate the Curland woman was the Arab's call, you know what they're like, it's only a secret if everyone who knows about it is dead. If it had been my call, we'd have spoken to you, made sure you and your friends were on side, but the world has turned since then. We had a Republican in the white house, an ex-director of the CIA, now we have a Democrat, who's knocking doors and asking questions. The only reason I have this job now is because I was the black sheep during the last regime; always questioning, always erring on the side of caution."

“Is it us Tom? Is this how a post ‘cold war’ America carries on?”

“This is bigger than countries Warren. You know, the whole damn system is corrupt.” He walked over to the massive mahogany fireplace dating back from before the Civil war which dominated his office. He reached onto the tall mantelpiece and took down an ornate gold inlaid wooden cigar box. Taking out a fine cigar, he bit the end off the dark cheroot. Looking Warren straight in the eyes, he said, “Cuba’s finest!” Tom Berrington looked down, stared for a few moments at the intricate design on the label of his cigar, contemplating how forthright his next revelation should be. “It’s not the politicians you see Warren. Generally speaking, they’re in it for the right reasons, and it’s certainly not the people of the land of the free and the home of the brave, no, this plan was hatched by the real rulers of the world, the corporations, those people who operate in the shadows, in every country the world over, regardless of their politics or their heads of state; the money men, the oil men, the industry heads. Sure, the CIA’s corrupt, the NSA’s corrupt, the Senate, Congress, even the White House, all watching each other, spying on each other, waiting to strike when the moment's right and the enemy's not looking. But you know what, it works. We muddle along, cancel each other out if you like, somehow the circus plays to a crowded big top and the audience applauds.” Tom sat back down on his sumptuous leather chair and faced Warren. “I’m only in this job because the electorate disturbed the status quo. This President has asked me to ‘clean up’ this nest of rattlers, but I doubt that I’ll have the time in office to get the job done. I doubt that he will have time to get the job done; he's already making powerful enemies. A twist of fate and it could soon be another Dan Ruthers sitting in this seat."

"Will they press ahead with the Middle Eastern idea now or do you think they'll run for the hills?"

"Well Warren, strictly off the record, it doesn't look like they've put all their money on the one horse. Alongside your Bahraini Sheik, the money men and their pawns have been nurturing ties with a Saudi family, they're oil rich, and they have a hot-headed son who's seen hands-on fighting with the Mujahidin. Coincidently, the family have a personal relationship with the former President and his son, who by the way, is well on his way to becoming your next Governor of Texas. The Republicans are grooming him as their next great white hope, so chances are, they'd have backed the Saudi in the long run anyhow."

"Be careful Tom. If there's one thing my friends have taught me about the Middle East, it's that when you think you've got someone dead to rights, sometimes you find out all you've got is a pocketful of pudding."

"The whole of the Middle East is a powder keg Warren. If it proves to be in my power to extract us from the whole sorry mess, be assured, I'll do just that."

"Well, you know I've always been proud of my country Tom, damn proud to be an American. I hope my part in this didn't cause the 'stars and stripes' too much bad will."

"If anything Warren, you've done her a great service." Tom laughed. "If you want my two cents, I think that the money men are making a huge mistake. They think they can take over the world's oil, and then gain a stranglehold over populations by manipulating the banks and the money markets. It won't work."

"The Cold War kept us all focused Tom," Warren mused, "all pulling the same way. Democracy was the best hope for the world. Now that the East has fallen, greed has risen; they think that they can ride in on the vacuum."

"Eloquently put Warren, but politics is changing on a day to day basis. This President is way more popular with the people than the previous one. If he lives long enough and manages to stay in office, who knows where his reforms may lead, what changes he might implement. Maybe with him in the White House, and me here, we can weed out the 'bad apples' and throw a spanner in the works of their objective."

"You're the right man for the job Tom; you're the most straight shooting honest man I know."

"Thanks Warren. I've got you and the affair with Dan Ruthers to thank for this appointment; I don't forget my friends in a hurry."

"What of the girl Tom? Can any reparations be made to her family?"

"I feel your pain my friend, really I do, but my office can't acknowledge any involvement in her death. Besides, she was chosen because she had no kin, no one to mourn or miss her. What I can and will do is power up some of our pet lobbyists, see if we can't get the President onside, and petition congress to allocate more funds in the fight against drug abuse and homelessness. That's the best legacy she can leave I'm afraid."

"Please make sure that happens Tom, I'd like to think that her life and death meant something."

"Sure thing Warren."

EPILOGUE

Consequence

The time was 08.14 on the eleventh of September. The year was 2001. It was a beautiful morning over the US Eastern seaboard, the sky was bright blue without a cloud to be seen. The weary controller at Boston Air Traffic Control Centre had been on duty since 06.00 hours. He was staring at a series of blips and transponder codes on his radar screen. His coffee was rapidly cooling on the desk in front of him as his attention was focused on the screen and on the information coming to him via the sophisticated radio set. He tried in vain to make contact with a plane which had just abruptly stopped responding.

"American Eleven Boston. American One One, the American on the frequency, how do you hear me?" The Boston controller made a quick call to his next nearest ATC neighbour at Athens Ben-Epps Airport. "This is Boston, I turned American Eleven twenty left and I was going to climb him, he will not respond to me now, at all."

Athens ATC: "Looks like he's turning right."

Boston ATC: "Yeah I turned him twenty right."

Athens ATC: "He's NORDO (no radio) Roger."

At 08.46 American Airlines Flight Eleven crashed into the North Tower of the World Trade Centre.

The rest is history.

OTHER TITLES IN THE BITTERSWEET SERIES

By Nicholas P Boyland

Published by Rhino Trikes

Bittersweet Sacrifice

The seminal book in the 'Bittersweet' series.

Published April 2013

Paperback ISBN Number: 978-0-9576285-0-2

ebook ISBN Number: 978-0-9576285-1-9

Neil Curland is languishing in an Indian summer heat wave when the worst storm in three hundred years throws the Country into a post-apocalyptic turmoil.

Caught up in his own personal hell, Neil finds himself unceremoniously dumped at the feet of the exotic Natasha. What begins as a labour of lust soon migrates into a deeper, darker erotic attraction, but Natasha comes with a dangerous past which just won't lie down and die!

Fate smiles on Neil Curland in the exotic Natasha, but life can weave a convoluted journey of jealousy, betrayal, kidnap, and violence when love is usurped by lust!

When her deranged ex kidnaps Natasha's child, Neil is forced to re-visit his former life in the armed forces; bringing together a task force with the skills to challenge the Provisional IRA at the height of the 'troubles'.

Obsession and erotic brinkmanship weave a convoluted path between misunderstanding and

coincidence. Cruel twists of fate see the couple separated by customs, religion and continents as their lives and loves veer off in opposite directions.

Will they ever see each other again?

What does fate have in store for Neil and Natasha?

Be careful what you wish for!

Bittersweet Humiliation

The second book in the Bittersweet series.

Published December 2013

Paperback ISBN 978-0-9576285-5-7

Ebook ISBN 978-0-9576285-3-3

Recently reunited. Wealthy beyond their wildest dreams. Newly-weds, Neil and Natasha Curland are enjoying the romantic honeymoon of their dreams in a modest coastal town on the sun drenched island of Crete. Back home, business is booming. Exciting new opportunities loom on the horizon, in America; the land of opportunity. As if the future could possibly get any brighter; Natasha has missed another period and is quietly confident that she is expecting the couple's third child.

Just a short three hour flight away, a storm is brewing deep within the troubled mind of a vicious psychopath. Unbeknown to the happy couple, their lives lie directly in the path of the storm.

www.ingramcontent.com/pod-product-compliance
Lightning Source LLC
Chambersburg PA
CBHW020819180626
46814CB00001B/30

* 9 7 8 0 9 5 7 6 2 8 5 7 1 *